JUSTICE IN THE MIND

DOCTOR WISE BOOK 11

ARJAY LEWIS

MIND
BENDER
PRESS

Justice In The Mind: Doctor Wise Book 11
Copyright ©2023 Robert J. Lewis

Cover Design: Marianne Nowicki, PremadeEbookCoverShop.com
Editing: Libby Broadbent

ISBN-13: 978-1737838180
ISBN-10: 1737838184

Published by:
Mindbender Press
474 South Main Street
Phillipsburg NJ 08865
www.mindbenderpress.com

DEDICATION

To Benjamin Corey
Magician, adviser
and all-around good guy

.

"It is the spirit and not the form of law that keeps justice alive."

—*Earl Warren*

"Justice is a certain rectitude of mind whereby a man does what he ought to do in the circumstances confronting him."

—*Thomas Aquinas*

PROLOGUE

Hunched under the harsh gleam of a desk lamp, Alex Worling conversed on the phone. It was one of twenty telephones, their wires snaking across the dim floor of his office.

"Honestly, Mrs. Henderson — I wish there was something we could do." His voice was sickly sweet. "Unfortunately, you have an outstanding tax debt of five thousand dollars, and we have to start enforcement proceedings. This may require police intervention, and we may have to foreclose on your assets, like your home."

As he listened to the elderly woman's rising panic on the phone, a smile graced his lips. She spoke of her deceased husband and the constraints of her income. Her gullibility and naïveté were evident.

Perfect.

"I understand, Mrs. Henderson," Worling said, sympathetically.

This was just too easy. His computer made random phone calls. In an automated voice, it claimed the recipient had unpaid taxes. The recording demanded immediate contact with an agent or face police intervention. Most people just hung up, but now and then he got a live one.

"I could use Form 2289—" Worling said, making up the number, "—for extreme situations, like yours. If you can pay the first five hundred dollars on a credit card, I might clear this up for you today."

"Oh? Can you do that?" she responded hopefully.

Of course, he could take her money. He would demand the five-hundred-dollar fee. Then he would produce a copy of her card to use for several days. Eventually, the credit card company would detect the forgery and deactivate the account.

Who was he hurting? The credit card company had insurance, and the elderly woman would hopefully learn to be more cautious.

"I'm authorized to commit to a settlement right now, and we can clear this all up."

"Well, my husband took care of all this, but since he died…" the old woman said.

An unexpected knocking on the office door made Worling look up and furrow his brow. No one knew he would be here, and visitors were exceedingly rare.

"As I was saying, all I need is your credit card number—"

A second knock echoed through the room.

"Excuse me, Mrs. Henderson, my supervisor is knocking on my cubicle. I have to make sure he will approve this settlement before I continue. Let me put you on hold, please."

He placed the receiver on the desk. This was his skill, the adeptness of a seasoned swindler. He seamlessly incorporated an unexpected interruption into his narrative and used it.

A master of his craft, that's what he was.

He cautiously opened the door, limited by the constraints of the security chain.

"Yeah, who is it? Whaddya want?"

The hallway was not well lit, and the man was tall, in a long dark leather coat with a black felt fedora perched on his head, leaving his face in shadows. He spoke in a deep voice, "Mr. Worling?"

"Yeah, I'm Worling. What about it?"

"You killed Willard Johnson eight years ago, during a robbery."

"What are you, a reporter or somethin'? Look, that was manslaughter, and I served my time for it."

"Five years for killing a man," the tall guy said.

Worling was glad he'd gotten the heavy-duty security chain. This guy was creeping him out.

"Go complain to the judge. I'm busy here," Worling said as he closed the door and turned the heavy deadbolt in place.

An explosion ripped through the middle of the thick oak panels, shattering the door.

It threw Alex to the ground, as pain shot through his back and he cried out in agony. With trembling hands, he touched his back and his fingers came away with a gory display of blood.

Three men surged into the room through the broken door. One of them wore a ski mask and the other one was bald and chunky, carrying a heavy-duty battering ram. The one in the fedora stood over him, holding an enormous gun with a suppressor on the barrel.

He aimed the gun at Worling's face. It looked like it was the size of a cannon.

The man with the gun spoke again. "After murdering an innocent man, you now steal from people with your scams. And we know about your other plans."

"What… the…" Worling said, struggling to breathe. "I need… a hospital."

"You don't need a hospital. Your time is up."

"What do you want?" Worling begged.

"Justice," said the big man as he squeezed the trigger.

1. UPRIGHT MAN

"I t's time to get up, Doctor." The sultry voice blended tantalizingly with the aroma of coffee.

Jyanette stood by my bedside in a silky robe, holding a steaming mug. Her gleaming eyes, striking against her dark complexion, beamed down at me joyfully.

She had been my fiancée for almost two months.

Grinning, I accepted the mug and took a grateful sip. Leaning in, she gave me a quick peck on the lips.

Standing up, I grumbled, "That's it?" I wrapped my arms around her, proffering a far more satisfactory kiss. She purred contentedly, but after a moment or two, stepped away from me.

"Don't get yourself started," she chuckled. "I have to shower and get to work."

I smiled. It's great to stand eye-to-eye with a lady when you're six-feet-four like me.

"I'm spoiled. I've gotten used to nookie in the morning."

"Nookie? Where did you get that expression? The 1970s?"

I kissed her throat. "What do you prefer? Lovemaking? Going all the way? The old rumpy-pumpy?"

"I prefer you control your libido until this evening," she chided me playfully. "Besides, you have a class, so you're in the shower as soon as I get out."

"We could shower together," I suggested. "It would save time."

"It would take more time because you would attempt some — what was it? Rumpy-pumpy?"

"It's British slang. It has a certain ring to it."

She shook her head. "I have to get ready, so I get the shower first. You should take a cold one."

"How quickly the romance is gone," I said.

"You haven't married me yet, Len." She headed for the bathroom off the bedroom. "Then the romance will be gone."

Taking my cane, I followed her into the bathroom as she shed her robe and revealed her nightgown. Once facing me, she let out a sigh and asked, "What do you think you're doing?"

"Just watching," I told her, attempting to sound innocent.

"You can look, but don't touch," she ordered. "I need to focus on going back to work at the county prosecutor's office."

"It was nice they gave you your old job back," I said, as Jyanette slid the nightgown up and over her head, revealing her striking, uninhibited form. Her skin shimmered with an ebony glow, inherited from her African mother. Every inch of her was stunningly beautiful and irresistibly entrancing.

"Will you please let me get ready?" she demanded, though I could tell she was glad I enjoyed looking at her body. "And it's not my old job. I'm a temporary assistant district attorney helping with the backlog they're facing with that woman on maternity leave."

"Can I watch you shower?" I said, grinning.

"Out!" She pointed toward the bedroom as she stepped into the tub and closed the shower curtain.

With a deep breath, I headed out to grab my morning caffeine fix, stealing a quick glance at the nightstand clock. She was right. I had a class to teach, but I still had a bit more time than she implied. I navigated my way to the kitchen, opting to grab a bite to eat so she could get ready without me leering at her.

I left my cane next to the bed. I used it much less after my recent surgery for my fused right leg. The surgeon gave me a new knee joint of metal and plastic, allowing the stiff leg to bend again. After two months of physical therapy to strengthen the damaged muscles of the weakened limb, I still needed it. Not all the time, but in case I got tired and my leg needed the extra support.

For years, the wooden cane with its metal cobra-head handgrip had been a constant companion. Going without it felt strange.

Following our engagement in February, Jyanette and I embarked on a journey to Virginia. Our purpose was to retrieve her belongings and transport them to New Jersey. Jyanette was residing with her family in Virginia while she was working at the Department of Justice in Washington, DC. We opted to place her previous apartment's furniture in storage, as Jyanette and I lived in a quaint two-story stone house belonging to my close friend and landlady, Mrs. Margery Higgins.

Mrs. Higgins acquired the property using her savings earned as a cook for affluent families over several decades. It was a mother/daughter setup with a spacious wing that had a distinct entrance.

It was a good-sized house for suburban norms, but considered a humble abode in this part of Mountainview where vast mansions were everywhere.

Since I assisted her in locating the property, she kindly offered to rent out the separate wing to me at a rate well-suited for a professor in their second year of teaching.

My unique psychic abilities came in handy when I advised her about the optimal time to place an offer on the house, leading to a great bargain. My mental talents proved useful in many situations. I gain insight into simple matters like purchasing homes to solving cases involving criminal investigation.

Over the past two years, I've aided the Mountainview Police Department. My friend Lieutenant Bill McGee asks me to consult to resolve perplexing cases. Although I've garnered several substantial rewards in recent months, I've always provided my help for free.

I'm currently documenting my cases as fictional novels with anonymous characters, and the book sales have been promising, though I'm far from being a best-seller.

Every bit helps. After all, I'm getting married.

I swung through the door into the kitchen. To my surprise, Mrs. Higgins sat at the breakfast table, savoring a cup of tea from a dainty porcelain cup and saucer.

"Well, hallo there, Doctor," Mrs. Higgins said with her Irish lilt and smiled. "Ye have a class this marning, don't ye?"

"Yes, I do," I said, topping off my coffee from a nearby glass carafe. "And Jyanette is off to the Essex County Prosecutor's office."

"It's so noice to see ye happy, Doctor."

I paused and smiled. "It feels good."

The house has an impressive kitchen: oversized refrigerators, multiple stoves and ovens, and an industrial mixing machine. For a former cook like Mrs. Higgins, it proved to be a dream. I helped myself to some cream for my coffee.

"I'm cooking dinner for the three of us tonight," she announced.

"Mrs. Higgins, that's really unnecessary—"

"I know, but we'll be celebrating Jyanette's first day at work, and I figure we should have a meal together before the trouble starts."

I frowned and met her eyes. "Trouble, what trouble?"

"I'm certain I don't know," she replied innocently. "But in case ye get busy."

As a parapsychology professor and a psychic, I am usually the one with the heightened abilities. However, Mrs. Higgins possesses a remarkable talent for predicting occurrences. She calls it her 'woman's intooition'. As someone who takes paranormal phenomena seriously, I value and trust her insights deeply.

"Okay, dinner would be nice. I have a mentoring session with Anna Sokolov in the afternoon, but I should be here by the time Jyanette gets home."

"How is the lass doin'?"

I sighed. "Anna is a gifted psychic, possibly better than I am. But she's seventeen and can be difficult."

"And she has a crush on ye," Mrs. Higgins pointed out.

"She's been better about that since I told her Jyanette and I are getting married. Hopefully, her attentions will turn toward someone her own age."

"T'will be difficult. It's hard to make a relationship work when ye can read the other person's mind."

This surprised me. "Jyanette and I have no secrets."

"Aye. But in any relationship, ye need to have a private place. All of us have things it's best not to share."

I lifted my coffee cup in salute. "As always, you are wise, Mrs. Higgins."

She waved away the compliment. "Joost common sense. Now, I've made some scones. Why don't you take one fer yerself and one fer Jyanette? She can eat while she dresses."

I carried the two freshly baked scones to the bedroom, where I found Jyanette. She was putting in her earrings, in front of the bathroom mirror, in nothing but a bra and panties. My mind, and other parts of me, wished for an extra thirty minutes to spend with her. Jyanette happily received the scone and requested a sip of my coffee before proceeding to apply her makeup.

Jyanette's presence in my life became familiar in no time. Her physical appearance, her scent, and just having her around were all captivating for me every day. Everything Mrs. Higgins said was true — I was content. Our journey had been arduous, but we finally earned some well-deserved happiness.

My smartphone chimed, and I went to the sitting room to retrieve it.

"Morning, Bill."

Bill McGee's voice was gruff. "Len, what have you got today?"

"A class in about an hour. Then I'm working with Anna Sokolov after three."

"Can you fit in a visit to Bloomdale between those?"

"Bloomdale? Isn't that outside your jurisdiction?"

"It's a homicide. Bloomdale contacted my captain at the Mountainview PD and asked for our help."

"Sure, I can be there after noon. Do you have any leads?"

Bill chuckled. "Not a one. That's why I'm calling you."

"Anything I need to know about the victim?"

"Just a two-bit grifter — there must be about a hundred people who wanted him dead. I'm hoping you can give me some direction."

"Text me the address and I'll be there," I assured him.

"Thanks, Len," he said as he hung up.

I sent a quick text to Anna, letting her know I might be a few minutes late for our training session that afternoon. As a high school student, she didn't carry her phone during school hours, but I knew she would see it later.

"Was that Bill?" Jyanette said, stepping into the room.

Wearing a black pant suit accompanied by a white blouse, she exuded the look of a professional.

"Yes, he's calling me in on a case in Bloomdale."

A strange expression appeared on her face.

"What's wrong?" I asked.

She immediately forced herself into an unreadable facade. "Nothing. It's just he hasn't called you in weeks. I thought maybe he wouldn't be calling you in on so many cases."

I gently took her hand. "We talked about this, and you said you understood why I have to do it."

"I do... in principle," Jyanette insisted, not meeting my eyes. "After all the things that happened to you... to us... it's hard not to get emotional about it."

"It's just a consultation," I promised her. "And don't let it upset you. After all, Mrs. Higgins is making dinner in your honor tonight."

Jyanette smiled. "What would we do without that woman?"

After planting a kiss on my lips, she mischievously gave my rear a playful squeeze.

"No playing with the merchandise if you're not buying," I scolded.

"Oh, I'm definitely buying," she smiled and gave me a quick pat. "Tonight."

2. IMPARTIAL DECISION

After my class ended at eleven thirty, I made my way toward the destination Bill texted me. As I departed from Mountainview and entered Bloomdale, the businesses became less luxurious. There was an increase in the number of liquor stores and convenience stores selling lottery tickets and cigarettes.

My GPS navigated me away from the bustling thoroughfares toward the dilapidated warehouse district. Here, neglected storage facilities stood in stark contrast to weathered office buildings that had clearly seen brighter times. A seedy liquor store stood next to a dingy pawnshop, and I pulled over.

The address was a five-story building. It was brick with concrete cornices, and arches built above the windows, but everything was dirty. No one had cleaned the outside of the building in a very long time.

With cane in hand, I made my way across the street to the front door, where a uniformed police officer was checking IDs. I presented him with my laminated 'Consultant' card, issued by the MPD. He informed me I needed to head up to the third floor. The elevator was out of order, or perhaps it simply did not exist.

I took my time ascending the stairs.

Since January, after I underwent leg surgery and dedicated myself to consistent exercises, I had gained strength in my leg. However, climbing three flights of stairs remained a daunting feat. I was grateful for the handrail and my cane as, between the two, they provided the support I needed.

The stairwell was dismal, as the lighting was insufficient, and the stench of urine was overwhelming. My grip on the metal handrail caused layers of paint to flake off, leaving an unsightly mess on my hands. Upon reaching my destination, dark green specks of paint dotted my skin.

I wished I had brought a moist towelette or some hand sanitizer.

On the third floor, a uniformed officer manned the entrance to the office, and I heard the booming voice of Bill McGee as I drew near. When I entered, Bill turned to me, as did Casey Latrell, the regional medical examiner, and Doug Millbank, the county forensics chief.

Bill was a towering figure, standing at my height, or perhaps a little taller. He has the bulky frame of a football linebacker, although his hair had greyed. Casey was a complete contrast, standing at five foot six, not too thin nor too chubby. I knew well that he always upheld the dignity of the deceased. And then there was Doug, a slightly plump figure sporting a pencil-thin mustache. Covered head to toe in white plastic coveralls, he wore a hood and a plastic shield to guard his face as he searched for evidence.

Two morgue attendants were taking out a body bag, and I felt bad for them carrying the former resident down all those stairs.

"Hey Len," Bill said, and Casey and Doug both nodded at me.

"What do we have?" I asked, watching the body bag leave the room.

Bill checked his notebook. "The deceased is Alex Worling, aka Bill Sykes, aka Alex Josephs, aka — well, a lot more. Numerous arrests for larceny, phone scams, forgery, identity theft, and a slew of other crimes. He did five years for manslaughter in New York a few years back."

"A fine upstanding citizen," I said and focused on remembering just the name Alex Worling.

"I'm done," Doug said, lifting the plastic shield from his face. "We got photos of the scene, dusted for prints. Nothing useful — the only prints were his."

Upon entering the room, it was dark as there was only one window with the blinds up. Even so, It did little to cut through the gloom, as the view from the window consisted of the brick wall of the building next door.

A scarred and cluttered desk flaunted multiple landline phones, an open laptop, and a heavily used office chair. Next to it was an extended table constructed from scratched white plastic, home to three antiquated computers. A thick wire emerged from the wall, connecting to boxes that led to the computers.

"Are those… phone lines?" I asked, pointing at the cords.

"Trunk lines," Doug answered. "Yeah, he had a bunch of phones coming in."

"We played some messages the computers were sending out," Bill said. "Galland was here earlier, and he cracked the passcodes and got us in. The computers are all doing robocall scams."

Bill was speaking of his aide-de-camp, Officer Ben Galland, who was also MPD's resident computer expert and white-hat hacker.

"He was doing it old school," Doug commented. "These are actual phone lines. These days, most phone scammers use voice over internet protocol, and all they need is an internet connection."

"Perhaps the phone lines were already here when he rented the location," Casey said, peering around the room. "It doesn't look like he invested much in the upkeep for this place."

"Galland downloaded the lists of phone numbers each machine phoned in the last 24 hours. He's calling people to see if anyone spoke to an actual person, and if so, when."

I turned to Doug. "What happened here?"

This made Doug smile. "I thought it was your job to tell us." He walked to the door, which had a large hole in the middle and a busted lock. "Pretty straightforward. The vic is on the phone. The perp shoots through the door with an armor-piercing round."

"That's pretty heavy duty," I said, stunned.

"The first bullet hit the vic in the back," Casey said, taking over. "Our guess is that he answered the door without opening it, and the shooter shot him through the door as he returned to the desk."

Doug was nodding and pointing. "Then they hit the door with a battering ram. From the marks, I have to say it was a two-man model like the MPD uses. The shooter gets in, bullet in the head and he's done."

"How many perps were there?"

"Our victim—" Doug checked his notes "—Mr. Worling — wasn't much of a housekeeper. We tracked three sets of footprints. Male, one size ten, and two size twelve."

"Well, that means I'm above suspicion," I kidded. "My shoes are size fourteen."

"They left little to go on," Doug went on. "Gloved up, in and out, didn't take five minutes."

"Anyone hear gunfire?" I asked.

Bill smiled. "That was my first question. No report of gunfire, and no calls to the police. The perp could have used a silencer."

Doug shrugged. "If so, a very prepared perp. Between the battering ram, and the quick in and out, I think we can assume they were pros." Doug removed the face shield and pulled his white plastic hood off. "Anyway, I got other crime scenes. You'll get my report, Bill."

"Thanks, Doug," Bill said.

"I'll head off as well," Casey said. "I want to get the vic on my table and see if there's anything we didn't see in the initial exam."

"I guess my timing was good," I said, as Casey left. "I got here just as the scene clears out."

Bill pushed the door shut and stood next to it. "Are the conditions okay for you to do your thing?"

This made me smile. "The usual — a crime scene with no leads. I would say the conditions are the way they usually are when you call me in." I indicated the office chair. "Is it okay if I sit? The stairs wore me out."

"Sorry, I forgot you're still in recovery. How's the leg?"

The chair creaked as I sat. "Still weak compared to my left. Sometimes it just gives out on me, but I still have my cane."

"With its surprise inside?" Bill noted, with a lifted eyebrow.

My cane contains a very useful twenty-four inch sharpened sword connected to the metal cobra head at the top.

Since I carried the cane, which is classified as a weapon, and illegal in the state of New Jersey, Bill was one of the few people who knew I had the hidden blade.

"No surprises with what I'm about to do," I told him. "I'll put myself in a trance and tell you what I see."

"And I'll push you for more detail. I know the drill, Len."

I rolled the office chair to the beat-up desk.

"Doug said the victim was on the phone, so this might have been where he was sitting when he went to answer the door."

I put my hand on top of the desk and closed my eyes, focusing on my breath.

In… out, in… out.

I moved swiftly into an alpha state and opened my eyes to find myself in a very dark office, the brightening effects of the sunlight gone. Everything was in sepia tones, giving it the feel of an old Film Noire movie. I was seeing it as it was when a strong emotional experience occurred, and my mind interpreted that as a vision.

I saw a hand that was not mine put the phone handset onto the table and then a figure rose from my chair and moved toward the door.

I receive visions in many forms, but in this case, I heard nothing, even though the man I saw going to the door was moving his lips. This vision was limited to just images. Sometimes, I receive a vision with the full spectrum of sound and color, but at other times, it's like watching a silent film.

"What are you getting?" Bill asked.

Occasionally, I become so engrossed in the moment, I forget to keep talking.

"A man, I think the victim, is going to the door. I guess there was a knock or someone talking."

"No sound?" Bill asked, familiar with my different visions.

"No," I said, and watched the translucent man check the chain on the door, then open it a crack.

"Worling is opening the door — only a little, and it appears he's talking to someone in the hall."

"Do you see who he's talking to?"

I pushed myself up and moved so I could peer out the small door opening. "No, I only see someone in shadows. Tall, and from his build, a man."

"Fat or thin?" Bill asked.

"On the thin side. From his silhouette, I guess he's clean-shaven."

He shut the door, and I got a good look at our victim. Even in the sepia tones, I could see he got little sun, and had small eyes that took in the room as he turned. He had dark hair with a receding hairline, and coffee stains decorated his white shirt.

Everything appeared to slow down as a bullet smashed explosively through the heavy door. I saw splinters and smoke from the discharge. The bullet's impact left a ragged, charred hole in the door, indicative of its force. It hit the man in the back, and I watched his descent to the ground in agonizing slow-motion, blood staining his shirt as he crumpled forward.

I saw the door shake from repeated blows against it. The forceful strikes continued until the door finally gave way as the lock shattered and the safety chain snapped.

As the victim hit the floor, three men pushed their way into the office, one carrying the heavy steel battering ram.

"The killers burst in," I said to Bill.

"Can you see their faces?" Bill asked.

I tore my gaze away from the fallen victim and stared at the three men looming over him. The tallest of the trio, who wielded the gun, remained shrouded in darkness, concealing his features. His accomplice, who stood a few inches shorter, wore a black ski mask, hiding his identity. The victim and the man grasping the battering ram were the only individuals whose faces I could see. The latter had a brutish appearance, standing at a meager height of five-foot-five with a bald head and robust shoulders. He clutched the battering ram as though it weighed nothing, a toy in his gloved hand. I scrutinized his thick eyebrows, heavy jowls, and closely shaved head. I wanted to remember him.

"I can only see one of them."

As I watched the con man's last moments unfold in slow motion, the first man's gun fired once more, illuminating the surroundings. Even in this prolonged replay of events, the flash was brief. Yet, in that momentary glimpse, I studied the shooter's appearance. He had a clean-shaven face, cropped brown hair, a strong jawline, and a sharply defined nose. His visage stirred a sense of recognition, but I couldn't place him.

The vision abruptly ended.

I was sitting in the sparse office with Bill still near the door. Dappled sunlight came in through the dirty window.

I took a deep breath. I felt light-headed, as if I hadn't been drawing in enough air for a full minute.

"It's gone," I reported.

"Anything useful?" Bill asked.

"I got a good look at one man, and a quick glimpse of another. Doug Millbank was right. They used a police style battering ram, four handles, black. The guy I could see held it like it weighed nothing."

Bill shook his head. "Those things are at least twenty-five pounds. Two sets of handles, huh? They'd need a pair of men to get through that solid wood door. Anything else you can tell me from what you saw?"

"It went down very much like Doug and Casey speculated. The victim went to the door, opened it a crack and on his way back, the perp shot him through the door. I would guess that the other two swung the battering ram, and it broke the lock and the door chain. Then they moved in, shot the victim in the head, and left."

"Nice to know our forensic chief is so accurate."

"There was one thing," I went on, not sure if I should share this part with Bill. "The other two were in shadow, but when the gun went off for the kill shot, I got a brief look at the shooter from the flash."

"Can you describe him?"

"No, the flash went by too fast. But there was something familiar about the guy."

"Would it help to go through the mugshot database? See if it is someone you've seen before?"

I shrugged. "I'll be honest with you, I don't think I will find him there."

"How come?"

I frowned. "Because wherever I saw this man, it wasn't from a crime."

Just after three, I made my way to Mindy's Diner for my lesson with Anna Sokolov. Hurriedly, I ascended the stairs of the single-story brick building surrounded by a sprawling parking lot.

Inside, Carl Sokolov, the diner's owner, stood behind the cash register. With an average build, dark hair, and a prominent widow's peak, he sported a bushy mustache and thick stubble on his chin from a few days without shaving. As usual, food stains besmirched his sleeves, given his role both running the diner and assisting with its culinary endeavors.

"My wonder man," he bellowed in greeting and came around the counter to shake my hand. He lowered his voice. "I want to thank you for getting Anna a scholarship to your college."

I hesitated. "Mr. Sokolov—"

"Carl, call me Carl."

"Carl, I am doing everything I can to get her in my program, but it's not all completed yet."

He put his hand on my back as he escorted me to the separate room in the diner, usually reserved for large groups and private events. "You are also getting her a job, a paying job as your assistant on top of it! I wish her mother were alive to know she is going to college. She would be so proud."

I was familiar with Anna's home life. Her wanderlust had allowed her to be abducted by a group of men who planned to use her as a prostitute. It was her unique psychic ability reaching out to me that allowed McGee, myself, and the FBI New Jersey Task Force to save her.

"I must tell you, last few months, working with you, things are better. She don't have those headaches no more, and she don't complain like she used to. And, you are getting her a scholarship to your college—"

I nodded at this and worried. I hope that scholarship will come through.

He went on. "I just want you to know you have made life much better."

"I'm glad to hear that, Carl."

"Now, go, she waits," he said and headed back to the register as I went through the door to the party room.

Anna was a gifted psychic of such sheer power, I stood in awe of her. I finally understood why my mentor, Doctor Kohl, became so excited when he met me. When you find someone with so much raw talent, you become enthused about who they will become and how they will use such abilities wisely.

I wanted to get Anna to major in parapsychology under my tutelage, and offer her a stipend as my assistant. This allowed me to help her and monitor her as she struggled to control her gifts.

Anna was sitting at a table with a stainless steel carafe next to a teacup on a saucer and a small container for cream.

Anna met my eyes and smiled, raising the carafe. "I know you like coffee in the afternoon."

I smiled as I sat. "That's very thoughtful of you, Anna."

She blushed and looked away. This shy seventeen-year-old had a problem accepting compliments.

I filled the teacup with steaming coffee from the carafe and added cream. "I want to commend you. You're not leaking your thoughts all over the place. I detected nothing as I came into the room."

She smiled and blushed a deep scarlet. "I've been practicing every day, like you said."

"It shows. I'm glad you're taking our lessons seriously. I had to fight you in the beginning."

"I realized that if I want the scholarship and to be your TA, I need to be responsible. Acting like a kid won't work. I have to be a grown-up."

"Well, you can still be a kid now and then."

She raised her chin and looked at me with the seriousness only a teenager can possess. "No, I've got special gifts, and it's my job to learn to use them. Like you do."

I didn't want to burst her bubble and mention how dramatic she was being. Instead, I merely said, "That's very flattering, but I just do what I'm needed to do. Let's get started."

I took her through a simple guided meditation and some of her thoughts 'leaked', which meant I received them. However, she did very well.

"How were your grades this quarter?" I asked after she was back to full consciousness. Since Anna was a senior in high school, she received her grades four times a year instead of twice a year, like a college student.

"I just got my third quarter report card," she gushed. "All A's."

"That's excellent. Once again, I'm impressed."

She met my eyes, and a thought came to me.

I love you...

I felt the best approach would be to respond in kind.

Anna, I can hear you...

She lowered her eyes and flushed red.

Sorry...

I continued projecting my thoughts, not bothering to speak.

Your mental barriers are the most important skill you can learn...

She grimaced. *I know, I know...*

I spoke aloud. "Okay, so we should figure out next week while you're on vacation from school. Same schedule?"

Anna fixed her eyes on mine, and I saw she was concentrating. *Why do we have to talk at all...?*

I frowned. *What do you mean...*

I mean, we can talk like this, completely, freely and no one can hear us but each other...

I smiled and said, "Because it would look weird to see the pair of us staring at each other and not saying anything."

Despite her efforts to maintain a serious demeanor, she couldn't help but let out a giggle.

"Besides," I went on, "when you communicate in a purely mental conversation, you may reveal more than you intend. That's why we're working on your mental barriers. You need to shield your mind. Our innermost thoughts are the only private thing we truly have."

"I understand. Thank you, Len."

"Doing anything fun for the break?"

She shook her head and sighed dramatically. "Working here at the diner, which will help my dad, what with Easter coming."

"I know. We have the Passover seder on Thursday."

Her eyes widened. "Will your brother the magician be there?"

"I'm not sure, he has shows in Las Vegas." Standing up to go, I added, "I'll see you Monday, Anna."

"Oh, can I ask you about something?"

I paused. "Sure. What's up?"

"A lady was here asking about you. She said she was from the DOJ."

"An agent from the Department of Justice?" This got my attention. "What did she look like?"

"Well, she was tall and—"

I held up a hand. "No, Anna. Send it to me. Picture her in your mind and then share it with me."

As Anna nodded and closed her eyes, I felt her dredging up a memory. Soon enough, I too visualized it vividly in my mind's eye. The recollection was that of a woman, early thirties, looking pale with edgy facial features. She wore her long, dark tresses tied in a sophisticated ponytail. She wore a black pantsuit, and from the cut of the garment, I was sure she carried a weapon in a shoulder holster.

"I see her," I said. "What was she talking to you about?"

Anna opened her eyes. "She wanted to know about those men that abducted me and how you helped save me."

I must have looked concerned, because Anna quickly added, "Oh, I didn't tell her about you and I reading each other's thoughts."

"Which is how I found you," I said.

"I figured you didn't want anyone to know about that. I mean, I've never even told my dad."

I relaxed. "That's good. But that incident was years ago, and I worked with the FBI to find you. Why is the DOJ interested in that case now?"

"I don't know, but she made my dad real mad."

"Why?"

Anna couldn't meet my eyes, but I felt her thoughts leak through.

She suggested that you... messed with me...

"She what?" I bellowed.

Anna looked stricken. "I told her the truth, that you've tried nothing, ever. My dad was so mad, he told her the interview was over."

I was still livid. "Did you get a name?"

"Yes, she even gave me her card." Anna reached into her pocket and pulled out the small white cardboard rectangle.

I took it from her. It held an address and cell phone number:

Agent Harper Montgomery
Department Of Justice

"I'm going to have to find out about this Agent Montgomery person," I muttered, as I put the number into my phone and handed the card back to Anna.

3. EVEN-HANDED

I drove home fuming. I wanted to phone the agent immediately and demand she explain why she was asking about me and give her a piece of my mind. It was cruel to bring such things up with Anna. She had come close to being sexually assaulted, if I hadn't found where they were keeping her and the other abducted girls.

To suggest that I would take advantage of her made me furious.

Once home, I took time to meditate and calm down, deciding to contact Agent Montgomery tomorrow. Jyanette was finishing her first day in the DA's office, and Mrs. Higgins was going to a lot of trouble to make dinner.

I could clear up any problem with the agent the next day.

By the time Jyanette pulled into the circular drive, I was back to myself.

Mrs. Higgins outdid herself, presenting a full turkey dinner, with stuffing, sweet potatoes, and even dessert. She and Jyanette each had a glass of wine, while I stayed with the water.

Alcohol deadens my psychic abilities. For years I used it to quiet my mind — until I became a full-blown alcoholic during my years living in California. I learned to master my psychic gifts and avoided drinking, as one drink would only lead to another and another.

I watched Jyanette and Mrs. Higgins have their one glass of wine without a twinge, and we talked of our day, joking and laughing.

"How was it going back, really?" I asked.

She sighed. "I forgot that the politics of the DA's office aren't any better than the Department of Justice."

"Do folks want to involve ye in their wee dramas?" Mrs. Higgins asked.

"Not yet, but I can see it coming. This job is only for three months, so I hope to stay out of the personality issues."

"How did the District Attorney feel about you returning?"

"He was grateful, as he needs the help, and was really glad to see me. He knows I can do the job." She paused. "You have said nothing about the fresh case you're on with McGee."

"A murder — three men broke into an office and shot a con man. I could see one man clearly, and I'm meeting Chuck Norman in the morning to work on a sketch."

"How excitin'," Mrs. Higgins said.

"You're not involving yourself in anything dangerous, for once?"

"Not so far."

"How was yer lesson with Anna?" Mrs. Higgins asked. "That was today, wasn't it?"

"She's making progress," I said. "I still don't have an answer on her scholarship, but I'm hoping it will all go through."

"Oh, it's a kind thing ye're doing, helping her," Mrs. Higgins said. "Her father works so hard, and him not having to pay for college will be a help."

I grew serious. "A weird thing today, though."

"Isn't weird what you do?" Jyanette said, amiably.

I smiled. "Usually." I grew serious. "But an agent from the DOJ met with Anna and her father to ask about her abduction."

"That was years ago," Mrs. Higgins said. "Aren't those criminals all in prison?"

"By any chance, was it Harper Montgomery?" Jyanette asked.

I turned to Jyanette, surprised. "Why yes, but how do you know?"

"She contacted the DA's office today and left me a message to get in touch with her," Jyanette said, taking another sip of wine. "She used to work with Marcus."

"Marcus Calvin?" I said. "That FBI agent you were dating?"

During a terrible time in our lives, Jyanette moved back to her parents in Virginia and took a job with the DOJ. She also dated FBI agent Marcus Calvin, until the DOJ enlisted my aid to stop a group of white supremacists.

She was also on the assignment, in fact recommended me.

During that case, our passion for each other was reawakened. We decided we wanted to be with each other, and Agent Calvin went back to DC without her.

I frowned. "You think this is a revenge thing for getting you to come back to me?"

"I don't know what it's about. I didn't have time to talk to her," Jyanette said.

"Anna got the impression that Agent Montgomery thought I did something inappropriate to her."

"What?" Mrs. Higgins gasped, and I saw the anger in her eyes. "Oh, the nerve!"

"I'm sure Anna was mistaken," Jyanette said. "Why would a DOJ agent claim that?"

After dinner, Jyanette and I headed for the bedroom and into each other's arms. After the teasing in the morning, we were both quite ready. Jyanette and I were getting into sync in our lovemaking, becoming experts at tantalizing each other in just the right ways.

Immediately afterwards, both of us still panting from our exertions, we lay in the big bed staring at the ceiling.

"So, worth the wait?" she sighed.

"Always," I gasped. "I wanted to run something by you, but I don't know how you'll react."

She rose on her elbow. "You want to ask something I won't like, and you wait until after we make love to tell me? Just like a man."

"I'm serious," I said, though I couldn't help but smile. "It's about the case. In my vision, I caught a quick glimpse of one man, and he seemed... familiar."

"Any chance you can figure out who it was?"

"I have an idea, but I wanted to run it past you, to make sure it won't bother you."

"Why does that sound so ominous?"

"I'm thinking I could do a hypnotic regression with Kate Yearling. She could help me focus on the face, figure out who it is."

It was silent in the bed, our breathing the only sound.

Finally, she spoke. "Kate Yearling, who was your lover while I was in DC?"

"Come on, Jyanette. You know she's an experienced hypnotherapist and an FBI profiler," I explained. "You and I were broken up when she and I had our... thing."

"Is that what you're calling it? A thing?"

"I didn't know you were the jealous type."

"I'm not, but we've been living in a very peaceful bubble the last month and a half," she complained. "Now I'm back in the DA's office and you want to work with Kate again?" She rolled away from me to stare at the ceiling. "I still have nightmares about the night that monster imprisoned us. I can still hear her screams when he... when he..."

The previous year, a madman imprisoned her and Kate. He removed Kate's scalp with surgical tools while Jyanette listened helplessly. Kate almost died. In fact, it was a miracle she was alive and functional.

I held her tight, her firm body next to mine. "Shh, it's okay."

Her eyes were damp. "I know. I know you have to do what you do, but that doesn't mean I don't get scared about it."

"I'll be fine," I said. "Should I make an appointment with Kate?"

"If it will help," she said and then flashed me a small grin. "If she makes a pass at you, I'll break her arm."

"Are you marking your territory?"

"Damn straight," she whispered, and kissed me firmly. She pulled the light blanket up to her neck. "Now, I'm going to get some sleep. I have a busy day tomorrow."

I rolled over myself and closed my eyes, dropping into a peaceful doze.

It didn't stay peaceful for long.

One problem I have when I take on a fresh case is that although I assume I let the situations go when I go to sleep, my mind does not. I spend my day with protective boundaries up to prevent unwanted thoughts and impressions from constantly bombarding me. But when I'm asleep, my protective walls are down, and my psychic abilities continue to reach out to find answers to the situation in which I am embroiled.

I found myself in that dreary office again, looking at the body of Alex Worling lying on the floor.

I moved to the broken door and looked out to see the three men walking quietly away down the hall. They moved as a group, casually, not in a rush. In silhouette, I noted that the gun still in the man's hand possessed an extra-long barrel, and I realized something I had missed in my psychic vision.

The gun had a silencer. That explained why no one called the police about the sound of gunfire.

The team of men reached the door for the stairway and were gone.

I turned back to see that Worling was no longer on the floor, but sitting in the wheeled chair at the desk, the very one I used that afternoon. He still had the bullet hole in his head. In fact, they blew off half of his face. I saw the bone of his damaged skull and blood dripping from the awful wound. His one good eye watched me as I stepped back into the room and stood gawking at him.

"So what do you do?" he asked, his voice was strong and undamaged.

It's amazing how much everything feels real in a dream, and you have an overwhelming need to play your part.

"I'm an investigator," I said. "I'm trying to find out who shot you."

"Good luck with that," he replied, amused. He turned back to his desk, his hand going to the headset of the phone.

I saw the gaping wound in his back and the hole that went through his head.

"Do you know who those men were?" I asked, trying to focus on him and not the injuries to his body.

"I don't have a clue," he said as he picked up the receiver.

"They were pros. Do you owe money to the mob or someone who might go this far?"

He hung up the phone and revolved in the chair to look at me. "I don't owe nobody nothing. I do scams, that's my gig. Getting money anywhere I can." He gesticulated at the surrounding office. "It's not like I got high overhead."

"But someone wanted you dead. Who was it?"

"How do I know?" he responded with a shrug. "I know I want a lot of people dead. I sometimes think what it would be like to be way up high, pointing down at people with a rifle." He leaned forward and held his arms as if he held a rifle in them, miming looking through a scope. "Man, that would be amazing. Looking down a scope and knowing you could just take out anyone you saw with a pull of a trigger. Maybe those guys just liked that feeling."

"There must have been some motivation for them to go to all this trouble," I suggested.

He shrugged. "Maybe they're the sons of some old lady I ripped off. Maybe they worked for the phone company and tracked me down."

I nodded. Officer Galland was looking into the phone records on the computers. Maybe this was an angle that would help him.

"I tell you one thing, though," the animated corpse went on. "I ain't going to be the last one."

"No, he won't be," a voice said, and I turned to see the silhouette of the shooter as he pushed the door open and raised the gun to point it at my face.

I jumped up in bed, my breathing ragged, my heart racing as adrenaline coursed through my body.

I was grateful for the sun behind the bedroom shades and the sound of the shower running. Jyanette's side of the bed was empty and a glance at the clock informed me it was after seven.

As I fought to calm down, I was glad I hadn't exploded awake in the middle of the night, as I had so often in the past. The last thing Jyanette needed was me waking her up.

I pulled myself out of bed, threw on pajamas and a robe, and peeked into the bathroom. Behind the semi-transparent shower curtain, I saw Jyanette's silhouette. Even with the distortion of the curtain, her taut body was amazing to behold.

"Should I get you coffee?" I yelled, to be heard over the sound of the running water.

"Len, you're up!" she said enthusiastically. "Yes, please."

I strode down the hall to the kitchen, where Mrs. Higgins was having a breakfast of baked beans and eggs.

"Ooh, Doctor, ye're up early," she said.

"Having an Irish breakfast, Mrs. Higgins?" I smiled.

"Not a full Irish," she replied. "But I had a hankerin' for eggs and beans this morning. Would ye or Jyanette like some?"

I smiled as I poured two mugs of coffee. "Not for me, Mrs. Higgins. I don't get the bean thing with eggs."

"It's actually quite lovely."

I paused as I added cream to my mug. "I had a troubling dream last night — or I guess it was this morning."

"About the case ye're working on?" she asked. "That's not unexpected now, is it?"

"No, except I was talking to a man with his head half blown off."

"It's the usual, then?" she observed with a grin.

"In the dream, the killer got the drop on me, and was about to shoot me when I woke up."

"Ah! I would interpret that to mean that ye have to be careful and watch yer back."

I took a sip of my coffee. "I didn't think this would be a dangerous case. You know getting injured on cases is what broke up Jyanette and me the first time we dated."

"Aye," she said and nodded. "So ye'd best be aware of when your abilities be warnin' ye, Doctor."

I took the mug of coffee and headed back toward my end of the house.

Mrs. Higgins was right, of course. Maybe it wasn't the best solution for me to run headlong into situations where I could get hurt. I had to remember that my job was as a consultant and give up the idea that I needed to play hero.

I walked into the bathroom and paused. Jyanette was bent over the sink, stark naked, looking at herself in the mirror. My heart — as well as other body parts — jumped in appreciation.

Primly, I placed her mug on the sink, but once my hand was free, I couldn't resist patting her amazing rear end.

"None of that," she chided. "You got yours."

"That was hours ago," I said, continuing my caress, as lustful thoughts entered my brain.

She turned around and kissed me with a passion that would have awakened a dead man. "I love you, but you know how long I take to do my hair. Please get out."

I sighed and left, returning to the bedroom. I grabbed my tablet and went to a local news site as I sat in bed and drank my coffee.

My case was all over the news with blaring headlines:

MURDERED SCAMMER!
BLOOMDALE MAN SHOT EXECUTION STYLE!

There was very little information, as Bill and the Bloomdale Police kept a lid on most of the facts.

One reporter on the site for the NJ Times-Ledger had quotes from anonymous sources. These claimed that "mob enforcers cleaning up for their bosses" murdered the man. The reporter's overall conclusion was that if criminals are killing criminals, who cares?

I frowned at this. From my vision, I didn't get the impression the men I saw were with the mob. Considering the gun with the silencer and the battering ram they used to get in, perhaps they could be. They were professional and were in and out quickly. Didn't that suggest paid killers?

Why go after a cheap grifter like Alex Worling? Yes, the guy was ripping off people, and possessed some strange ideas of using a sniper rifle on anonymous strangers. But why would the mob care enough to send hired killers?

Jyanette came out of the bathroom, her hair finished.

She dressed in a light blouse, knee-length dark blue skirt, and matching jacket, looking every bit the lawyer. She was ready to go into court and face any judge.

I got out of bed, and she kissed me quickly.

"Don't forget, we're having dinner with the Baines' tonight," I told her. "Call me if you're running late."

This made her lift an eyebrow. "I'm the one with the steady schedule. Best if you call me if you're running late."

As she strode towards her car, I stood at the doorway in my pajamas and robe, watching her drive away. It was one of those warm April days, with the sweet scents of spring filling the air and the sweltering heat of summer still a distance away.

It filled me with a peculiar sense of peace. Losing my fiancée, Cathy Garber, nine years ago had been a crushing blow. We'd just graduated from medical school and planned to tie the knot before starting our medical residency at Rutger's Medical Center.

It was the night when my abilities manifested.

Becoming a surgeon like my father was my goal, but when I developed powerful psychic abilities, it left me unprepared. I grew up in a household with Conservative Jewish parents. My childhood was quite ordinary and my fascination with my father's profession motivated my ambition to pursue medicine. Filled with excitement, I pushed myself to graduate high school a year ahead of schedule. I then completed pre-med courses in a mere two years, followed by medical school in just three.

On a wet evening, while returning to Mountainview from a party on Schooley's Mountain, everything took a turn. I witnessed an enormous demon standing in the middle of the road, compelling me to dodge it, resulting in a collision that took Cathy's life and severely injured my right leg.

It wasn't the end of the strange occurrences. As I recuperated, I realized I could tune into other people's thoughts. It was like a constant murmur of whispers encircling me at all times.

When I went to Cathy's funeral, still in a wheelchair pushed by her brother, Terry, I saw an old woman walking around the room during the service. She seemed out of place in the funeral home with all those mourners listening to the preacher as he spoke fondly of Cathy. Everyone ignored the poor woman as she came up to me and asked if I could help her.

The pastor was in the middle of the sermon, so I quietly said, "I can't help you now. Maybe after the service."

The woman smiled. "I'll wait in the hall." She walked away.

Terry bent close and whispered, "Who are you talking to?"

"The old woman," I whispered back. "She was lost."

He glanced around the room quickly. "What old woman?"

That was when a chill ran up my spine.

She was a ghost.

When we left the service, Terry pushed my wheelchair. I kept my head down and my eyes closed so as not to see her. I hoped people would assume it was my grief.

Faced with the unsettling ability to hear thoughts and see spirits, this made me question my sanity. I resolved to pursue psychiatric studies in a fellowship program in California. One night, I was fortunate to be at a speech delivered by Doctor Fritz Kohl. He spoke about parapsychology and talked of people who had unique gifts that allowed them to see and hear things most people could not.

I spoke with him after that speech, told him what I was going through, and begged to join his program. It was only there, under his tutelage, that I trained my abilities to make them a useful tool instead of a burden.

My old friend, Jon Baines, brought me to Garden State University for a speech and then helped me create a parapsychology department. It was during this time that I began using my unique talents to assist Bill in putting a stop to criminal activities.

I also met Jyanette.

Our love story took a dark turn when a monster abducted her. The man who held her captive was no longer human — he succumbed entirely to the sinister influence of a demon. The traumatic event shattered our bond, and she found out she was pregnant while I was working on a case in California.

It all came to a head when a woman seeking vengeance caused Jyanette to abort with so much internal damage, the doctors told her she could never have children. She left Mountainview and me, and I thought it was all over.

I started drinking again once she left.

When we ended up working together for the Department of Justice, it was impossible to deny that the sparks were still there. She finally accepted my request to marry her, and the last two months were the happiest I'd been in years.

During those two months, our usual routines didn't consume us. I was not working on any cases, and she had recently lost her job. It felt like a blissful honeymoon, with endless moments spent together. There were no thoughts of terrorism, perplexing criminal dilemmas, or her responsibilities as a lawyer. It was simply the two of us.

Now, we had to start real life again, both working jobs and me working with McGee. I understood that taking on cases might trigger all of her fears.

With my innate abilities, I could help to bring justice to the victims while also thwarting the murderers' plans. It was imperative that I trust in the purpose of my unique talents and use them to make a difference.

I had to find out about this DOJ agent who was looking into me.

I headed into the shower to get ready and head out to the MPD.

I'd worked with Chuck Norman, a talented police sketch artist, in the past. He was a former art student at GSU, then got hired part time by MPD. In just the last few months, he'd worked with Officer Galland to create an app anyone could use to do sketches of suspects. Chuck was now in great demand, flying all over the country and teaching police departments how to use his app.

"The nose is a little smaller," I said, as Chuck and I sat in front of a large monitor while he manipulated the image on a tablet computer. "And the face is a little rounder."

Chuck made changes, and the image shifted right before my eyes. The software combined his talent at capturing the look of a suspect with the ease of a flexible computer program.

"There, that's it," I told him and he completed the image, sending it to a nearby printer. "How's the launch of your software going?"

He continued to look at the screen. "Good. Lots of traveling. It's a limited market, but I make it up with the training sessions."

Chuck was a shy guy, and this was one of the longest string of words I'd heard him put together. I guess that having to go meet people and explain the software was actually getting him out of his shell.

"Are you enjoying yourself?" I asked tentatively.

"I have more time for my art," he said. "And the money is better. But I still like to come here and help."

"Well, it's great. You and Galland built the program?"

"I created the concepts of how the different body parts should look and how the user can adjust them. Galland wrote the code, and both of us are doing well off it, but I mostly go do the training because Galland prefers to stay here."

I nodded. Ben Galland was a cop, through and through. Even though he could make more money going around the country teaching software, he would be unwilling to give up being an officer.

"What kind of art do you do?" I asked, realizing that I'd known Chuck for two years, and did not know what he did in his own time.

"A mix," he said as he closed the laptop and put it into a bag. "Oils, watercolor, even some murals."

"I hope I get to see it sometime."

"I have a show coming up this weekend," he said and pulled a postcard out of his bag. It showed Chuck in front of a large painting of a sunset on the beach. The water was foaming onto the sand in the foreground, an incoming wave further back. Beyond that was the sinking yellow ball of the setting sun in the distance. He'd colored the sky in flaming reds and oranges, fading into the darkening blue above. The painting looked more like a photograph than the work of an artist's brushes.

The caption read: The Art of Charles W. Norman.

I think my jaw fell open, because the painting was so beautiful, and I was so unaware of my associate's talent.

"This looks amazing," I said, impressed. With his short hair and boyish good looks, Chuck seemed very young, yet he had mastered such powerful skills and a sense of composition.

"Come to the show if you can," Chuck said, and pointed at the dates. "The opening night is Saturday, and it's a wine and cheese thing." He made a note on the tablet in his hands. "I'll get you on the list of invited guests."

Jyanette and I had not been out in weeks. I was pretty flush from the sale of my novel and a recent reward I received for the capture of a criminal mastermind. We were watching our money as we had a wedding to plan and pay for.

"That would be nice," I said. "My fiancée and I would love to come."

At that moment, the printer spat out the finished rendering of the face Chuck and I created using his program.

He wheeled his chair over to the printer and held up the print. Chuck was good when he'd been a sketch artist, but the computer-generated image almost looked three dimensional.

"Is this your guy?" Chuck asked.

I nodded, and a shiver ran down my spine, as well as the feeling that I would stare into that face again far too soon.

4. IGNOBLE INTEGRITY

After I made copies of Chuck's drawing, I took a moment to call Kate Yearling. Our communication ceased in February, when we realized we didn't match well. Noticing the way I gazed at Jyanette each time she appeared, Kate decided she wanted to find someone who would look at her the same way.

That person wasn't me.

As we went our separate ways, we left behind no ill will. Our relationship provided her with the support she needed during her recovery to help her move past her self-doubt. She helped me by being brutally honest about my drinking.

She also was right — Jyanette was the one who sent my heart spinning. I liked Kate, certainly respected her and enjoyed her company, but it wasn't love, and both of us knew it.

"Well, hello Doctor Wise," Kate said as she answered her phone.

"And hello to you, Doctor Yearling," I replied. "Am I calling at a bad time?"

"No, just working on a profile for a suspected serial killer in South Jersey."

Having once been a rising star as an FBI profiler based in Washington, Kate now worked with the FBI New Jersey Task Force in Morris Plains. Her previous career took a dangerous turn when she barely escaped with her life during a confrontation at Blackshale Asylum. The man surgically removed her scalp and left her for dead.

The doctors in New Jersey saved her life, and the agency transferred her here to remain under their care. A year later, in what some might call a miracle, she was back to her full-time status and had kept the brilliance that made her an exceptional profiler.

"I need a favor if you can fit me in," I said.

"What's it about?"

"A homicide in Bloomdale with the MPD. Pros gunned down a con man."

"Sounds like a case of a syndicate wanting to remove competition."

"Might be. In a vision, I got a good look at one guy, but I saw another in the flash of his gun, and he seemed familiar. I was wondering if you could hypnotize me and help me recall the face."

"Hm, an interesting idea. Do you have any classes today?"

"No, it's Friday and I'm off."

"I could squeeze you in about three. I have an hour then."

"How's the work going?"

"Very well. I'm feeling like myself again. And as you know, there is no shortage of murder and mayhem."

Upon finishing the call, I retrieved the copies of the suspect and headed to Bill's office. As I approached, the door swung open, and out stepped Dan Harris, captain of the MPD. Harris is an African-American man with grey hair and a physique that resembles that of a power lifter, and he exudes a sense of authority that commands respect.

Harris spoke harshly. "So we have to make space for someone out of town and give them all our files?"

"Afraid so, sir," Bill said.

"It's the last thing we need," Harris complained. "Stay on it and let me know what happens."

Without acknowledging me, Harris strode towards his corner office and forcefully slammed the door.

Bill saw me, and I held out the sheet with the drawing of the suspect. He took the paper and scowled at it. "This is the guy you saw at the scene?"

I nodded. "The one that was in the light."

Bill screwed up his face. "I'll get it in the system, see if we get any hits from facial recognition."

I stepped close and glanced at Captain Harris' office. "Is everything all right, Bill?"

"We have someone from Washington coming in with a warrant to go through our files," Bill growled. "Captain Harris doesn't like it."

"Wait, is it someone from the DOJ?" I asked.

"Yeah, did you get one of your psychic flashes?" Bill said.

"No, there's been an agent who contacted Jyanette and talked to Anna Sokolov," I said. "Her last name is Montgomery."

Bill nodded. "Yes, Harper Montgomery. What's it all about, Len?"

"I don't know," I said. "I was hoping it was nothing, but if she wants to come to the MPD, it can't be good."

"She has a warrant to go through all our records for the last two years."

"A warrant?" I paused. "That's about how long I've been working with the MPD."

"Yes. Harris isn't happy about it, and neither am I. What is she looking for?"

"I have no idea."

"She setting up shop here in the next few days. What's on your plate today?"

"Kate Yearling has made time for a hypnotic regression session, to see if I can recognize the man I saw in the muzzle flash."

Bill nodded. "Good. If we can get more information, maybe we can find who did this."

"If these guys were out-of-town pros, they could be long gone by now," I offered.

McGee's jaw became firm, and he shook his head. "I don't think so. I have a hunch."

"Go easy, Bill. I'm the psychic on the team," I joked. "Let's see if Kate can help me."

With a nod, Bill went back into his office and I headed out to the parking lot and into my van.

Why did this Montgomery woman want to go through the MPD files? Our case files were complete with my involvement if I worked it. However, the files contained no mention of my abilities, as that information wasn't relevant.

I started my custom van, a gift from a grateful client, and got the vehicle into traffic. The vehicle was state-of the-art, and equipped with hand controls, because in the past my paralyzed right leg couldn't work pedals. Even though my leg had a knee joint again, I was used to the hand controls and preferred them.

I had time before my meeting with Kate, so I headed to GSU to check in at the main office. I wanted to look over the plans for the graduating class, as well as the upcoming fall semester.

I drove slowly, relishing the fresh spring air and the delightful vistas that even busy Mountainview offered. I pulled in the main entrance, which took me on a long winding road through this former estate. Stone walls bordered the roadway, with vines and greenery hanging from them. I passed newer parking lots and newer buildings side by side with older ones. They all maintained the classic architecture of the early twentieth century.

I reached Alumni Green and College Hall, the business and administration building, and pulled into a convenient handicap parking spot. College Hall is the original structure from the estate, with fine marble floors, carved wood doors, and soaring stone archways. Making my way through the impressive entrance, my cane tapped the floor, giving my right leg any support it might need.

I wanted to visit my Teaching Assistant, Teddy Santos, but first stopped by the Associate Dean and my best friend, Jon Baines. As I stepped into his outer office, Trisha Heywood looked up from her desk. Trisha was Jon's assistant and the one who kept the entire university running like clockwork.

"Hey Trisha, how are you?" I said.

"Surprised to see you. I thought the only time you were here was during classes," she said with a smile.

I rubbed the back of my neck. "Jyanette and I have been getting… um… reacquainted."

She rose. "You don't have to make excuses for me. Though you should check in now and then. The only thing I've seen from you are emails."

"I promise to be more visible as the semester ends. Is Jon in?"

She moved to the door. "Let me check on Dean Baines."

That was Trisha, always so proper. She could have called him Jon in my presence, but she wanted to maintain the formality.

She opened the door and said, "Are you available for Doctor Wise?"

"Who?" Jon boomed. My old friend had a voice made for the stage. Considering he spent a lot of time making speeches and begging for money, it suited him. "Do I have someone on staff named Wise?"

"Hilarious, Jon," I yelled back.

Trisha smiled at me. "You may go in."

I stepped past Trisha with a nod and walked into the wood-paneled room of Associate Dean Baines.

Jon stood up from the piles of papers on his desk and put out his hand. "Hey, Len. Sit down."

I took his hand in a firm handshake. "Sorry I haven't been around as much as I should—"

"We're still on for dinner tonight, right?"

"Yes, Jyanette and I will be there."

"Good. We can catch up then. Now, as far as not being around the campus, you've kept up with your classes. That was the important thing. The operation on your leg and that incident with those terrorists kept you pretty busy. I know you can't talk about it, but how much danger were we really in?"

"As you said, I can't talk about it."

"All right, but if Jenny ties you to your chair and tortures you until you talk, don't blame me," he responded. "So, we heard about your engagement. I'll have you know Jenny did a happy dance when she heard."

Jenny was Jon's wife, as petite as he is large. She has been my one-woman cheerleading squad since we first met two years earlier.

"Yeah, Jyanette and I have mostly been keeping to ourselves and staying home."

"With you in recovery, you couldn't spend your days running around. At least you don't have that wheelchair anymore. We had to move so many of your classes."

"I prefer my regular room, even with all the stairs. Look Jon, I wanted to stop by to talk about the paperwork I submitted for Anna Sokolov."

"Yeah, I saw that. You want to promote a full scholarship and give her the Teaching Assistant position? I know Santos is graduating this year, but Anna will be a freshman. Don't you want a junior or senior if they have to take over your classes to cover for you?"

"Jon, Anna is one of the most gifted psychics I've ever met. I think I can learn from her as well as teach her."

Jon shook his head. "I don't know, Len. I mean, you sent her grades from Mountainview High School, and they're good enough, but I don't see her at the level you set."

"It doesn't take a genius or someone as driven as I am to be a good parapsychologist. I think she needs some real-world experience and practice, but I—"

"Len, why don't you send her out to Doctor Kohl and the University of Southern California for her first year? Kohl could take care of any rough edges and train her like he did you."

"She needs to be close to home. She's all her father has, and she works in his diner on the weekends."

Jon raised his arms in frustration. "Seems like you've decided."

"Teddy's willing to work with her this summer, get her up to speed on running my office."

"How are her computer skills?"

"Not nearly as good as Teddy's."

Jon exhaled out a long breath as a hiss. "I can't say that I agree with your choice, but it is your department, and if she can do the work, I don't have any objections. I'll have to bring her name to the scholarship committee. It's possible we could get her the Presidential Award Scholarship."

"That sounds great, Jon."

He shook his head. "Len, I should warn you, those scholarships are highly competitive. The requirements include high academic achievement and community involvement. Believe it or not, psychic ability is not the requisite."

Now it was my turn to sigh. "Jon, she's a bright kid and had a tough life. She and her father moved here from the Ukraine, her mother's dead. She mastered English and excelled in school, but she had to work at the diner to help. Plus, after the abduction two years ago…"

"I remember that."

"I'm working with her one-on-one a couple of times a week."

"But once again, a hard-luck story doesn't replace academic performance or community service," Jon said. "I'll see what I can do."

"Thanks Jon, I appreciate your help."

I headed out of his office, waved at Trisha, and went back into the hall to get to my little office on the same floor. Trisha was right. I hadn't been to my office for a while, because of the bulky wheelchair and rushing home every day to be with Jyanette.

Trisha and Jon didn't mention the DOJ agent, which I was glad about. Maybe she hadn't contacted them. I decided it was time to take the bull by the horns and speak to her.

The entire situation annoyed me.

I sat down behind my oversized desk that took up much of the room. Jon got the desk because it was the only one I could fit my paralyzed leg under comfortably. Now that I had more flexibility, perhaps I could exchange the massive wooden contrivance for something sleek and more useful.

I booted up my desk computer and pulled the agent's number up on my phone. After two rings, it went to voicemail.

Great.

"Hello Agent Montgomery, this is Doctor Leonard Wise. I understand you've been looking into my background. I would be happy to speak to you and clear up any misunderstanding about my work."

I recited my number and ended the call, more annoyed than before.

"Hey, Doc," a voice said from the doorway.

I looked up to see my Teaching Assistant, Téodoro Santos, in the doorway. Teddy had long, straight hair that hung to his shoulders and thick glasses that magnified his eyes, making them appear much larger than they truly were.

"Teddy!" I exclaimed. "How are you doing?"

He sauntered into the room. Teddy gained a lot of poise and self-confidence since I met him almost two years earlier. I was glad to see it. He had become a man who was comfortable in his own skin.

He smiled at me. "I think I might make the Dean's list for graduation."

"That's great, Teddy," I said, genuinely pleased. "If I can do anything to help, let me know."

He looked me over from head to toe. "Are you back now? I mean, you know, no wheelchair, able to get around and everything?"

"Yes. I'm sorry I haven't been more communicative. Are you still available to help Anna get up to speed this summer?"

"Yeah, I have a full-time job that starts in the fall."

"That's good," I said, and turned.

"By the way, Doc, I gotta call from this lady who says she's with the Department of Justice—"

I felt my jaw clench. "Harper Montgomery?"

Teddy brightened. "Yeah, that's the name. She said she wanted to talk to me about you. What's it all about?"

I shook my head. "She's been contacting everyone I know. To tell you the truth, I don't know what she's looking for."

"Should I avoid her?" Teddy asked, concerned.

"No, you should speak to her. I just wish I knew why the DOJ is looking at me."

"That's simple," Teddy said and shrugged. "You just solved a big case when they couldn't and you made them look bad. This is about payback."

I met his eyes through his thick lenses. "I certainly hope not."

As I parked my van in Morris Plains across from the train station, I glanced up at the two-story brick building that harbored the FBI New Jersey Task Force. The lower level held a retail drug store and a dry cleaner. Treated windows shrouded the bureau's offices on the upper level, undecipherable from the exterior.

With its innovative surveillance gear, the imposing structure could detect a visitor well before their ascent. Technology scanned people on the stairs for weapons or listening devices. They could also disable any audio or visual apparatus before you even reached their offices. Knowing this always made me feel concerned.

I entered the secure space through a weighty door equipped with hydraulic locks in case of a breach. I headed past a research room sealed off by a sizable pane of glass. Through the glass, I saw a male and female in white lab coats and surgical masks diligently operate a multitude of machines. These devices could scrutinize evidence obtained from crime scenes spanning the entire state.

I made my way around the corner towards Kate's office and knocked on the door before stepping in. The space held its crimson leather sofa reserved for her patients. Kate used it for her hypnotherapy sessions to help agents recall events more clearly. Next to the couch was an ample green armchair. The room featured a window with the blinds closed during her sessions. Today, they were open, though the privacy glass restricted the natural light that filtered in.

Kate sat at her desk behind an overlarge computer screen, her piercing green eyes studying the data with a fierce intensity. Kate was a natural redhead before her attack and now wore a wig that matched her lost hair perfectly. Despite her scarred scalp, Kate carried herself with a quiet confidence and an air of determined resilience.

She stood and gestured for me to go to the divan.

"Do I have to?"

"Don't be petulant, Len. You know it works better if you're lying down. How's Mrs. Higgins?"

I moved to the divan, taking off my sports coat. "Great! She asks about you. We should have you over for dinner."

She took the coat and put it on a hanger behind the door. "I doubt your fiancée would approve."

"Jyanette knows we were just a temporary situation," I hedged, thinking fast. "She respects you."

"Let's just focus on this session for right now," Kate said, grabbing a pad of yellow lined paper and sitting in the green leather chair. "You're trying to recall a face you saw. Was it in a vision?"

"That's right."

"Okay then. Lie back and listen to the sound of my voice…"

With a soothing tone, she led me into a state of relaxation by guiding me through a straightforward exercise. I followed her guidance, relaxing every muscle as she expertly directed me into an alpha state using her voice.

"You are going back to yesterday, when you were at a crime scene. Tell me what you see."

I painted a picture for her of the run-down office, complete with the scratched-up desk, the row of computers, and the lifeless body of Alex Worling.

She led me through my arrival in the room, when I sat down and moved into the vision of the killing. I saw the entire scene again. This time, the images were clearer, the details more vivid. However, when Kate walked me through the events, everything seemed to slow down to a crawl. When the man in the corner came into view with the light shining on his face, I observed something peculiar.

His face appeared different.

I paused, feeling perplexed. What caught my attention was the apparent fluctuation in his face. Not an obvious transformation, but there were subtle dissimilarities from the portrait that Chuck created for me earlier that day. As I observed, his features seemed to be in a constant state of flux, continuously altering and changing as I watched.

I wanted to keep observing it, but Kate kept me moving ahead. "Think of the moment you saw the flash from the gun, that one moment when the man with the gun had light on his face."

I moved along mentally as Kate led me, seeing the silhouette looking down at the fallen con man, the pistol outstretched. At a pace where each moment lasted a full minute, the hand dragged the trigger and the gun flash brightened the surrounding area.

It was happening so slowly that for the first time; I noticed the man standing between the shooter and the bald background man. I couldn't see his face because he wore a ski mask, but I knew he was there, watching the gunman as he killed the unarmed grifter.

Refocusing on the assassin, I observed the muzzle flash. It revealed a chiseled jaw, taut lips, cheekbones resembling those of a movie actor, symmetrical ears, piercing blue eyes, and chestnut hair.

As I suddenly realized, I could no longer remain at ease and quickly sat up. I gasped for air, taking deep breaths to dispel the lingering effects from my mind. My eyes widened in surprise at what I had just discovered.

"Len, why did you do that?" Kate chided me. "Coming out of an altered state like that is not—"

"I know who it is," I panted. "I know who the shooter is."

"You could have just waited and told me when I brought you out!"

"You don't understand," I began, likely appearing unhinged with a crazed glint in my eyes.

"I understand that pulling yourself out of a hypnotic state is not good for—"

"He's a cop."

"What?" Kate said, leaning back in her chair.

"The man I saw was a cop!"

5. RUINOUS RIGHTEOUSNESS

"Tom Harrigan?" McGee said, as I stood in front of his desk at MPD. "Are you sure?"

"As sure as I can be," I explained.

"What the hell does that mean?"

"The image of the man Chuck drew? His face keeps shifting."

"Shifting?"

I paused. "It was strange. I've had nothing like it happen before."

"But you think you saw Harrigan firing the gun?"

I nodded. "Yes, Bill, I do."

Two years ago, Tom Harrigan was an up-and-coming officer with the MPD, a decorated veteran, and a good man.

Tragically, Dr. Anika Vanya, a psychopathic hypnotherapist, obtained control over him, compelling him to follow her every command. Under her direction, he launched a vicious assault on the MPD and attempted to blow up the building. During the chaos, he shot Chuck Norman in the leg and killed Lieutenant Butler, Bill's predecessor. The only reason we stopped him was because I fired a Taser and incapacitated him.

Afterward, we deprogrammed him from the hypnotic controls. A panel of judges decided he was not responsible for his actions and they brought no charges against him. However, he lost his position as an officer with MPD, and word had gone out so that he could not get another job in law enforcement.

I testified on his behalf and was grateful that he didn't end up in prison, as he truly was not accountable for his actions.

This situation was different. If it was him, he was doing it by his own choice — no one was forcing him.

"Do you know where Tom lives now?" I asked. "Is he even in New Jersey?"

"Word on the street was that he was working security at Newark Airport. Not with Homeland, just a security guard. But I also heard he'd left that position a while back." Bill shook his head. "This seems so out of character. Tom was a guy who followed the rules. I can't believe he would become a hit man, for the mob or anyone else."

Gazing at the floor was my only response as I struggled to come to terms with the notion that the man I once knew could have become a hired killer.

"Could your vision be wrong?" Bill asked. "Could someone be playing with what you see?"

"I don't know how it's possible to affect what I receive," I said. "Bill, the visions I experience are the emotional residue of an event in a location. I picked up on the last moments of Alex Worling's life."

"Yeah, I know, you've told me."

"Plus, how would anyone know I would be involved? I only become part of one of your cases when you invite me, and that's sporadic."

"I understand," Bill said, and rubbed the back of his neck. "Well, it's a starting point, if nothing else. I'll try to see if I can find out about Harrigan. If we can track him down, we can find out if he has an alibi for that night."

A woman knocked on the frame of the open door into the office. She stood about 5'9", with a lean, muscular physique. She carried a folder with her.

I immediately recognized her from the mental image sent to me by Anna. This was DOJ Agent Harper Montgomery.

I was so surprised that my mouth fell open.

"Lieutenant McGee," she said, sharp eyes going from Bill to me. "And Doctor Leonard Wise, I believe."

Bill stood. "Can I help you?"

"This is Agent Montgomery," I said, my jaw tight.

Her eyebrows went up. "You looked me up online?"

"He wouldn't have to," Bill said, looking annoyed. "So, you're the one who hit us with that warrant. What's this all about?"

Her eyes went to me. "I cannot discuss this in front of Doctor Wise."

"I'll leave the room," I said. "But Agent, I want to talk to you when you're done with the Lieutenant. I want to know why you're contacting my friends and students."

"I am not at liberty to speak about an ongoing investigation," she snapped.

"You're investigating Len?" Bill bellowed. "Who the hell do you think you are, coming in here—"

Harper spoke sharply. "I have a legally issued warrant, and I will go wherever my investigation takes me—"

"Hold it!" I said, even louder than the pair of them. I turned to Bill. "Talk to her, Bill. Agent Montgomery, all I ask is that you take a few minutes and explain to me what you can. It may be an active investigation, but if I can clear up anything, it might help make sense of all of this."

Montgomery glared at me, but I saw her face soften. "Very well. Once I tell Lieutenant McGee my requests, I'll give you five minutes."

"I'll be in the conference room." I walked out the door, closing it as I went.

The conference room boasted a massive table stationed in the center of the room, surrounded by a dozen chairs. In addition, there were ten more chairs discreetly arranged along both walls. After settling into one seat, I placed my cane on the table and massaged my throbbing right leg. I really had not done all that much but the muscles were still weak. I could see that I would still need my cane for a while.

I was finally coming face to face with this agent. I couldn't fathom what could concern her. With my extensive experience working with MPD, the FBI, and even the DOJ, my work had effectively thwarted criminals and ultimately saved lives. I received generous rewards in the last few months and was even gifted my van by a wealthy family. All of which I duly reported on my taxes, as I had nothing to hide.

On the other hand, I'd often bent the rules, and even taken the life of a killer when my life and Jenny Baines were in the balance.

Bill accompanied Agent Montgomery to the room after twenty minutes.

I stood as they came in, and Bill did not look happy.

"Please sit, Doctor," Montgomery said, and I returned to my seat, as Bill excused himself from the room.

I chose to be the aggressor. "Why did you ask Anna Sokolov if I attempted anything inappropriate with her?"

She didn't bat an eyelid. "It was an obvious line of investigation, considering your arrest for attacking a student in your office two years ago."

I am sure I turned red. "They dropped all those charges. There was video evidence that I did nothing wrong, and that the student was being influenced."

"Still, if there was an accusation, it made sense to pursue it with Ms. Sokolov. I was trying to understand your strange interest in the girl."

"She's gifted," I said, but my explanation sounded lame.

"I am sure she is, considering you 'work with her' two to three times a week." Montgomery glared at me.

"She has unique abilities that require one-on-one guidance," I shot back.

"As a psychic?" The sneer was clear in her voice.

"Yes. It can be frightening when you receive unwanted images and impressions."

She leaned forward to address me. "Doctor, I'm curious to hear your insights on a known crime boss, Anthony Marconi. What can you tell me about him?"

She shifted the conversation so completely that for a moment my mind went blank. "Marconi?" I tried to gather my thoughts and stammered, "I — uh — helped rescue his niece from a cult."

She opened the file, holding it so that I could not see its contents. "Is that all?"

"No," I said, as sweat broke out all over my body. "I met him in Maine."

"On his private island?" There was accusation in her tone. "Where he ran an import export company that may not have been legal?"

"Yes, his — uh — son was killed, um, murdered in a haunted house. I was called in to investigate."

She examined the pages in her folder again, letting the silence grow. "You assisted the Portland Police Department and helped reveal the killer?"

"Yes," I said.

"And then a few short months later, you were working for Mr. Marconi on his niece's abduction?" she said, as if she already knew the answer.

"I — uh — wouldn't say I was working for him," I blurted. Why did I sound so guilty even to my own ears?

"You worked with a private investigator named Darren Ward. Is that correct?"

"Yes," I admitted, afraid of where this was going.

"It seems Mr. Ward has a history of engagements for Mr. Marconi. Then there was another incident last year. An escaped felon named Emma Truesdale kidnapped you. You testified a sniper shot both her and her partner, Doctor Anika Vanya?"

"Yes," I said.

"Even though there was no police sniper at the location. Do you have any idea where that sniper came from?"

"Um… no. At the time, I was fighting for my life."

"And now you're involved in a case of a con man assassinated in Bloomdale?"

I frowned. "You think Anthony Marconi was involved with the murder in Bloomdale?"

She closed the folder. "No, Doctor, I am interested in you. You show up here from California, and suddenly you're working with the police and known criminals, like Mr. Marconi. I have to wonder — what's the connection?"

"I-I try to help."

A smile appeared on her lips, but not in her eyes. "Yes, and you've received several substantial rewards. You can understand why I am interested in your background. I mean, you were working to be a surgeon, then a psychiatrist, then you're a professor of parapsychology. Yet you end up working with the police." She leaned forward in her chair. "What is it you bring to the table?"

"I have a unique perspective that helps in an investigation," I said, giving the line I always used when asked.

"You're a psychic?" she scoffed and sat back again. "I don't believe in psychics. When I see someone who works with criminals and the police, it is my job to investigate." She observed my reaction. "Let me be clear, Doctor. I will find out everything there is to know about you. From the reports, I believe you are involved with the criminals who do these acts or you gain information from illegal sources."

I glanced at the clock on the wall, and my heart sank. It was almost six o'clock. I was supposed to be sitting down to dinner with the Baines' in a half-hour.

"I have an appointment," I said, rising. "Am I free to go?"

"For now," she said in such a way that I could only interpret it as a threat. "I'll be in touch, Doctor."

"Jenny, you truly outdid yourself," Jyanette said as we sat at the Baines' dining room table with a pair of candles lighting our plates. She took another forkful of the Mushroom Rigatoni.

Jenny beamed. "Thanks, Jyanette. You guys pick a date for the wedding yet?"

I glanced at Jyanette, but she was chewing and expecting me to answer. "My brother is getting married this summer in Las Vegas. We figure we'll pick a date once all of that is done."

"Don't wait too long," Jon announced. "Once Jenny finally agreed to marry me—"

"Oh Jon, don't make it sound like that," Jenny said.

"I married her fast before she changed her mind. Didn't give her a chance to think about it," Jon said and took Jenny's hand.

They both looked happy. I looked over at Jyanette, and she was smiling as well. It was good to see her enjoying herself.

Soon we finished dinner and went out to their living room as we had a dessert of a homemade Tiramisu and coffee. Although Jon and Jyanette had wine and now coffee, Jenny had water during dinner and was only having the sweet, creamy confection, and a small portion of it at that.

I brought up Agent Montgomery during dinner. She would soon go after my records at GSU anyway, so better to let Jon know about it in advance.

"I can't believe it!" Jon stormed as he cut a piece of the dessert with his fork. "Especially after you worked with the FBI and the DOJ to stop that group of white supremacists who were about to release that virus all over town."

"I think that's how I got on their radar," I said. "This is why I always prefer to stay in the background."

"The university will give her any records she subpoenas, but if she interviews me, I am not telling her a damn thing," Jon said.

"That will only make her more adamant to find what you won't tell," I attempted. "Jon, just give her whatever she asks. It's the only way to make this go away. I have nothing to hide."

Jyanette shook her head. "Len, you're damn stupid if you don't think that innocent people don't end up charged with crimes. A prosecutor can indict a ham sandwich if he wants."

"A ham sandwich has some meat in it," Jon said. "This stuff about Len is all just conjecture."

"It's a series of coincidences that together form a pattern," I said. "Can we change the subject? I'm tired of talking about this."

Jenny glanced at Jon again and spoke up. "I think we should let you know — Jon and I have good news."

Jyanette smiled. "We could use some."

Jenny and Jon took each other's hand and shared a look that reflected pure love. Jenny turned to us, her eyes bright, and said, "I'm going to have a baby."

Both Jon and Jenny were watching my reaction. Jyanette was at an angle to them. I was the only one who saw her face fall at the news.

"That's great!" I exclaimed and got up, went to Jon and Jenny, and hugged them.

Jyanette recovered enough to smile and say, "That's wonderful. Excuse me, I have to use the bathroom."

As she left the room, I saw her eyes were wet.

"You two will make wonderful parents," I said.

"We're both really excited," Jon said. "Took us a couple years, but we did it!"

I nodded. "I noticed Jenny wasn't drinking wine or coffee tonight."

"Always the detective," Jon chuckled.

I paused at this, but Jon was right. Since working with Bill McGee, I was more observant of things, and scrutinized them more than in the past.

After conversing for a brief while, Jyanette returned from the restroom and it was apparent that tears had streaked down her face. Sensing her distress, I promptly feigned exhaustion and made apologies and we soon departed.

On the ride home, Jyanette sat in silence as she gazed out of the window. The news had clearly impacted her deeply, and although I wanted to comfort her, I couldn't think of any words to say.

We soon arrived at home, and after we went in through our separate entrance, Jyanette went through our sitting room and into the hall of the main house to the kitchen.

"I'm getting another drink if it won't bother you."

"No, it's fine," I responded as I trailed after her. I felt foolish for being unable to help.

Upon reaching the kitchen, she extracted a bottle of Chardonnay from the fridge and poured it, not into a wine glass, but a large tumbler. Seating herself at the kitchen table, she took a substantial swallow.

I placed my hand on hers. "Look, Jon and Jenny didn't mean to upset you. They're just excited."

She gazed at me. "They should be. I didn't know that the news would throw me like it did." She sipped her wine and watched me. "It threw you, too, didn't it?"

I met her eyes, wanting to lie, but I couldn't. "Yeah, I guess it did. After... what happened to you... to us..."

Despite her stoic exterior, her eyes welled with tears as she spoke. "You thought about the fact that I can't have children."

"We're not sure of that," I blurted. The last thing I wanted to do was send Jyanette into a dark pit of depression.

"The doctors were pretty sure," she said, not looking at me, fighting to hold back the tears. "If you want kids, you can still back out, because I might not be the lady for you."

I got down on one knee in front of her. "I don't want anyone else but you, Jyanette."

"You say that and I believe you," she said, fighting not to cry. "But I don't want you, years from now, to think you got cheated, because... because..."

I pulled her close and held her as she broke down and wept. It was difficult to see a woman who I know is so strong, weakened by her grief.

I whispered, "I want you, as you are, as we are. We still have time. If we want kids, there are ways. It's us — as a team — that really matters."

She pulled back, and I saw she was forcing herself to take control. "But you thought about it today, and it hit you hard, didn't it?"

"Yeah, but that doesn't mean I don't want to be with you," I explained. "It's not your problem, it's our problem, and we can find solutions."

"Sometimes, my dear man, there aren't any."

That night, we held each other as we fell asleep.

I was floating, resting easily, when my vision cleared and I stood before a pleasant house, well-maintained on a quiet street. I looked about, trying to figure out where I was. It could have been Bloomdale or even Mountainview. Or it could have been in another state, out in the middle of the country for all I knew.

I had a sense that it was... close.

Gazing at the house, a vehicle's headlights approaching drew my attention. I almost attempted to move out of the street and had to remind myself that I wasn't physically there. Although it resembled a dream, my experience told me this wasn't ordinary slumber.

This was astral projection.

One of the training exercises I learned from Doctor Kohl was to separate my physical and spiritual bodies. This technique proved extremely helpful in my investigation of hauntings and supernatural activities. Although I could employ it through conscious effort, sometimes it happened involuntarily during sleep.

The vehicle came to a halt two houses away. With the sound of the car doors opening, my senses heightened as three men emerged. They drew closer to my position. I recognized the distinct outlines of the shooter and his two associates from the previous evening.

They headed right to the door of the house.

I drew closer to them and tried to get a good look at their features, but it was too dark. All I could see were their damn silhouettes.

Why were they here? What were they doing this time?

The three men framed the door on both sides, and the heavy-set man knocked very quietly.

There was the sound of the door unlocking and opening a crack. No one turned on the overhead light.

"Jamie?" a man whispered hoarsely from inside. "Is that you?"

The large man spoke in a treble voice, like a young man in the middle of shifting into a lower register. "Yes, I got here as soon as I could."

As the man opened the door a little wider, the big man on the side smashed his shoulder against it, throwing the man behind it to the floor. The other two followed him in, and they quickly stepped in and closed the door.

I walked up to the front of the house and passed right through it — one advantage of being insubstantial.

Inside the house, the heavyset guy and his friend picked up the fallen man from the floor. I hoped that inside the house there would be enough lighting so that I could get a good glimpse of the three men. It frustrated me that there was only one lamp on in the room. It had a piece of red cloth hanging over it, leaving the space dark and tinged in scarlet.

The living room had a couch facing a big screen TV, and video game controllers were out on a coffee table in front of the sofa, along with bowls of popcorn and chips. It was apparent that the resident was expecting company.

I focused my attention on the man being held. He was thin, wearing a dress shirt and khakis, and clean-shaven. His brown hair was thinning on top, and he appeared to be about fortyish. He was panting and looked frightened.

"Who are you?" he demanded, raising his voice. "What are you doing here?"

The tall silhouette that I believed to be Tom Harrigan raised his hand, revealing the gun with the extended barrel.

"Be quiet, or I'll end this," he growled, and pointed the pistol at the ceiling. It was two years since I had seen Tom, but to my ear, it sounded like him.

The frightened resident looked pale and like he was about to pass out. He glanced at the gun and then at the two other men. "What do you want with me?"

"It's what you want that worries us," the man I thought was Tom said. "You know convicted pedophiles aren't supposed to communicate with anyone underage." He pointed to the heavyset man, who was still in shadows. "You thought my friend here was a young boy?"

He looked at the three men, desperate and hoping for any escape route. Seeing none, he fell to his knees and began weeping loudly.

"I can't help it," he sobbed.

"It's your other plans that worry us," the man said, looking down at his victim. "The things you've been buying and collecting."

The kneeling man's eyes grew wide and then tears were streaming down his face. "I-I don't know if I'll do it. Buying those things — it was a compulsion."

Although he was still in silhouette, the big man looked down at his pathetic victim and said, "Then I will relieve you of your compulsion."

He lowered the gun, so it pointed at the man's face. The whimpering man covered his head with his hands and screamed.

I leapt up in bed and yelled, "No!"

Jyanette bolted upright and gasped, "Wha — what is it?"

I sat there covered in sweat, staring into our darkened bedroom.

"Bad dream," I told her, and rose out of bed.

"Len, are you going to do this every night while you're working this case?" she moaned.

"I just had a bad dream," I reassured her. "Go back to sleep."

"Every damn time you get a case," she mumbled, "I end up losing sleep."

After using the bathroom and getting a glass of water, I tiptoed into the sitting room, where my phone rested on its charger. I quickly sent a text message to Bill:

Saw a murder by our trio again.

Private home, possible pedophile.

Gun with a silencer.

Let me know if you get a hit.

I returned to bed, where Jyanette was peacefully asleep.

I thought about what I'd seen. I'd recognized what appeared to be the identical group, although I still could not confirm their identities as I did not see their faces. Their approach remained consistent — find a felon and execute him. They executed the act with remarkable expertise. It was a swift and inconspicuous operation that did not disturb the surroundings. Undoubtedly, they left immediately.

The assailants' motives didn't seem like a case of mob-style retribution. It was more like the work of self-proclaimed enforcers seeking to administer their own version of justice.

This idea suggested more than ever that the shooter was Tom Harrigan. If he felt he was fighting crime, he might have convinced himself he was doing a service. It would appeal to his sense of duty.

Having a background in psychiatry, I testified at Tom's trial, which was the last time I saw him. I was a witness to his destructive actions. I informed the three-judge panel they could not hold Tom accountable. His actions were because of Doctor Vanya's hypnotic programming.

According to Tom, my testimony saved him from being sent to prison.

But now what?

If Tom was indeed involved in this group's violent acts, it signified a disturbing shift in his character. He had been someone inherently upright and honorable. How did he succumb to the temptations of vigilantism, failing to distinguish justice from vengeance?

As I lay in bed, hoping for sleep to return, I worried about just what kind of man Tom Harrigan had become.

6. QUESTIONABLE ETHICS

I pulled myself out of the bed Saturday morning to answer the phone at seven AM as Jyanette murmured in her sleep.

"Yeah," I said, unable to articulate any better.

"Len, it's Bill. You were right on the money."

That woke me right up. "There was another murder?"

"Yes, in Mountainview, near the Bloomdale border. It's a private home, two bullets to the head. Can you come over and verify that it was the place you saw in your vision?"

"Give me the address. I'll come right over."

I quickly entered the information into my phone and rushed into the shower. I dressed just as Jyanette woke up.

"You heading out?" she muttered from the bed.

"Yeah, crime scene. I've got to meet McGee."

"On a Saturday? Yuck!" She lay back and waved.

"Oh, I forgot to tell you. We're going to an art show tonight."

She sat back up. "We are?"

"I mean, if that's okay," I said, realizing that my darling might have other plans.

"No, that's fine. I just didn't know, and I thought I was dreaming — Len Wise doing something social?"

Jyanette was aware of my inclination to steer clear of crowded spaces. In groups, my mental barriers can't completely stop the flow of other people's random thoughts, and that sometimes overwhelmed me.

I smiled and tried to make light of it. "Yeah, Chuck Norman is having a show, and I want to see his stuff. He invited us to the opening night party. It's local, just over in South Orange. Besides, I want to show you off."

"Really?" she said and her hand went to her messy hair.

"Yes, really," I said and kissed her.

"I wouldn't mind getting all decked out for an evening with my man," she said. "If you're going to show me off, I have just the dress."

"It starts at eight."

She nodded. "I think I can be ready by then. Should I plan dinner for six?"

"I'll be home long before then," I replied. "So I can help."

She looked at me slyly. "Hm. If you make dinner, and not leave it to Margery, I'll get really dolled up for you."

"Sounds great," I said, inspired by the thought of my lady dressed to the nines, which was sure to elicit envious stares from every male present.

Before I stepped outside, I hastily grabbed a jacket. Despite the forecast predicting a cloudless day, raindrops sprinkled down on my van as I navigated through town.

As I journeyed down the less-frequented paths, the continuous heavy rain acted as a musical backdrop, stirring up a sense of foreboding.

I parked on the curb exactly opposite the intended destination. As I surveyed the house, I confirmed it was exactly as I saw it the night before. In the light of day, I saw it was a two-story brick house in a simple Colonial style, with a sidewalk leading up to the front door.

The door stood open, with a short, uniformed officer in a black hooded poncho standing outside. There was a bevy of people inside standing about, which I saw through the open door. As I approached, I saw the flash of a camera strobe.

I wished I had worn my raincoat or brought an umbrella.

The officer in the rain gear at the door was Tylissa Booker, and I was glad to see her.

"Tylissa," I beamed. "How are you?"

She smiled up at me. She was an African-American woman, about 5'2" and chunky, but mostly muscle. I'd seen her take down a six-foot-tall man with little trouble. "Hey Doc, ain't seen you for a while. Heard you finally got engaged to that ADA you were dating."

I smiled. "I did, after she spent a long time saying no. How's Darren? You guys still seeing each other?" Darren Ward was the private investigator who had connections to Marconi, who Harper Montgomery was concerned about. I didn't care what the DOJ agent said. Darren saved my life more than once and was a friend.

"Damn straight," she crowed. "He knows that I'm the best thing that ever happened to him. Maybe we'll be announcing an engagement before long."

I chuckled. "Glad to hear it. Give him my best."

I went inside and looked around. Bill was standing next to Doug Millbank. Suited up in the white coverall, one of his forensic team was taking photos of the body. I recognized the victim from his clothes, which I'd seen in the previous night's vision. That was the only way I could've known who it was, as he lay face down with half of his head blown away.

Doug nodded at me, and Bill stepped close.

"From the look on your face, I take it this was the place you saw?"

"It's odd," I said. "It feels like I've already been here. Do you have a name?"

"Clyde Barton, aka Carter Brown. The state of Ohio convicted him of child molestation. Served two years, and they must have been rough, because prisoners don't treat pedophiles nicely. This guy liked teen boys, preteen if he could get them." Bill looked down at the body and went on. "Moved to NJ and changed his name. He was supposed to register with the New Jersey Sex Offender Registry but failed to do so."

"Didn't Ohio follow up on him?"

"He was on probation for six months. Once it was over, he was free to go anywhere he wanted."

I looked down at the body and the pool of blood that covered the wood floor, seeping into an oriental carpet.

"How did the killers know?" I asked.

With a nod of his head, McGee guided us to the corner of the room, away from the others. "Walk me through what you saw, step by step."

I nodded and closed my eyes. Speaking quietly, I recounted what I'd seen: the men coming to the house, getting in, and what they said before the shooting.

"Any idea what the perp meant by what our victim was 'buying and collecting'?"

"Not a clue."

McGee turned away from the others and murmured, "You're sure it was the same men?"

"Not totally. The lighting was bad, and I only saw them in shadows, but it was three men, and they were the same height and size. The gun was the same one used to shoot the con man in Bloomdale."

"That you recognize?" he snorted.

"Yes. I forgot to tell you that the weapon had a unique silencer. It makes the barrel a lot longer than a regular pistol, even in silhouette."

"You holding out on me, Len?"

"Just an oversight. Looking at the damage to the victim, is it the same armor-piercing bullets?"

"I have to let Casey tell me if they are the same that he removed from Mr. Worling." Bill shifted his eyes to me. "Do you know what they call those bullets?"

"No."

"They call them cop-killers," McGee said grimly. "Because they can punch their way through everything but the top of the line bulletproof vests."

I paused at this, shocked. "Not good."

"Doug's team found a heavy duty safe in the bedroom closet," Bill said.

"Really? What's in it?"

"They don't know. We have to contact the manufacturer and send them a death certificate, and they'll send someone to open it. It'll take a few days."

"One more thing, Bill, when I heard the shooter talk. He sure sounded like Tom Harrigan to me."

Bill nodded at this, his eyes on the forensic team in the bedroom. "I've had no luck finding him."

I nodded. "Tylissa used to be his partner. Maybe she knows where he is?"

At that moment, a pair of men stepped into the room, carrying a black body bag. McGee stepped over to Doug. "We have the guys from the morgue, Doug. Can we clear the body?"

Doug sighed. "Might as well. There is nothing we can get from him here." He glanced over at me. "Unless you can get him to rise from the dead and tell us who shot him."

I moved closer. "He doesn't know."

This made the forensic expert smile. "And how do you know that? Did you talk to the ghost?"

"No, I was here when they shot him," I said simply.

He frowned, studied me, then shook his head. "You're a riot, Wise. Good thing you're not out doing stand-up comedy, you'd starve."

As soon as the men entered the room, Doug signaled to them, prompting his team to move away from the corpse.

"Do you want to try a reading?" Bill asked. "See if you get anything?"

I shook my head. "I doubt I'll get anything more than I saw in my dream."

"I get that. Let's talk to Tylissa." We stepped outside into the rain, and McGee said, "Hey, Tylissa, have you heard from Tom Harrigan lately?"

She looked surprised. "Tom? I used to, I mean, after everything went down. He moved out of state, like Ohio or something. I haven't heard from him for at least a year."

"Do you have any way to get in touch?" Bill insisted. "A phone number or an email address?"

"Let me look," she said and produced a smart phone from her poncho and went through it. Once she located the contact, she sent it over to McGee, and both of us thanked her.

McGee looked up at the rain falling from the sky. "Tylissa, why don't you head back to the precinct? Forensics is almost done, and I can seal the place."

"Fine with me," Tylissa said and stepped out from under the overhang and headed for the MPD police vehicle parked on the street.

"Okay, now that it's just us," McGee said. "Tell me about this dream or vision or whatever it was last night."

I went through my vision, and Bill interrupted with questions. We had to stop when the two men from the morgue loaded the body bag on the gurney they left outside, and the forensic team departed.

"When he pulled the trigger, I woke up, the vision gone," I said as I brought the story to an end.

Bill shook his head. "Unless we get some useful forensics or a lead, the only thing we have is that sketch and your belief it was Tom Harrigan."

"Afraid so, Bill."

"You're thinking they're a team of vigilantes?"

"That was the impression I got."

He looked back into the house. "We only got the call because the victim had a cleaning lady who showed up bright and early this morning. She let us in."

"That made things easier," I suggested.

McGee shook his head. "Nothing is easy about this case."

He walked down the sidewalk to his unmarked MPD vehicle and came back a moment later, carrying a roll of yellow crime scene tape. "Can you give me a hand with this?"

"Sure, Bill."

He took one last look inside, then shut the door and pulled out a key to lock it. "I mean all of this — execution of bad guys? Vigilantes? I gotta wonder, how did our trio even know that this guy was a sex offender?"

I held one end of the tape as he stretched it across the top of the closed door.

"I have no idea. From what I overheard in my vision, they lured him in, pretending to be a young kid."

He pulled the tape taut and cut it with a small penknife. "How do you think? Internet?"

"Probably for the initial contact. Then they spoke over the phone, probably a burner. For all we know, they'd been pursuing him for days."

"Back to the initial question," Bill said as he put a strip of tape up one side of the door. "How did they know he was a sex offender from Ohio?"

As he cut the tape, I took the roll and did my side of the door. "Didn't Tylissa say that Tom Harrigan went to Ohio? Maybe he found out about this Clyde Barton guy there."

McGee put two strips in an 'X' across the front of the door. "Another place to start. Maybe he found work in public records."

"What do you want me to do?"

McGee finished cutting the tape and turned to me. "If you wouldn't mind seeing these murders before they happen, so we could stop them—"

I smiled. "I'm afraid I don't have that much control, Bill."

"Work on that when you get a chance," Bill chuckled. "What's the point of having a fortune teller if he doesn't see the future?"

I looked out at the puddles forming on the lawn, my tone serious. "Bill, I think I see a future of more of these murders if we don't stop these guys."

Bill followed my gaze. "Sad to say, my gut instinct agrees with you."

7. NEGATIVE NEUTRALITY

As I drove the van into the parking lot of the North Jersey Museum of Art in South Orange, I couldn't help but feel a sense of awe. This was the perfect location for an artist's debut, with its elegant atmosphere and prestigious reputation.

As I disembarked from my van, its automated system lowered my seat down to the ground, allowing me to stand upright with my cane in hand. My attire of choice for the event was a sleek navy blue suit, paired with a stylish tie gifted by Mrs. Higgins the previous Christmas. I hoped the ensemble made me look polished.

The machinery hummed as I watched my seat return to the driving position. I really didn't need it to raise or lower me anymore. I was at the point where I could just step up into the van.

I guess I was nervous about letting it go.

My paralyzed right leg limited me for a long time. That I could soon drive any vehicle and soon would no longer require a cane was challenging to grasp.

I moved to the passenger door to assist Jyanette. Her sky-high four-inch heels required a little extra support. In that moment, she was a vision of elegance in a stunning, dark blue sequin dress that hugged her curves perfectly. The fabric had a slight cling and sported a daring slit up one side. She braided her hair, and it flowed down past her shoulders, unlike the tight bun she usually wore in court. We linked arms and walked toward the entrance of the building, which was cloaked in panels of smoky, dark glass.

I focused my mind, calling on my training to maintain protective mental barriers which would keep other people's thoughts out of my head.

As we entered the lobby, we noticed a poster that was an enlarged rendition of the postcard Chuck handed over to me.

We queued up at a table, where they verified our names on a list. The lobby was bustling with people, and I spotted many familiar faces. Among the crowd were several individuals from the MPD, along with members of the local art community from our New Jersey region.

Moving into the party, a tall thin man with graying hair crossed my path — Sergeant of Detectives Joseph Tice. We had a prickly history at the MPD. He was not my biggest fan, and I frequently found him to be unpleasant and argumentative. Upon noticing me, he scowled, but immediately changed his expression when he glanced at Jyanette.

"ADA Emery," he said, all smiles. "Nice to see you back in New Jersey."

Jyanette flashed her dazzling smile. "Nice to see you again, Joseph."

She leaned to him, and he kissed her cheek.

I was a bit stunned. "You two know each other?"

"Of course," Jyanette explained. "The sergeant has testified in several of my cases."

"Which you always handle with your usual skill," Tice said, still grinning. "I heard you and the swami are engaged."

"Now Joseph," Jyanette said sweetly. "Len isn't a swami. He's much more of a witch doctor."

Both of them laughed as I stood there, still surprised they knew each other.

"Well, congratulations," Tice said and looked at me. "You are one lucky man, Doc."

"I know that."

As Tice sauntered off, I glanced towards my lady friend. To my surprise, her high heels seemed to make her tower over me, forcing me to tilt my head upward.

"Joseph?" I said. "You're on a first name basis?"

She shot me another smile. "Of course. I had to prepare him for his testimony. Oh, he's very funny."

I suddenly realized there was an entire side to Tice I didn't know.

As we headed for the bar, Bill and his wife, Laura, came through the crowd.

"Len, you made it," Bill said. "You both know Laura."

Laura was a statuesque woman with jet-black hair cascading down to her shoulders. She wore a shimmery evening gown and perfectly coifed hair and makeup, radiating pure sophistication. Extending her hand towards Jyanette, she introduced herself.

"Jyanette Emery, isn't it? We briefly met before, and I've heard nothing but wonderful things about you."

Jyanette frowned. "Have we met? You look very familiar."

Reluctantly, I had withheld the truth from Jyanette. Anika Vanya held Jyanette and Laura captive in a building about to be blown up with them in it. Jyanette was in a hypnotized state, so she hadn't really 'met' Laura McGee.

Laura shook her head. "I'm not completely sure. But I've seen photos of you, especially after the capture of those awful white supremacists."

"Let's not talk business tonight," Bill said. "What are the plans for the wedding?"

Thankfully, my beloved was unperturbed when probed. "We're still ironing out the details, and we'll announce the date as soon as we decide." She squeezed my hand tenderly, gazing at me affectionately. "It won't be long."

"The sooner the better," I stumbled.

Laura smiled at this. "Well, Bill and I did it on the fly and then had a party afterward. It was incredibly romantic, which, with Bill, is saying a lot."

"Hey, I'm romantic," Bill said.

"As a toothache," Laura laughed. "But I do love you."

It was good to see the pair of them out as a couple. Because of Bill's job, he often had to work overtime and miss out on important family occasions. Raising young children left them with scant opportunities to go on dates.

As they ventured off, we carried on toward the bar, where Jyanette requested a glass of champagne while I settled on ginger ale. The bartender furnished us with matching champagne flutes, and the liquids were alike in appearance.

We went to one of the several arranged tables. Each showcased a delightful spread of cheeses, crackers, and artisan breads. It presented these delectable treats on wooden boards, inviting guests to indulge and savor the array of flavors.

I saw the star of the evening, Chuck, circled by a crowd eager to engage in conversation and take snapshots with him. He wore a tuxedo, and he didn't look bad in it. He wasn't wearing his thick glasses, and I guessed that he put in contact lenses for this event.

As we reached a secluded nook, I scanned the area cautiously. Other people's thoughts were seeping into my consciousness like brief whispers.

All this hype for some drawings? He'd better be good or I'm leaving…

These things are always so dull…

That black lady is gorgeous. I wonder why she's with the geeky guy with the cane…

That one made me smile. I leaned closer to Jyanette and said, "Somebody noticed you."

With a narrowed gaze, she looked as though I was a dullard. "In this dress? A lot of people noticed me."

It was undeniable. She stood tall in her heels, a stunning ebony goddess in a magnificent dress that stressed her every curve. "Whoever it was, they were wondering why you're with the geek with the cane."

"Obviously, you must be my bodyguard," she said, taking a sip of the champagne. "Will you guard my body, Len?"

I grinned. "Every inch, carefully."

With a gentle smile on her lips, she turned her gaze toward me, her expression now reflecting a hint of worry. "Are you all right? I know how hard it is for you with crowds."

"I'm doing okay. I'm better at shutting out the mental chatter than I used to be."

A lady approached the double doors and tapped a spoon against a glass, garnering the attention of the room. Clad in a stunning pink lamé dress, she commanded the gazes of those around her with her silver locks and commanding presence.

"Greetings everyone, I am Gilda Renquist, the curator here at the North Jersey Museum of Art, and your host for this evening. In a few moments, we shall open the doors to the gallery and see the work of our featured artist, Charles W. Norman."

As she raised her arm in a grand gesture toward Chuck, he stepped forward and waved, his face flushed as the crowd clapped politely.

She went on. "Before we go in, I would ask Charles to say a few words about his work."

Chuck reached Mrs. Renquist and extracted some index cards from his tuxedo pocket as the audience continued to applaud.

Chuck, or 'Charles', looked about and waited for the room to be quiet before he spoke.

"I'm… uh… very glad to see all of you here tonight," he focused on his index card. "Art is expression, and I hope you sense the emotion and the feelings I brought to each piece you see tonight. I want to thank curator Renquist and everyone here at the museum for making this possible. Thank you, and I'll see you inside."

Mrs. Renquist yanked open the doors and secured them to reveal the expansive rotunda of the gallery. A throng of people surged inside.

I was grateful it wasn't a long-winded speech. Then again, Chuck was never much of a talker.

"I'm going to go look around," Jyanette said.

"I'll get more ginger ale," I told her.

She handed me her empty glass. "Well then, a little more champagne would be nice."

I smiled as she joined the crowd heading into the display in the museum.

As the bartender prepared our drinks, I placed my cane under my arm. I grasped a glass in each hand and turned around.

"Len? Len Wise?"

I looked at the man in front of me. He was close to forty, so not one of my students. But he was familiar...

"Terry?" I blurted. "Terry Garber? Is that you?"

Terry, the brother of my deceased fiancée. We hadn't crossed paths since Cathy's funeral nearly a decade ago. Back then, he helped me with a wheelchair because of my crippled leg. Terry had filled out since then and regarded me curiously. He didn't offer a hand to shake, but with me balancing drinks and my cane, he probably could see I couldn't return it.

"Yes," Terry said. "I didn't know you were back in Mountainview."

"For about two years. I teach at GSU."

He frowned. "What do you teach? Premed?"

"No, parapsychology. I'm the head of the department."

"Parapsychology? Isn't that ghost-hunting?"

"It's the study of the paranormal, and I prefer to keep it science-based. What are you doing in Mountainview? I thought you planned to move to the west coast."

He grew solemn. "My parents passed away. I came here to clean up the loose ends and settle their estate. I got a job in New York City and I've been here ever since."

Cathy was years younger than her brother, the eagerly expected girl. When she was born, her mother was thirty-nine and her father was forty-five. At the funeral, Mr. Garber was a septuagenarian, and his wife was in her late sixties. Mr. and Mrs. Garber had been very kind to me.

"Sorry to hear that," I murmured.

Jyanette approached us because of my delayed return.

"They never really got over losing Cathy," he said.

"Who's your friend?" Jyanette asked as she drew near.

I turned to her. "This is Terry Garber. He was Cathy's brother."

She considered this. "Cathy? The woman you were going to marry?"

Terry's eyes met Jyanette's. "How do you know Len?"

"I'm Len's fiancée," Jyanette stated proudly.

"Going to marry him?" Terry retorted, and his jaw became tight. "I'd be careful of that. Women who want to marry Leonard Wise end up dead."

"I beg your pardon," Jyanette warned, her smile gone, and a threatening tone in her voice.

"That was uncalled for," I said, a bit surprised.

"Why should it be?" Terry shot back. "She died in the car you were driving,"

"Terry, I never knew you felt this way," I said, trying to calm the situation.

"My only sister dying? While you walk away with a bad leg?" He looked down at me. "From the looks of you, even that has healed."

I attempted to explain. "Cathy meant the world to me. A day doesn't go by—"

"Save it for someone who cares, Wise. The point is, you're out in the world, getting married, while my sister is in the ground."

My mouth hung open in disbelief as Terry made his way to the exit.

To my surprise, Bill McGee materialized beside me. In a gruff voice he said, "You okay Len? Should I go after that guy?"

"No, no," I said. "He was just… venting." Setting the glasses upon the adjacent table, I got my cane under me. My leg throbbed with discomfort, and I was cautious not to put too much weight on it, afraid it might collapse under me.

"He had no right to talk to you that way," Jyanette fumed.

I shook my head. "Sorry, I don't much feel like a party anymore. Jyanette, why don't you catch a ride with the McGees?"

"No way. If you're going home, I'm going with you."

By now, Laura had joined us, as did the guest of honor.

"What's going on?" asked Chuck.

"One of your guests just insulted Len," Jyanette said, obviously still quite angry.

I raised my hands defensively. "Look, I don't want to spoil your night, Chuck. Bill, Laura, I'm just going home."

They murmured their regrets as I headed for the door. Before I got there, Jyanette reached me and took my arm. "You're my date. Don't you try to run out on me."

"I'm sorry," I said as we stepped outside into the cool spring air.

"For what? Not letting me punch the jerk who insulted you?"

I couldn't fight the smile. "I wouldn't put it past you."

"Damn straight."

"I wanted to take you out, show you off, not make you have to deal with anything from my past."

"I guess your dead fiancée's brother insulting you is better than my ex-husband kidnapping you."

"That wasn't your fault."

"We can't deny it happened," she stated as we arrived at the van. She leaned in to kiss me, and it was a beautiful moment. "Our pasts are in the past. We both made errors during our previous relationships. However, we're now looking towards the future... as a team."

"I know. It's just frustrating that when I think I'm ready to move on, something like this happens. And he's right, you've seen it — being around me is dangerous."

"Len, I know that if things had been different, you'd be married to Cathy, have a bevy of kids, and be a famous surgeon, like your father. But, it didn't work out that way. I think that your destiny was us getting together, and the universe had to go through a lot of crap to make that happen."

"I guess you're right," I sighed.

"I am. Now take me home and make love to me until we fall asleep in each other's arms."

That sounded like a great idea.

As we settled into the van and I started the engine, my eyes wandered to the parking lot. The sight of a dark SUV immediately grabbed my attention, its presence enhanced by the illuminating parking lot lights. I easily saw into the vehicle, where I glimpsed someone sitting in the driver's seat, holding a camera with a sizable lens.

It was Harper Montgomery.

She pointed the camera in our direction, as I put the car in gear and drove away.

8. PREPARED PROCEEDINGS

I woke up the next morning feeling refreshed and invigorated. Jyanette's advice to make love with her wholeheartedly had done wonders. As we lay in each other's arms, we were completely content. It was a lazy Sunday, and I had no plans other than to unwind and enjoy the day. Jyanette was still lost in slumber — a serene sight, lying on her stomach, delicate shoulders on display in the dawn.

As I made my way to the kitchen for coffee, the sweet aroma of freshly baked pastries wafted through the air. Mrs. Higgins was leisurely sipping on a mug of robust Irish tea while seated at the breakfast table.

"Mornin' Doctor," she said. "I brewed coffee. I was expecting you to get home late last noight."

I poured myself a cup. "So did I. We ran into a problem, and I didn't feel like being at a party afterward."

"Oh? Is it somethin' ye can talk about?"

I sighed. "I ran into Cathy's brother, Terry."

"Oh! That couldn't have been pleasant."

"I thought it was going to be. At first he asked me what I was doing in town and I told him about teaching at GSU."

"When did it go bad?"

"When Jyanette introduced herself as my fiancée…"

I went through the tale of what happened, and even Bill's offer to defend my honor, as well as Jyanette and me leaving. She listened as she sipped her tea. When I finished, she remarked, "Oh now, this reminds me of a story."

I smiled. "Another one of your stories, Mrs. Higgins?"

"Aye, and you'll not be so dismissive when ye hear it. Duckett's Grove was an estate, and William Duckett built Carlow Castle upon it in the 1800s."

"A modern tale, I see."

"Hush now. His family owned the land for nearly two centuries. As the family grew in wealth and social standing in both Carlow and Dublin, William felt the somewhat ordinary family home did not meet his needs. So, he married an heiress to further his aspirations."

"The old 'marrying for money'?"

"Aye, but you see, he was having an affair with a simple town girl."

"And if the heiress found out, she might reconsider."

"Indeed. So, the girl and William are off riding one day and the girl falls from her horse to her death."

"Or someone pushed her?"

"We'll never know. The grieving mother of this young woman calls down a piseóg—"

"A what?" I interrupted.

"A curse. She calls it down upon the Duckett family. Once he marries the heiress, they heard wild noises comin' from the woods. It t'were the cry of a Banshee."

"I thought Banshees were portents of a coming death."

"Aye, that they be. But this one was the very spirit of vengeance. They heard the Banshee screaming from the towers every night and disturbin' the sleep of the entire clan. They get no rest and no peace, and one by one, the family dies before their time."

"Pretty potent curse," I pointed out.

"It doesn't end there. The untimely deaths filled the castle with disembodied voices, bangs, floating balls of light, and spectral shadows. Also, apparitions of members of the Duckett family, including what they believe to be the ghost of William Duckett hisself, riding a horse on his estate. No one would buy or maintain the castle, and it eventually fell to ruins."

"I don't get the point of the story, Mrs. Higgins."

"Don't you see? Pursuing vengeance only leads to ruin."

"A moral lesson, but I don't see how it relates to my situation," I told her as I moved to the coffeepot, topped off my cup, and poured one for Jyanette.

"Not now," she said and smiled innocently. "But ye will."

I was back in the sitting room when I noticed a message on my phone. I headed into the bedroom and found Jyanette sitting up in bed.

"Your phone was ringing, and it woke me," she muttered.

I handed her the coffee, kissed her forehead, and said, "I'm sorry."

"Well, you brought me coffee. I guess I can't be all that mad," she said and took a sip.

I went out to the sitting room to my phone and saw that Bill called. Without listening to the message, I called him back.

"Len, is that you?"

"Yeah, sorry. I was getting coffee."

"Can you meet me at a crime scene?"

"A new one?" I blurted, shocked. "What is it?"

"I think it's our trio again. Busted in a door, no sound of gunfire, and the victim looks like they shot him with the same type of bullet."

I sighed. I had received nothing, in fact was unaware it even happened. "What kind of criminal this time?"

"Not a criminal — well — a crooked lawyer. Seems that if they are indeed vigilantes, they are expanding their definition of lawbreaker."

"Text me the address. I'll get there as fast as I can."

It surprised me to discover that the address was not a residential home. Instead, it was a towering five-story structure on Bloomdale Avenue. It was an office building boasting a magnificent view of the town's lower region and the bustling train station. The ground level comprised various shops. The entrance to the office suites were conveniently around the corner from the retail establishments.

The place triggered a strong sense of déjà vu.

At the entrance, I met Tylissa Booker again, who was securing the scene. She nodded, pointed to the elevator and said, "Fourth floor."

Upon entering the elevator, I realized this was a familiar place, and I was returning to an all-too-familiar office.

Officer Galland stood at the end of the hallway on the fourth floor. Even though I recognized the office from my previous visit, it was a good two years since I set foot there.

Someone nicely furnished the suite. Its walls were adorned by numerous bookcases, housing an extensive collection. A tastefully designed Oriental carpet lay on top of the linoleum. A laptop sat open on a traditional roll-top desk from an older era.

I recognized the man lying in a pool of blood on the ground. He had an unremarkable face with craggy features, thinning hair, and thick jowls. He wore a black turtleneck and suit jacket.

Bill came over to me as I walked in.

"That's Jacques Hallman," I grunted, looking down at the dead lawyer.

The corner of McGee's mouth twisted up. "You remember him?"

"Sure! On the case of the…" I paused and looked around the room. There were two forensic team members working in their white coveralls. "… of people burning to death."

I was talking about my initial case with Bill. It was during this investigation that I uncovered the perpetrator's ability to manipulate fire with his mind, making him a pyrokinetic. However, in Bill's official documentation, he referred to the culprit as an arsonist, concealing the truth from the public eye.

I faced Bill. "Do we know what happened here?"

"Same MO as the other murders," Bill said and looked at the door, which was broken in the middle. "TOD about midnight. Best as we can tell, either Hallman was working late, or someone persuaded him to be here. The attackers used a police-style battering ram on the door. Hallman moves to the door, and that's where the first shot hits him. He falls, and they put a second bullet in his head. Once again, armor-piercing cartridges. From the looks of things, it matches the others." He turned me away from the pair of crime scene agents. "Did you get anything about this?"

"Nothing. Your phone call was the first I knew about it."

Bill glanced at the pair, still working in their white suits. "Once they're done, do you think you can do a reading?"

"I'll try."

"Have you had breakfast?"

"No, I ran right over."

"There's a diner across the street," he said and led us into the hallway where Galland stood. "Hey, Galland. Can you text me when forensics is done?"

"Yes, Lieutenant," Galland said, still watching the hallway.

Bill nodded, and we headed to the elevator.

We made our way across the street to a charming one-story brick building with a vibrant blue awning bearing the name Mountainview Diner. The exterior featured two empty tables beckoning passersby to take a seat and enjoy the cozy ambiance. Stepping inside, it had the look of a classic diner with a bustling counter with stools boasting bright red vinyl seats.

We took a booth at the rear of the restaurant. I watched Bill peruse the menu.

"Any leads on locating Tom Harrigan?"

"Not a one. Galland is doing an internet deep dive, but we keep being distracted by new murders."

The server came, and I ordered two eggs over easy and Bill ordered banana pancakes, of all things.

"Are you serious? Pancakes?" I asked once the server left.

"It's an occasional vice, Len. Besides, they really make them great here. Whole wheat pancakes with sliced bananas and they use real maple syrup."

"Okay, okay, I'll accept your indulgence. Have you had any hits from Chuck's sketch?"

"We got a couple of potential matches. Of the three we found, two are in prison and one is on parole in California."

"It's weird," I snapped. "That was the face of the man I saw, and yet, it wasn't."

"What does that mean?"

I shook my head. "I wish I knew. So far, I'm not much help on this case."

"Hallman's death is going to ratchet everything up. Politicians get nervous when people bump off lawyers."

"I thought everyone knew how crooked Hallman was."

"Hallman always skated the line. The biggest thing we caught him on was helping the Nova Corporation, when all those warehouses were burning down. He had his fingers in some illegal situations, but we could never convict him of a crime, or even get him disbarred." He picked up his spoon and twirled it between his fingers, nervously. "If this trio is out killing people, they decide who's guilty, and without a proven crime, we have no way of knowing who they might strike next."

"It seems like they have their own ideas about who deserves to be executed."

"And that's not a good thing," Bill intoned.

Our food arrived just as he finished speaking.

"As you said, this ratchets things up," I went on, glancing about to make sure no one was sitting too close. "Add to that, we have no way of predicting who their next target will be. It could be a proven criminal or a person skating the line between legal and illegal."

"Exactly our problem," Bill said as he put a forkful of pancake into his mouth and chewed thoughtfully. "Is there any way you can get ahead of this?"

"Bill, you know it doesn't work that way."

"Come on Len, you've sometimes gotten peeks of a crime before it happens. Isn't there any way you can do that now?"

I sighed. "If I can get a fix on the person, maybe."

"Well, focus that brain of yours on Harrigan. Len, all we need is one place where they're planning to go and we can stop this."

As we finished up, Bill got a text.

"Galland says the forensic guys are leaving," Bill said. "I'll stay with you while you try to get a vision, and then Galland can seal up the place."

I nodded in agreement. "Bill, I have another thing bothering me. Last night when I left the art show, Harper Montgomery was sitting outside in an SUV with a big camera. Is she following me?"

"She has a warrant, and is probably at the MPD right now, going over every case you and I ever did. There's really nothing I can do about that."

"Great, I have my own DOJ stalker."

While Bill grabbed a coffee and soda for the road, I opted for a bottle of water to sip on after my reading. I learned the hard way that using psychic abilities often leaves me dehydrated. Now, I always carried extra bottles in my van to replenish my fluids after visiting a crime scene.

Once up in the office, Bill asked Galland to wait outside and shut the door.

"Have there been any usable forensics from the other locations?" I asked as I moved to a chair that was away from the desk, probably reserved for clients.

Bill shook his head. "No fingerprints. The bullets match, so we have that. From the damage to the door at the first scene, we've isolated the make of the battering ram." Retrieving his notebook from his pocket, he flipped through a few pages. "A Blackhawk, very common. You can get them from multiple police supply houses, and even on Amazon. We've reached out to a couple of companies, but I think it's a dead end."

"Anything else?"

"A couple of loose hairs that are being run for DNA. But if it is Harrigan, we don't have his DNA on file, so I don't know if it will help."

"Let's see if I get anything," I said, and sat back and shut my eyes, focusing on my breathing.

In… out, in… out.

With ease, I shifted into an alpha state. As I surrendered control, my mind loosened and my defenses slipped away, prompting me to open my eyes.

Jacques Hallman sat at the desk, all sepia tones. The scene was lacking color, and Jacques looked like an old black-and-white movie, as he typed away at the laptop.

As a knock sounded at the door, I realized that this vision would include more than just sight, but also sound. Perhaps it would provide a crucial clue to the identities of the mysterious trio.

Jacques rose at the sound of the knock, cursed, took a couple of steps toward the door and said, "Yeah, who is it?"

With the deafening boom of the battering ram, the door flew open. A towering figure charged in, brandishing his gun with a sleek silencer extending from the barrel.

Only — his face was not Tom Harrigan.

The man before me boasted a rugged handsomeness, with short, spiky black hair and chiseled features. A defined chin and full lips completed his striking appearance. And yet, something felt off about his face, though I couldn't quite put my finger on what it was.

Jacques froze in fear as two more men barged into the room. One of them had a bald head and a round face, just as I described for the police sketch with Chuck. The other man, tall like the shooter, had brown hair and a mustache that gave him the air of a bookstore owner rather than a vigilante crew member.

As the weapon fired with a dull 'thuk,' Hallman attempted to turn and run, but was struck by the bullet at close range, and he collapsed to the floor. Through the well-lit office, I plainly saw the gunman stand over the fallen man.

"Why — why are you doing this?" Hallman said, lying on the floor. He was obviously in pain from the first bullet.

"Justice," the man declared in what sounded like Tom Harrigan's voice. He fired the gun, and with a second 'thuk', the vision vanished.

I closed my eyes, cleared my mind, and slowly stood up, trying to get used to being in my body again.

"What did you see?" Bill asked.

"The room was well lit, and I could see them all," I reported, as I opened the bottle of water and took a sip. "I've been wrong the entire time."

"What do you mean?" Bill said, frowning.

"The shooter isn't Tom Harrigan. In fact, the three men I saw were totally unrecognizable to me."

Bill hissed out a breath. "That puts us back to square one."

9. MORAL AMBIGUITY

As I recounted the situation to Jyanette and Mrs. Higgins over dinner, I voiced a concern that I hadn't mentioned to Bill McGee.

"Could it be that my abilities are — I don't know — losing their accuracy? I mean, I was sure the man I saw in the muzzle flash was Tom Harrigan, but then when I saw the same man in the well-lit office, he looked completely different."

Jyanette spoke first. "Len, you know more about your abilities than anyone else. You should know if something is wrong."

"That's just it. I know the faces I saw and yet I feel that they're just not right."

"Well, ye know," Mrs. Higgins expounded, "sometimes things aren't what they appear."

"Were they wearing disguises?" Jyanette asked.

"How? I mean, one man was bald, and the other had a receding hairline. I just can't get my head around it."

"Are you meeting with Chuck?" Jyanette asked.

"Yes, tomorrow after my morning class. Jyanette, if these guys are targeting lawyers, I have to ask — are you armed?"

"I renewed my concealed carry permit as soon as I received the job offer from the prosecutor's office," Jyanette said. "But I haven't felt the need for my handgun."

"Please start carrying it again," I said.

"It moight be a good choice dear," Mrs. Higgins added.

Jyanette sighed. "Okay, I'll clean it after dinner and get it ready. But Margery, I'm not in my office late at night like these victims have been."

"No dear, but ye'll make the Doctor worry less. Ye know how he gets."

"What do you mean?" I grumbled. "How do I get?"

"She means you overthink things and you're a worrier," Jyanette explained. "However, considering all the situations that have happened to us since we started dating, you might have a good reason to worry."

"Ye both went through far too much," Mrs. Higgins lamented. "The pair of ye need to be careful."

Jyanette eyed me. "We should get you a carry permit as well."

It was my turn to sigh. "I wouldn't be comfortable carrying a gun."

"Dammit, Len," Jyanette complained. "Will you at least carry that taser of yours?"

She was talking about a small Taser Bolt Two I owned that resembled a flashlight more than a gun. It had interchangeable cartridges and I could quickly reload it for a second shot before the battery ran out of power.

"If it will make you feel better," I replied.

"Requesting that you carry a taser isn't too much to ask," Jyanette insisted, her temper rising. "I've seen how beat up you get playing hero."

"I'll just poot away the leftovers," Mrs. Higgins said, grabbing a platter and ducking into the kitchen.

I was now in a situation. Jyanette was getting angry, and this was our old argument that split us up in the past. I decided not to get defensive, even though emotionally that was how I felt. Instead, I tried a different tack.

"You're angry," I said.

She looked at me, and I saw the fire in her eyes dampen down. "Not angry… worried and upset."

I got up and, with the help of my cane, got down on one knee next to her seat. "I'll be cautious, but the deal is that you have to be careful as well."

She gazed at me intently. "Just please don't get hurt. You know how it tears me apart to see you like that."

"I do," I said. "I promise I'll be more watchful. After all, I am about to marry the love of my life."

She touched my cheek. "I guess I'm afraid of that, too."

I returned to my seat. "What do you mean?"

She touched her napkin to her eyes. She wasn't crying, but she had gotten teary. "Cathy."

"Cathy?" I asked. "Are you concerned about a woman who's been dead for nine years?"

"Damn straight," she said, and her mouth curved in a sad grin. "I can compete with any living woman, but Cathy is the one person I can't win against."

"I still don't—"

"She died! A month before you two were going to get married. She was smart, a talented doctor, and pretty and a great lover, and so on. How can I compete with that? Len, do you really mean it when you say I'm the love of your life?"

I struggled for words. "I feel like I'm being put into a no-win situation."

"Really? I've been married, and at the beginning, I thought Antoine was the love of my life — I was wrong, dead wrong. There are times I think of him, and now that he's passed away, I think of what we could've been if he hadn't done the drugs and treated me like crap. I need to know if you really believe I am the love of your life."

"Jyanette—"

"No, don't give me a pat answer. Think about it. I'm going to get a glass of wine. Once you know what you want to say, meet me in our sitting room."

She went into the kitchen through the swinging door.

This annoyed me. Why couldn't Jyanette just take me at face value? It was hard to admit she was right. When we started dating, I was aware of her ex-husband, Antoine Powell. It took a while for her to admit just how badly he'd treated her. I then met the man and knew that driving away Jyanette filled him with regret.

How did Jyanette compare with Cathy for me? I guess she'd been living in the shadow of my long-dead fiancée since I first met her. Running into Terry Garber didn't help, as he was a living reminder of my former love.

I stacked the dinner plates and went into the kitchen.

Mrs. Higgins glared at me. "And what do ye think ye're doing?"

"Um… helping you?"

"With the lady ye're about to marry wondering if she's the love of your life, having wine and thinking all sorts of bad thoughts," she said, incredulous.

"W-What should I do?" I said.

Her jaw tightened. "Honestly, it's a miracle you ever bedded the woman at t'all." She pointed at the door. "Go to her, speak from yer heart. Tell her ye'd die for her and then take her in your arms." She put her hands on her hips. "Ye're a smart fellow, Doctor, but sometimes ye don't have the good sense the Lord gave a fly."

Properly chastised, I went out the other kitchen door and headed down the hall.

Now I wanted a drink.

Both Jyanette and Mrs. Higgins had a point. I overthink things, make everything too cerebral. In my heart, I knew what she wanted to hear.

I stepped into the sitting room, and the lights were out. In the bedroom, there were two large candles lit, one on the bedside table and one on the bureau. These were the candles we lit when making love.

Mixed messages? Or was she thinking I would sweep her off her feet? I not only had to tell her how important she was to me, but do it in such a way that she would melt into my arms.

Great, more pressure.

I stepped into the room and Jyanette was sitting up on the bed against several pillows, the wineglass in her hand. She had changed into diaphanous lingerie she would wear on sultry nights, with an equally semi-transparent robe, both in a light blue. Although dressed, the garment hung to her every curve, and I knew from experience that I could get it off her with one quick motion.

It was still cool in the room, but I was sweating.

She looked at me, and I swear she batted her eyelids, like a damsel from an old movie.

Why does the woman I love like to make me squirm?

I stepped into the room fully and went to the end of the bed opposite her.

I reached out and took one of her feet in my hand and started to massage it.

She groaned. "Ohhhhh! That's cheating."

"So is the negligee," I pointed out.

"It's not a negligee, it's a silk sleep shirt," she corrected, and pulled her robe closed tighter. "You can't see anything."

I continued to massage, in the ways I know she likes when she has spent a day on her feet, and she leaned back and moaned again.

"Ms. Emery," I began, continuing to caress her foot. "You showed up in my life at a bad time."

She frowned and looked up. "What does that mean?"

"Sh! Either you want me to tell you how I feel or you can add commentary. You can't have it both ways."

She leaned her head back, and another soft moan escaped her lips as I rubbed individual toes.

"You came into my life at a bad time," I started again. "I had just moved here. I was still trying to get my head around teaching classes, and I was involved in solving crimes, and also accused of a crime myself."

"I remember," she breathed.

"You were very attractive, and it surprised me I had the courage to ask you out, and even more that you agreed."

"Not bad, go on."

I started on her other foot, which elicited another gasp.

"We became lovers, and soon I fell madly, crazy, in love with you. But we also faced challenges. You dealing with my family—"

"They aren't so bad."

"And some terrible things happened to us, and I thought I lost you forever."

She raised her head, deadly serious. "I thought I had to get away from you, get away from the things you do."

"Then fate, supernatural forces or, I don't know, sunspots, put us back in proximity, and — there was no one else for me. I knew if I couldn't be with you, I would just spend the rest of my life alone."

She sat in silence as I continued rubbing.

"Fate didn't test Cathy and I the way you and I have been. If she had lived, yes, we would have married, and our own difficulties would have come at some point. You and I have faced the worse things that could happen to anyone, and I can say with certitude that I love you with all my heart, and I cannot wait until we're married."

I stopped rubbing and looked at her. She smiled, put down her wine, and applauded my efforts. "Very nice. Those could be your vows, Doctor Wise."

"And now, I want nothing more than to make love to you, Jyanette Emery, Esquire."

She sat up. "Well, the foot rub was pretty good foreplay, and it would be a shame to waste it."

She came into my arms, and the silky garment was soon an impediment no longer.

I was in Jacques Hallman's office, and the heavyset man was at the desk, the laptop open in front of him.

He glanced over at me. "You gotta do something. Those guys are going to bust in here and kill me."

"You can see me?" I asked.

He grew annoyed. "Of course I can see you. You're sitting right there."

There was the knock on the door. He blanched. "Come on, do something."

I stared at the man. "There's nothing I can do. I'm not really here. This is just a dream."

"So much for the Super Psychic of Scudder House," he grumbled.

That was a nickname a newspaper gave me after I had a tremendous success at a haunted house.

I always hated it.

The door burst open, and everything slowed down. I saw the battering ram as it smashed through the cheap wood of the door. I saw the door fling open and the shooter step in.

This time, the gunman was indeed Tom Harrigan. There was no doubt about it.

Whoever the face was before, the weird look to it was gone, and it was all Tom.

I looked at the heavyset man, and his face was entirely different as well. He was no longer bald with a round face, but he had a thin face, a good head of hair, and the physique of a bodybuilder.

My eyes then flew to the third man.

It was Terrence Garber.

Tom lifted the gun and shot Jacques, stepping into the office as the man fell slowly to the ground.

I moved from where I sat and stared at the men, trying to understand what I saw.

"Why — why are you doing this?" Hallman said, as he had before. Only now his eyes went to me.

"Justice," Tom said, and I knew for certain that it was indeed his voice.

As Tom shot Jacques a second time and the man stopped moving, Tom held the gun and turned to Terry. "You know where it is?"

Wearing blue surgical gloves, Terry nodded, but remained quiet. He went to the laptop on the table, powered it down, then unplugged it and flipped it over. Using a unique tool, he removed the screws holding the bottom in place.

With the gloves, he wouldn't leave fingerprints.

From the damaged doorway, the third man kept a watchful eye on the hall. He wedged his body against the door, which could not stay shut anymore. As I observed him more closely, I realized he was wearing an earbud, a detail I had not initially perceived.

Using a penknife, Terry expertly detached the bottom of the laptop. He then removed the hard drive by carefully undoing the small screws securing it.

Tom turned to the door watcher. "Anything?"

"Nothing on the police band," he said in a gruff voice.

"Not yet. Time?"

"Five minutes so far," the man reported.

Having disconnected the hard drive, Terry deftly slipped it into the pocket of his black cargo pants. Once he reattached the bottom, he carefully returned the screws to their original position.

"Make sure you put it back in the exact place," Tom warned.

"I know, I know," Terry replied.

It was unmistakably Terry's voice.

Struggling to make sense of what was before me, I couldn't help but question whether this was all just a figment of my imagination. While the individuals were familiar to me, they were not the same people I saw in my vision in Hallman's office. It all seemed too surreal.

On one knee, Terry gently restored the laptop, ensured it was connected to power, and left the screen exposed.

Tom looked at his watch. "Eight minutes."

"I'm done," Terry said.

The three men moved to the door and out into the hall.

The man who was shorter and well-built said, "You think the psychic helping the police will know it was us?"

Terry said, "We won't have to worry about him much longer."

I stood there, stunned. They knew about me. They were making plans to get rid of me as a threat.

As they headed through a door and down the stairs, Jacques Hallman leaned up from the floor, a large hole in his head. He opened his one remaining eye and said to me, "A lot of help you were."

I glanced away from the animated corpse and shifted my gaze toward the closing door as the men departed down the stairs.

I was more confused than ever.

10. EXCESSIVE EQUITY

"Good morning," Jyanette said as she placed a cup of coffee on the bedside table.

I lifted my head and rubbed my eyes. Jyanette was fully made-up, hair done, and dressed, looking ready to walk out the door. I glanced at the clock, which read: 8:00.

"I overslept," I mumbled.

A devilish grin appeared on her face. "No, I wore you out. Did I make it worth expressing all your feelings?"

"Yes, ma'am. Remind me to express my feelings more often."

She ran one finger up my cheek. "Chicks dig that."

I couldn't help but grin at her. "Now you're a chick?"

She smiled at me. "Sometimes, and sometimes I can be a bitch, remember that. See you tonight."

She grabbed her briefcase and hastily departed. I grasped my coffee and drank it with appreciation. Our progress the previous night was noteworthy, as I may have even sorted out some of my own feelings about our impending nuptials.

I tried to make sense of the dream, which I remembered vividly. It had to be complete nonsense, and yet it was as striking as my vision from Hallman's office. It was bad enough that I saw

Tom Harrigan and Terrence Garber in place of the men I'd seen in the vision. However, where did I get that entire scenario where he removed the laptop's hard drive? And they knew about me. What did they mean they wouldn't have to worry about me much longer?

I thought back to the laptop when I actually was in Hallman's office. The laptop was open, yet appeared inactive. In both my dream and vision, Hallman was typing on it. When I arrived at the location, the computer appeared to have simply entered sleep mode. Maybe this was something I should check?

I called McGee on his cell.

"Hey Len."

"Any murders last night?" I asked.

"None reported, but it's still early. I would be grateful if our assassins took a night off."

"Bill, I'm going to ask a strange question."

"Why should today be different?"

"Has anyone checked out Hallman's laptop?"

"Galland brought it to the MPD. I don't know if he's examined it. Why?"

"Could you call me after he looks at it?" I asked. "I have a feeling there might be something wrong with it."

"Care to elaborate?"

"I had a dream last night, where one of the three guys after the shooting took time to open Hallman's laptop and steal the hard drive."

"Really? Why do you think they did that?"

"I don't know, but it might help us find out why they targeted Hallman."

"I'll move that to the top of the list. Anything else?"

"There is something else, but I would prefer to talk to you about it in person. I'll be at the MPD this afternoon. I'm meeting Chuck to have him sketch the faces of the guys I saw."

"See you then."

I put the phone down just as it rang, and the name 'Darren Ward' appeared. I answered immediately. "Hey Darren, how are you?"

"What the hell did you do, Len?" Darren's voice snapped over the line.

"What?"

"The Department of Justice has served me with a warrant to turn over all files involving Leonard Wise and Anthony Marconi. What's it all about, Len?"

I sighed and spent the next few minutes bringing Darren up to speed about my interaction with Agent Harper Montgomery. I told him about the fact that she was talking to everyone, from Anna Sokolov and Kate Yearling, to Bill and the MPD.

"So, she's looking for a crime," Darren seethed. "She's got you in her crosshairs, and she'll take down anyone you've ever worked with?"

"Darren, we did nothing illegal."

"No, but you and I experienced things that were not normal. I just wonder how she will deal with those crazy women from the cult and you being attacked by Anika Vanya."

"She doesn't believe that I'm actually a psychic."

"Well, Len, if you ain't, you're the next best thing," Darren said.

"Just tell her what she wants to know, as best as you can," I advised.

"She has a warrant. What choice do I have?" Darren said and ended the call.

After a shower and shave, I drove over to GSU for my class. I wanted to get there early to grade some papers.

The possibility that the killers knew the police were using a psychic still worried me. If they knew that, why didn't they attempt to hide their faces? I mean, if they were afraid of a psychic, or even a video camera recording them, wouldn't they wear ski masks? One of them did at the first crime scene, but wouldn't all of them follow suit just to make it harder to figure out their true identities?

They hadn't done that — yet I had a feeling that I wasn't seeing their true faces.

In movies, they have things like a holographic face covering and the hero always pulls it off to reveal himself underneath. Could someone have perfected a similar masking technology? I doubted such a thing was possible.

Could it be Tom Harrigan and Terry Garber? My thoughts went back to Terry and the first time I met him.

It was the first dinner with Cathy's folks, and I was so very nervous. I was wearing a suit jacket my father lent me, and although the sleeves were long enough, he was much broader than my twenty-one-year-old skinny frame. I also borrowed a tie and wore the jacket with a white shirt and my best jeans.

I brought flowers and Cathy met me at the door. The Garber's were an older couple, and Terry was eight years older than Cathy. The dinner went well. It surprised Cathy's mother that I wanted to be a surgeon and deal with so much blood as Cathy was planning to go into Pediatrics.

Terry was fairly introverted until we brought up computer sciences. At which point he took over the conversation. He went on and on about what the innovative technologies were, and where they were going.

At the time, I followed about half of what he said, but many of his predictions about phones, tablets, and applications from the internet have proven correct over the years.

I left my memories behind as I pulled into my parking space behind Williams Hall. I thought it strange that Terry, so excited by computers and life, became that angry man I'd seen at the art exhibit. Cathy's death hit him hard.

It hit me hard as well, and I took years to come back from the dark place I had been. If I hadn't met Doctor Kohl and learned the techniques to control my psychic abilities, I would probably be dead now myself, just like Cathy's parents. I understood how losing his sister, then his parents, may have made Terry bitter.

But I found it hard to believe he became a killer.

"I'm returning your papers on Madame Blavatsky. I want to commend some of you on your ideas, and others for your clever interpretation of her writings. As this is your last class with me before spring break, I ask you to have fun and be careful. Also, take some time to think about the concepts Blavatsky considered in her writings on Theosophy. We will review some of those concepts when we next meet. Thank you."

My students sat in rows above me, looking down at my desk, which stood in front of a large digital whiteboard, which flashed: Enjoy the break!

They all rose from their seats, putting away laptops and pulling on backpacks. Every one of them pulled out their smart phones and stared at the screen, as if an hour without their dopamine fix was scrambling their brains.

I quickly packed my laptop and used my cane to help me up the stairs and out of the room. Freshman classes are the least interesting to me. It's a lot of history about different psychics, different studies about them, and the basics of what to do at the scene of a paranormal event.

In the second and third year of our curriculum, we focus on exploring psychic testing and equipping our students with the skills to utilize their minds. I instruct various techniques, including meditation, breath control, and inducing an alpha state. Many students expressed the significant improvements in their lives after acquiring these valuable abilities.

The liberation comes from calming their mind and dismissing the belief that thoughts simply arise in one's head. Discovering that they have the power to control their thoughts and intentionally choose what to think is truly empowering. Witnessing the transformation of many students through these methods has been a remarkable experience.

Unfortunately, it is often at that point I lose some students. To accept that you control your thoughts scares some of them. Others realize they can no longer claim they're victims of something out there controlling them. To some, that idea terrifies them so much, they just quit my class.

I had to learn to control my mind just to survive, and I've been able to channel those abilities in ways to help. Will any of my students be able to do what I do? The only one I've met whose abilities matched or exceeded my own so far was Anna Sokolov.

I drove over to the MPD lot. Chuck and I met in the computer room.

Chuck had his tablet computer with him again and was slowly piecing together the faces as I closed my eyes and described them. My problem was, I kept seeing the other faces from my dreams, Tom, Terry, and the other man. I really had to focus to stay true to the images I witnessed in the vision.

It didn't take as long this time, because I was more familiar with how the parts fit together to form a face and Chuck followed my instructions easily.

As he printed up sketches of the two drawings he created, I said, "Sorry I had to leave your art show so early."

"Yeah, I'm sorry that guy hassled you," Chuck said. "What was it all about? Who was he?"

"Terry Garber. I was engaged to his sister. She was the one who died in the car crash that messed up my leg," I said. "Do you know him?"

"I met him once. He does the website for the museum. Mrs. Renquist invited him. Were you and Jyanette okay? I'd really feel bad if you—"

"We're fine, and we'll come back to see the entire show during the run. What I saw, I thought, was brilliant."

Chuck flushed at this. "Thanks."

I thought about what Chuck said. Computer science was Terry's major interest. When I met him at that first dinner, we talked about his plans to make apps and create his own social media network. How had he ended up just being the webmaster of a small art center? Of course, if he did web design, he probably had multiple clients. He said that he came back to Mountainview to take care of his parents. That could have changed his situation. His family had money. I'm sure he could have hired help. Maybe he inherited and didn't feel the need to work anymore.

The big question was, what did he have to do with the trio of assassins?

Chuck handed me copies of the two men, and I nodded. Both sketches were the men I saw in my vision. So why did I feel they were wrong?

"Thanks, Chuck."

"Yeah, I'll be out of town for the rest of the week, if you need any other drawings," Chuck stated proudly. "I'm training a police force in Connecticut for the use of my software."

"Have fun — I mean, if you have fun doing that."

Chuck smiled. "I usually do."

I took the pair of sketches and headed for Bill's office. This took me into the executive area, where the police dispatchers have individual work stations.

CeeCee Carter, our regular day dispatcher, was in uniform. She is a blond, about thirty-six, and a sturdy lady. She is attractive, though not pretty and always a terrible flirt.

"Hey Doc! How's it hanging?"

I grinned. "As well as expected, I guess."

"Ain't seen ya here recently."

"You guys only call me when it's a tough one. Besides, you know I teach and also, I got engaged."

"Yeah, that I heard. The black babe who's an ADA?"

"Yes."

"Good for you, Doc. Me, I ain't the marrying kind. Oh, and Doc—"

She gestured me to come over, and I approached, looking right and left because she was also glancing about.

"That lady's here, Agent What'ser name?"

I frowned. "Agent Montgomery, here at the MPD?"

She put her index finger to her lips to silence me and spoke quietly. "She's in the conference room. We had to give her files for the last two years. What's it about, Doc? She says she's investigating you."

I sighed and tried to control my temper. "She has an idea that I'm involved with criminals."

CeeCee made a noise of derision. "She should talk to me. I'll straighten her right out. Maybe with a good right hook."

"I believe you would," I smiled wearily. "Thanks, CeeCee."

I went over and knocked on Bill's door.

His booming voice responded, "Come in."

I walked in and Bill was going over paperwork.

"I have the sketches of the two other men from my vision," I said and offered him the printed papers.

"Okay. I'll have Galland do a run with facial recognition," Bill said, and put them to the side of his desk.

"I need a favor."

This got his attention. "What's up?"

"They know about me, Bill."

He frowned, studying my face. "What do you mean?"

"They know you have a psychic on the case, and they are planning to eliminate him."

Bill rubbed the stubble on his chin as he gazed at me. "Are you sure they mean you?"

"I don't know. I mean, where did they find out that you use a psychic?"

"Maybe they read that book of yours?"

"Bill, I changed all the names and I write under a pen name. The only people who know I wrote those books are my agent and my publisher."

"And your friends and family," Bill pointed out.

"You know I try not to draw attention to myself or my work with MPD."

"Do you think you're in immediate danger?" he asked.

"Not yet, but I wanted you to know that it's a possibility."

"Len, you say the word, and I will have a police car outside your house every night."

I considered this. "Not yet, but it's reassuring that you have my back."

"Anything else?"

I sucked in a breath, and finally released it. "Can you do a run on Terrence Garber, see if anything pops?"

"Wasn't he the guy who hassled you at the museum?"

I nodded. "I think he has something to do with all of this."

Bill grabbed the sketches and looked at them. "He doesn't look like either of these guys."

"Just see what you can find out," I said.

Bill shrugged. "If you want a deep dive, you might have to ask that PI friend of yours out on Staten Island."

"He has enough troubles right now."

Bill frowned. "What's wrong?"

"Darren got a visit from the intrepid Harper Montgomery."

"What? Him too?"

"CeeCee says she's here right now in the conference room."

"Captain Harris assigned her an electronic pass card," McGee grumbled. "She can come and go as she pleases."

"This is ridiculous," I said. "I should go talk to her, make it clear—"

"Len!" Bill barked, and I stopped. "Keep away from her. You talking to her is a terrible choice, unless you have a lawyer."

I stared at Bill. "A lawyer? I've done nothing wrong."

"Len, you're being investigated. It doesn't matter if you were doing something wrong or not."

I stood in Bill's office fuming. "What the Hell? I've worked to help bring people justice, and because of that, the government is putting my life under a microscope? When did the government get such power that it could turn someone's life upside down?"

"The Patriot Act and other laws," Bill said. "Turns out they weren't about protecting your rights but expanding the government's right to snoop."

I turned to go, still angry, but Bill held up a finger, halting my progress.

"How did you know?"

"Pardon?"

"The hard drive was missing from the laptop collected at Jacques Hallman's office. Galland tried to run it this morning, and bingo — no hard drive. At the scene, you said you only saw the bad guys until they shot Hallman."

"I saw the hard drive removed in a dream," I said. "Sometimes that's how it works."

"You've told me. In a dream, your conscious mind doesn't limit your abilities."

"That's it, Bill."

"Anything else in that dream I should know?"

I hesitated. "Just look into Terrence Garber."

Bill shook his head. "Cryptic as always, Len."

"Worried, Bill. Seriously worried."

11. IMPERATIVE IMPARTIALITY

"No," I said, turning around the ESP card and showing Anna the image of three wavy lines. "You're not getting it at all now."

Anna Sokolov shrugged listlessly. She appeared to be having trouble concentrating.

"Anna, this test has always been easy for you, but you have to focus."

"I'm sorry, Len," she whined. "I'm distracted."

"You know, the more you hone your abilities, the more prepared you'll be when you need them."

"It's not easy now! I have to put up my mental barriers all the time at school," Anna said, and I saw she was upset. "I didn't use to have to do that, but now if I don't put up my barriers, I sense people's thoughts all the time."

I spoke in a calm voice. "That's because you're becoming more sensitive. It's a good thing."

She sat back in her chair; her face a mask of abject misery that only a teenager could pull off. "It's exhausting. Now I even have to have my mental barriers up here in the diner. Then I work with you and I have to drop them." She looked away, and I saw her eyes were wet. "Maybe I'm not cut out for this."

"What do you mean?" I said, concerned.

"Len, you've said it yourself. I'm like a leaky bucket. My thoughts just drip out all the time."

I smiled. "I'm the only one able to receive what you're thinking."

She paused and looked up at me, her eyes still wet.

You can only read my thoughts when we're close…

Her words appeared directly in my mind. I responded in kind.

No, when we first met, I read your thoughts from miles away…

Anna pondered this.

But that was when I was so scared. Do I need to be scared for you to hear me from far away…?

As you become better at using your abilities, you'll be able to do more…

"But we should get back to today's training," I said aloud. "Even distracted, you can practice."

"Actually, I think the problem is that you're distracted," Anna said, and she seemed completely recovered from her moment of sadness. How do teenage girls do that?

"What do you mean?"

"I mean, when you look at the cards, you're the one who's not focused," she explained. "You're thinking about that lady investigating you."

"What?" I said, surprised by this. "Has Agent Montgomery bothered you again?"

"No, but you were thinking about her each time you looked at the cards. You're worried and I can sense it."

Getting over my shock, I had to grin. "Maybe I'm the leaky bucket today."

"You're also worried about this case you're working. I keep getting images of the bodies," Anna said.

I immediately grew serious. "Sorry, you shouldn't see those."

"Because I'm a child?" Anna said, annoyed. "In case you haven't noticed, Doctor Wise, I'm a fully grown woman."

She was a teenager and acting like one, but telling her that would be counterproductive. "Not because I think you're a child, but because those bodies, those images, are horrific."

"If I work to become an investigator like you, I'll see stuff like that and worse."

"Maybe so, but there is no need to rush that part of your training. I am distracted and I guess I didn't have my mental barriers in place as strongly as I should. It's been a busy few days." I closed my eyes and took a deep breath, clearing my mind. "I'll try to do better."

I held up the next card, and Anna immediately said, "Circle."

I flipped it over to show the circle printed on the card. "Now that's what I'm used to with you."

Anna frowned. "Is that a problem for you, Len? I mean, if someone has troubled thoughts, does it stop you from reading them?"

I tried to put my experience into words. "No, because if I have a reason to push my way into someone's mind, I usually guide them to the information I need."

She smiled. "Show me!"

I purposely looked away from her. "You're not ready for that. And I don't just do it to impress people or show off. I only use that ability in a dire situation."

"Why?"

"When people think about random things that I pick up, it's not focused, it's just their mind putting out thoughts. But when I move into someone's mind, I try to take control, and for a moment, it takes away their free will."

"I see," she said, and looked at her hands. "I think I should know what it's like. If I ever need to do it to someone, I need to have the experience."

She had me there.

"Okay," I said. "I'll do it only for a moment. You should focus on something unimportant, a favorite toy or a blanket you had as a child."

She took a moment. "Okay, I have one."

"Very well," I said, preparing myself. "Look into my eyes."

She met my eyes, and I reached in. Her pupils dilated as she felt my consciousness as it moved into her mind. I was expecting to see a teddy bear, or a favorite blanket.

Instead, I found myself in a dimly lit chamber, surrounded by blood-red drapes. My wrists were bound and yanked upward, trussed to the headboard, while restraints forced apart my legs against my wishes. A male figure steadily advanced towards me, fixated with desire.

I immediately broke contact and turned away. I had activated the memory of a vicious gang that abducted Anna. She narrowly escaped a horrifying encounter with a client who had paid for the opportunity to deflower her, tied up and helpless. I was shaking as I experienced all of her sensations. I felt the incredible fear, the effects of the drugs they'd given her, and the helplessness of being bound to be abused in any way the man wanted.

Anna was openly weeping, as she had experienced the memory as I did. I got up from my side of the table and, using my cane, got down on my knees and hugged her as she wept on my shoulder.

"W-why did that memory come up?" Anna gasped between bouts of sobbing.

"I don't know," I said. "I shouldn't have made the attempt. You aren't ready for anything like that. That memory is still too close and your mental barriers aren't strong enough."

I held her as she calmed down and got control of herself. I had not intended to take her back to that awful place, and it surprised me it happened.

I returned to my seat as she blew her nose on paper napkins.

"You were right," she said, sniffling. "That's a terrible thing to do to people."

"Anna, I didn't know—"

"No, it's not your fault. I made you try. I didn't know that horrible place was still so close in my thoughts. Sometimes I go back there, or dream about it."

"That's all for today. I don't want to push you anymore."

"I think I'm done anyway, Len. I'll see you next week."

I got up and patted her arm. As I walked out of the room, I felt her thoughts touch my mind.

I love you…

I sighed as I got into my van. When I was in my psychiatry fellowship in California, I learned that a common situation a therapist faces is transference. That's where a patient thinks they are in love with their therapist. I literally saved Anna's life when she was sixteen, and I am the only person qualified to teach her to control her psychic gifts.

Her feelings reflected a classic case of transference. As her teacher, I represent the same role as a therapist. She thinks she's in love with me, and it's motivating her to want to please me. On the plus side, she's been working harder, getting good grades, and been easier to get along with for her father. But the downside of a patient in love with the therapist is that it allows the patient to think they can only become whole by being near the therapist. I wanted Anna to work with me, not make me the center of her world.

This made me think how we fool ourselves into believing what we want to. Maybe that caused my odd dream. Was I seeing Tom Harrigan and Terry Garber as the faces of the killers because both of them had been on my mind? It might have been my subconscious merely regurgitating them because of my interest in Tom and my confrontation with Terry.

However, despite my doubts, the hard drive was indeed missing from the computer. And in my dream, I saw Terry remove it.

I really needed to get a clear direction on the case before anyone else died.

As I pulled into the driveway, I received a text from Jyanette:

Hellish day.

Will probably be in a bad mood when I get home

Sorry.

I got right to it and made pasta primavera for dinner. I intended to greet Jyanette at the door with a glass of wine.

The second part was harder than I thought, carrying a glass of her favorite Chardonnay to our sitting room. I caught the aroma of the wine and had a wild compulsion to drink down the entire glass. It was a momentary impulse, and when I got to the sitting room, I quickly put it down on the coaster on the desk, and stepped back from it as if it were a savage animal.

There was no attacking animal, just my baser instincts. I recalled from my many Alcoholics Anonymous meetings that this is the classic situation for an alcoholic. They convince themselves that they have it under control. It's all easy now. Then they find themselves with a drink in their hand, and the desire for that drink is almost overpowering.

For me, it was a danger on more than one level. The slightest amount of alcohol or any recreational drug, and my psychic abilities become non-functional. In the years after Cathy died, when I didn't understand what was happening to me, alcohol was the only thing that allowed me to sleep through the night.

I reminded myself that I would have to attend AA meetings more often.

Reconnecting with Jyanette and the recuperation from my surgery had gotten me out of the habit. With a choice between sitting in a meeting while people tell their stories of how alcoholism ruined their lives, or staying home and making love to Jyanette, who can blame me for staying home?

But my desire to drink the wine was a wake-up call.

I started a bath for Jyanette.

She arrived in time for her wine to still be cool, and she was right. Her brow showed thunderclouds, and her mood wasn't good.

"I have a bath filling and I brought you a glass of wine."

I turned to get the wine, and just like that, my right leg gave out on me, tumbling me to the floor. It happened so quickly and unexpectedly that Jyanette cried out.

Fortunately, I fell on my side, and caught myself as I fell, but it still hurt.

"Len!" she said, concern filled her voice. "What can I do?"

"I need my cane," I said. I pulled out the office chair at my desk and she helped me sit.

"Does that happen often?" she asked.

"No, not much at all," I assured her. "Sometimes it just goes out on me. I should carry the damn cane, but then I get overconfident."

As I pushed myself up on my feet and made sure the cane was firmly in my right hand, I said, "Just need some more exercise. Do you know anything I could do lying down that's still aerobic?"

She caught the gist of what I was saying. "I recognize a trick question when I hear it."

She picked up the glass of wine.

"I made dinner," I boasted.

She grinned. "You're making me feel better all ready. I'll go check the bath." She stepped into the bathroom, and I heard her turn off the water.

"Why don't you soak and I'll put everything on the dining room table?"

"That would be nice," she said, and returned to the room.

I froze. Her skin was paler than it should be and an unhealthy gray color. The upper right side of her head was missing, and her right eye was gone. I saw the remains of her skull and the gray matter of her brain as it leaked out, and her other eye stared stiffly as if in death.

I staggered, raising my hand in terror, and in that moment, she was back to her undamaged self, looking at me quizzically.

"Len, what's wrong? Did the fall hurt more than you thought?"

Barely able to control my emotions, I pulled her into my arms.

She held me tightly and murmured, "Oh my God, you're shaking. What is it? What did you see?"

"I saw you," I whispered. "Dead."

She pulled back and met my eyes. "Was it a vision?"

"No, it was different," I said, tears streaming down my face. "I don't know... like a warning or something."

"I'm okay," she said and stepped back. "See, all in one piece."

"You've got to be careful," I choked, my emotions suddenly smashing past my defenses. She pulled me back into her arms and held me tightly, rubbing the back of my head.

"Shh, it's alright. I'm right here. If this was a warning, then we just make sure we listen to it. We have to be ready for anything."

"Right," I gasped, fighting to control myself. "I just don't want you to end up like… like…"

"Like Cathy," she said. "I know that's one of your biggest fears."

I stroked her face. "If anything happened to you…"

"Nothing is going to happen. We're home, we're safe. Now, I'll take my bath, and you'll get dinner ready."

I nodded, and she headed into the bedroom to undress. I went down the hall to make a quick salad dressing and get dinner on the table.

Was what I saw merely a warning, or was it something I was going to see in the future? My darling lying dead, the side of her head blown off? I had to believe it was a premonition. It also meant I had to find out who these killers were.

If they were targeting lawyers, why wouldn't they shoot an Assistant District Attorney? DAs were the ones letting criminals off easy so they could continue to prey upon the innocent.

I had to track them down. Finding and stopping these men was no longer simply an assignment.

Now it was a matter of life and death.

12. TWISTED MORALITY

"A really splendid meal, Len," Jyanette said and pushed her plate away as she retrieved her wine glass. "And the garlic bread was unexpected."

"It turns out Mrs. Higgins bought the french bread and mixed the garlic butter for us," I said. The meal had been good even with me as the cook. During the preparation and serving, I was able to calm down from my frightening vision. I leaned forward and took her hand. "Mrs. Higgins went out for the night."

"Oh?" she said, smiling. "Does that mean we can do naughty things anywhere we want in the house?"

I pulled back. "Hey, I'm marrying you. Nothing we do is naughty."

She laughed. "Technically, it's all naughty until we exchange vows."

"I would do that in a minute."

"I think we can wait until we have a date everyone can live with. Are we talking potential dates with your family on Thursday when we see them at the seder?"

"We can try, but not until we're eating. There is a lot of ceremony to do beforehand."

"I look forward to the experience," she said and sipped her wine.

I stood to collect the dishes when I felt the buzz.

Danger…

I occasionally get flashes of precognition, quick insights, warnings that come to me out of nowhere, and sometimes they have saved my life. I refer to these as a buzz.

Jyanette saw the change in my expression. "What's wrong?"

"I don't know," I said, and put the dishes down and grabbed my cane. I stepped to the light switch on the wall and shut it off, plunging the dining room into darkness.

Jyanette slipped from her chair in a crouch, pushed opened the swinging kitchen door, and doused the lights in there as well.

The hallway lights remained on, casting a translucent glow through the curtains that allowed outsiders a peek into the house. Jyanette and I retreated into the dark rooms. This rendered us invisible to anyone watching unless we stepped too close to the illumination from the doorways.

I stayed in the room's darkness and scanned the roadway beyond our driveway. I spotted something that drew my attention. Someone parked a white van at the top of our driveway on the street in front of the house with its motor running. It wasn't a minivan like mine, but a big full-sized one, with only two front doors for a driver and passenger, and a pair of back doors.

My heart skipped a beat.

It's the killers. They know I'm the psychic and they've come for us.

I took a step back further into the darkness and called out to Jyanette. "I see a van out on the street, a big one."

"I don't see them on the security cameras," Jyanette replied. When she entered the kitchen, she must have gone to the monitors for our house security system that hung over the breakfast table.

Months ago, a crazed gunman attacked the house, and he shot up the place. If it weren't for the fact that the house was mostly stone, he probably would have taken out me and Mrs. Higgins. After that, Galland, working with my teaching assistant Teddy Santos, set us up with a state-of-the-art security system. It included cameras for both entrances with microphones so we could watch and listen to people. We could watch either location from the kitchen, which is the most fortified room within the house.

"What's happening?" she asked.

I looked carefully, wishing I had a pair of binoculars. "Someone is sitting there watching the house."

Danger…

I went on. "I'm getting a bad vibe from it."

"Any idea who it might be?"

That's when it hit me. "My guess is it's that Harper Montgomery woman."

Jyanette came through the swinging door and moved to me in the darkness. "You're kidding! That bitch is doing a stakeout of our home?"

"I saw her in an SUV taking pictures outside the art museum on Saturday night."

"How does she even know where we live?"

I shrugged. "I don't know. The mortgage and the bills list Mrs. Higgins' name, but the MPD has this address for me."

"She's been going through the case files that involve you?" Jyanette said, disgusted. "We should go up there and tell her to stop it."

Danger...

"I don't think we should approach that van," I said and pulled my phone from my pocket. "I'm calling McGee."

"That's a good idea," she said and rose to look at the monitors, being careful to stay in the shadows.

He answered on the first ring. "Yes, Len?"

"Bill, I have a white van on the street outside my home that I got a very strong warning about."

"What? Why?"

"I have no idea. My first guess is that Agent Montgomery assigned a couple of guys to spy on me."

"She's following you?"

"She was at Chuck's show last Saturday. Could you send a police car to check on the van? It would make me feel better." I lowered my voice. "Bill, I saw something. Not a vision, but a warning. I saw Jyanette — dead."

"Jesus," he hissed, and the phone was silent for a moment. Finally, Bill said, "You think it was an actual premonition? When will it happen?"

"I don't know, but then this white van showed up and my psychic alarm bells started ringing. Maybe I'm just being paranoid."

"Look, I'll post an officer on the road outside your place tonight. Will that help?"

I exhaled heavily. I was unaware until that moment that I'd been holding my breath. "That would, Bill. I'd feel safer if you did."

"Okay, and I'll have the report about Terry Garber you asked for tomorrow. You can come by and see it then."

"I appreciate it."

"Expect a car within ten minutes. They will check the drivers of that van and get some ID."

"Thanks, Bill."

He ended the call, and I stood there, breathing hard, feeling my muscles quiver from the fight-or-flight response. After several minutes, I glanced out the window and watched as the van suddenly drove away.

"They're leaving," Jyanette said with a sigh.

"Yeah," I replied, frowning. "Not a good sign."

Jyanette turned to me. "I thought we wanted them to go."

"But why did they leave right after I talked to Bill?" I pointed out.

"You think they were monitoring the police band?" Jyanette said, seeing where I was going.

"Exactly. I'm sure Bill called dispatch, and dispatch used the radio to send a car. Then these guys take off. That points to law enforcement."

"Not necessarily, Len. Anyone can scan the police frequencies with the right equipment."

"They certainly didn't want to be here when the MPD showed up."

Jyanette shook her head. "It appears that they didn't."

We stayed in the shadows of the dining room until we saw the police car pull up and park at the top of the driveway. After that, I turned the lights back on and Jyanette and I cleaned up the dishes.

Between my vision of Jyanette and the appearance of the white van, the evening had taken on a much more somber tone.

We spent the night watching television in the living room, holding hands, and staying close to one another. I kept finding excuses to wander into the kitchen and check the video display of the exterior of the house.

We didn't go to our wing of the house until Mrs. Higgins arrived home, and we were sure she was safe.

The next day, after a restless night, I insisted Jyanette take her handgun with her. After the visit from the white van the previous night, she was willing.

At noon, I stood in front of my class of juniors. Together, we facilitated a dynamic conversation about real-life case studies of paranormal activity. I encouraged my students to share their thoughts on the experiences reported by witnesses. I got them to offer potential explanations for the phenomena. To aid in the discussion, I presented them with the investigator's notes but held back their conclusions.

My students offered everything from well-considered potential solutions to blurted ideas that came to them on a whim. I finally revealed the opinions of the investigators and discussed whether or not they had drawn the best conclusions. It was a really fun class, and I think everyone came away with a better understanding of just what being a field operator meant.

As I walked to my car, Teddy Santos pulled up in his large fire-engine red van, held together by duct tape, wire hangers, and spit.

He waved at me with papers in his hand.

"Hey Doc, I brought you the report on that Terrence Garber guy. Galland said you'd want to see it right away."

"That's great, Teddy. How did you get it?"

"He emailed it to me from the MPD, and asked me to print it up and catch you after your class."

I took the papers. "This is a big help. Thanks, Teddy."

"That lady from the Department of Justice finally interviewed me," Teddy said.

"Agent Montgomery?" I said, feeling my back stiffen. "How did it go?"

"It was weird, to be honest. I mean, she started with questions about you, but then switched to questions about me."

I frowned. "You? Why did she ask about you?"

"She said I was spending time with an officer from the MPD."

I knew Teddy had an on-again/off-again relationship with McGee's aide-de-camp, Officer Galland. Galland did not want anyone to know he was gay or that he was seeing Teddy.

This outraged me, and I struggled to contain my anger. "That's an odd line of questioning. What does she care about your relationship with Galland?"

"I don't know, but it freaked me out," Teddy winced. "The last thing I want is my mom to know that I'm bi."

Through clenched teeth, I said, "No one will hear about it from me, Teddy."

"Thanks, Doc," he said, looking relieved. "Now, I've got a class."

"See you later," I said.

Why was Agent Montgomery asking my Teaching Assistant questions about his relationship with Galland? Teddy's or Galland's sexuality had nothing to do with either of their jobs. It also had nothing to do with the validity of my work. This invasion of privacy felt like an attack on Teddy's character, and an attempt to discredit my work by focusing on entirely unrelated aspects. It made little sense, except as a tool of coercion.

I worked to push down my temper and focused on the papers about Terrence Garber. The first few pages went through his schooling. He graduated with honors at the Massachusetts Institute of Technology with a degree in Computer Science. He earned his Master's at Carnegie Mellon University in Pittsburgh, Pennsylvania. These were both prestigious colleges which must have set his family back a bit, but as I recalled, they had more than enough money to spend.

The report listed that he was unmarried, living alone on his parent's estate. He built websites for non-profits in his free time. His major career currently was consulting for a Wall Street firm doing Cyber Security and Data Mining. All of that sounded very important, and very vague. I wondered what data mining might encompass. It sounded like he did number crunching that would advise brokers on what companies were up and coming, and which were on the downswing.

But it could be more.

If Terrence somehow was involved in this trio of vigilantes, how would data-mining help them? And how did they pick out their targets?

A phone scammer, a child predator, and a crooked lawyer didn't seem to be the most prominent people to pursue, yet those were their choices. I saw each one was a problem for society, but why those specific people?

Flashes of future…

I heard the buzz so clearly; I felt compelled to lift my head and gaze around my van, nervous that someone was sitting inside the vehicle whispering to me.

What did those words even mean?

I continued my reading, and I found several pages that made me pause and go back. There was an additional note from Galland. He noted that the last few pages were from a paper Garber published in the Journal of Computer Science and Technology. The article bore the title:

Data Mining Techniques for
Cybersecurity Predictions and Solutions

His treatise started by defining data-mining. It turned out that it was a process of finding patterns in events. Then sifting through the data to find the points that converge to predict future trends.

Terrence wrote of focusing on cyber security threats by setting up specific databases that included compiling the data. He felt he could transform it into specific guidelines, mine the information, and evaluate the patterns. It was his concept that with this information about cyberattacks in the past; it was possible to predict attacks before they happened.

The paper went on with a breakdown of the different techniques, but by now it was all just gobbledegook to me. I turned to the last page, which held the summary. I paused and found I was reading the last paragraph a second time.

"Data mining techniques can help us identify the characteristics of any malicious activity. We can even predict not only possible cyber-attacks, but almost any form of anti-societal behavior. We could use it to prevent crime and find criminals by delving into what I call 'flashes of future' to stop them. With the correct data-mining program, we can predict the plans of terrorists and even dangerous criminals. This could be a powerful tool to eliminate a threat before an illegal activity leads to a cataclysmic event."

There it was in black and white: flashes of future.

He was writing about the idea of creating a database that would go through all the records online. By sifting through thousands of gigabytes of data, his plan was to track criminals and remove them before they did something worse.

I considered the people the vigilantes had eliminated. What massive threat was a phone scammer, a pedophile, and a lawyer? I just didn't see it. Jacques Hallman's worse crime was creating phony businesses and maybe overcharging his clients. A guy who steals your credit card number might be bad for you, and annoy your credit card company, but his actions wouldn't kill anyone.

It was the same with the pedophile. Yes, he was vile, and his actions could cause a lifetime of trauma, but that didn't suggest danger on a massive scale.

Unless maybe it did.

My mind flashed back to the vision of the terrified pedophile.

"It's your other plans that worry us," the man said. "The things you've been buying and collecting."

The kneeling man's eyes grew wide and then tears streamed down his face. "I-I don't know if I'll do it. Buying those things — it was a compulsion."

What things was he buying? What was his compulsion beside young boys?

I called Bill.

"I thought you were coming by?"

"Have you seen Galland's report yet?"

"Haven't had the chance."

"Terrence Garber is in cyber security for a firm in New York. He looks for future threats by data-mining."

"That would make sense."

"It's more than that, Bill. He put out the idea that a sophisticated data-mining program could predict criminals planning to do something before they do it."

"That would come in handy. Might put you out of a job."

"That's the thing. He called this concept 'flashes of future', and I got a buzz of those very words before I read them."

"Flashes of future, huh? What do you think it is?"

"Terry has been a programmer since he was a kid. I think he may have written a program that does what he theorized."

"Len, that's crazy! You can't predict every criminal that's going to do something big in a country as large as ours."

"What if he kept it local?"

There was a pause as Bill considered this.

I went on. "Let's say he focused on Essex County, or even just crimes within the area around Mountainview? Terry's parents lived here, his sister died near here. What if he's testing this program to see if it actually works?"

"Are you suggesting that Terry Garber is the mastermind behind all of this?"

I sighed. "I don't know. We need more data ourselves."

"Forensics is still going through everything from the crime scenes."

"Can we follow up on the guy in Bloomdale? You said he had a safe in the bedroom. Have you gotten into it yet?"

"No, the manufacturer is taking his time getting someone out to open it."

"If either of those dead men were planning a major crime and we could find proof, it could show that Garber collected the information."

"I'll have Galland do a web search into the 'flashes of future' thing. Maybe that'll turn up something."

"That's good. Can we go out to the sex offender's house, Clyde Barton? I want to look at that safe."

"You think you can get into it?" Bill asked.

"I'd like to try," I said.

"Leonard Wise, safecracker," Bill said with a chuckle, then his tone changed. "Len, if Garber is involved in any of this, you know we'll have to arrest him."

Terry was already angry at me, and he might consider such an act another betrayal.

"I know. But let's not jump to any conclusions yet. I'll meet you there."

As I started up the van, I considered my situation. Terry blamed me for his sister's death — if he was guiding this trio to their next target, would he consider adding me to the list out of a sense of justice?

Or revenge?

13. INFECTED INTEGRITY

By the time I pulled up in my van, Bill had removed the crime scene tape from the door. If there was the possibility that Clyde Barton was planning a major crime, why hadn't my extra senses picked up on it? Looking back, when Bill asked me to do a reading at this house, I should have acted on it.

Doctor Kohl often corrected me about my assumption that my abilities should guarantee that I would know everything.

I heard his voice in my head. "Leonard, your mind is merely reading energy from a traumatic experience and interprets that as a vision. It does not reveal all secrets, but only vhat the person who left the energetic residue vas focused on. You can learn more, but you must get past the traumatic incident first."

Doctor Kohl's theory of energetic residue meant that I could find more information. To do so, I had to move beyond the strongest mental impression in order to find it. This could explain why I had been doing such a poor job in this case. I focused my attentions on the incident that ended each victim's life, but I hadn't gone through their files or touched their papers to get a reading. Maybe it was because the murdered men didn't evoke any sympathy from me. The people our vigilantes took out were the dregs of the earth.

I still had to do my job to the best of my ability.

The other thing that occurred to me was that maybe I trusted my visions too much. Since I saw everything that happened at the crime scene, I could just describe the perp to Chuck and he would make a sketch. But what if these guys fooled my ability to see them?

They knew a psychic was looking for them and expected my involvement.

That was not reassuring, and in fact, made me feel paranoid.

Inside the house, the victim's blood still discolored the carpet. The most important thing for me was not to touch the blood. Blood carries energy strongly, and anytime I have physical contact with blood, it overwhelms my psychic senses.

I was here to go beyond the murder of Mr. Barton, to find any secrets that he was keeping about a crime he may have wanted to commit.

Bill was looking down at the bloodstain. "So what's the plan?"

"Show me the safe," I said.

He nodded and led me to the bedroom. Walking in, an array of clashing colors and mismatched furniture assaulted my eyes. Garish wallpaper covered the walls, adorned with loud patterns of neon geometric shapes.

The centerpiece of this surreal chamber was a bed that screamed for attention. It had an eye-watering combination of pink satin sheets, sequin-studded pillows, and a neon fur-covered headboard.

Bill went to the closet door and pulled it open. With a loud creak, the closet doors revealed what lay within. Resting prominently in the corner, overshadowing everything else, was a gun safe. Its dull metallic finish stood out even against the already flamboyant backdrop of the room.

It seemed out of place, yet captured my attention with a mix of intrigue and discomfort.

"Was he allowed to own a gun?" I asked.

Bill shook his head. "There's no official record of him owning any weapons. That doesn't mean he didn't have an entire arsenal. You really think you can open this?"

"I said I'll try," I replied with a shrug. "I don't guarantee results. Besides, I might get a reading from it."

"As long as we're here," Bill agreed.

I pulled the drapes aside and let in more light, a terrible choice because it made the abrasive colors even worse. The window faced a tall white vinyl fence, blocking any view of the neighboring property.

"This guy liked his privacy," I pointed out.

"If you were up to something illegal and inappropriate, you wouldn't want people to see you do it," Bill acknowledged.

I peered through the open closet doors with clothing hanging from the closet rods, mostly shirts and pants with a few jackets. The tall, thin safe was built from black steel with a circular electronic keypad on the front. The whole thing was about twelve inches wide and twelve inches deep, shoved against the corner of the wall out of the way.

"If you cannot put in the correct combination within six attempts, it freezes up, so only the key will open it," Bill said.

I nodded, bending to look at the electronic lock more intensely. There was a residue of white fingerprint powder on the keypad. "Forensics dusted it?"

Bill nodded. "Yeah, in case we could figure out the combination from the keys he touched. They think the combination included the four, eight and zero, but several other numbers had fingerprints."

There was a small desk in the corner of the room opposite the bed. I grabbed the chair, returned to the closet, pushed the clothes out of my way, and sat facing the unit.

"Bill, I'm going to put myself—" I began.

"—into an altered state. Len, I know the drill."

I nodded and closed my eyes, focusing on my breath, and I lay my hand on the front of the safe. I willed myself to relax and allow anything that might come to me.

After feeling myself slip into a meditative state, I opened my eyes to see the room was in a sepia tone, superimposed over the sunlit room I was in.

"Bill, can you shut the drapes again? I can't really see what's going on."

The room darkened to the same dimness as my vision, and I saw the thin shape of Clyde Barton pacing the room. He walked to where I sat and his shadowy image pressed the keypad on the safe. I watched his fingers carefully.

4-0-5-8.

He opened a shadowy version of the door which passed through my leg and I looked down to see several reddish tubes in the bottom. I froze as Clyde reached down and stroked one tube lovingly.

He pulled something off a shelf in the safe and opened it up. It was a black-fabric vest covered in large pockets. Each pocket would fit the red tubes.

My eyes shot open, and I backed away from the safe.

I glanced over to see Bill staring at me, confused. "Did you get the combination?"

I nodded weakly, still backing away. "Bill, you need to get the bomb squad down here."

"Why?" Bill asked, suddenly alarmed.

"He was making a suicide vest and there's dynamite in that safe."

We waited outside the house for the Essex County Sheriff's Bomb Disposal Unit to arrive.

They pulled up in a large Humvee-style armored truck. Two men came out wearing standard uniforms, a one-piece jumpsuit. One was a thin African-American man, and the other a sturdy white man with a physique that suggested weight training.

Bill made introductions and referred to me as his civilian consultant.

"I'm Technician Moore," the black man said, as he shook Bill's hand. "This is Technician Carter. Tell us what's going on."

Bill explained the situation to the pair, as well as giving them the passcode for the safe that I discovered.

"Did you see if something connected the dynamite to any blasting caps?" Moore asked.

"No, the dynamite is just lying in the bottom of the safe," I volunteered. "I didn't see any blasting caps, but there was a small cardboard box on one shelf, and a vest that looked like he could use it as a suicide vest."

The sturdy man went back to the vehicle and pulled out a large helmeted padded suit, which he put on.

"You touched nothing, am I right?" Moore confirmed.

"Just the outside of the safe," I said.

With a nod, he headed back to his partner and helped him to put on the pieces of the protective suit. The upper body section had huge kevlar pads and a collar that went up around the face and around the neck. Moore put on kevlar pads that covered the front of his partner's legs, and once in place, he got the helmet for the suit.

Finally, the two men grabbed a heavy metal container, and the pair carried it into the house by a handle on each side.

Bill looked at me. "Are you sure he didn't booby-trap that safe?"

"When I saw him open the door to the safe, he just opened it. No tricks," I told him. "I'm not sure he had a plan to use the dynamite or if he ever intended to."

"Then why did he have it? More important, how did he get it?"

I sighed. "I don't know. Let's hope Galland can find out that information going through his computer."

Bill gritted his teeth, his attention focused on the house. "It looks like Clyde could've been a much bigger threat than we thought. I mean, an unregistered sex offender is dangerous enough, but a suicide bomber, right here in Mountainview?"

"Can you keep this out of the press?" I asked.

"I will seriously do my best. This is the last thing this town needs."

Moore came out, a walkie talkie in hand. He stood next to us and we heard his conversation with the man inside the house.

"Opening the safe now," came Carter's voice over the walkie-talkie.

I felt like I should cross my fingers or something. I'd been wrong about so much on this case, I hoped I was correct that there was no booby-trap on the safe.

We all waited. I was holding my breath.

The walkie talkie crackled. "Yeah, we've got dynamite in here. Also, a box of blasting caps, but not connected. Repeat, blasting caps are disconnected."

All three of us breathed a sigh of relief.

"I'm placing the explosives into the containment unit," Carter said, his voice echoed from the helmet.

"Roger that," Moore said into the radio, and then turned to Bill. "Thanks for calling us in, Lieutenant McGee. Whoever this guy is, you stopped a possible terrorist incident."

"Actually, we're investigating a murder," Bill told the man. "Someone shot the guy who owned the house, killed him."

Moore's eyebrows raised. "Maybe whoever shot him did us all a favor."

His partner called in an all-clear that the explosives were within the heavy metal disposal container. With a nod to us, Moore went inside to help carry it out.

"How does the prediction concept look now?" Bill asked.

I shook my head. "Like the program might have guessed correctly. But we still don't have enough evidence to prove that our trio of assassins knew anything about Clyde collecting explosives."

"What if they did?"

"Then they're still cold-blooded killers. If they had any inkling that Clyde wanted to blow up some landmark or kill people, they should have gone to the police."

Bill glanced at the house again. "If Barton had dynamite, it seems possible that Worling had some weapon as well."

I grimaced. "I have to agree with you. We should search where he lived. Did you track down his home address?"

"Yes, I can lead you there. It's a cheap lodging in Bloomdale, a rooming house. I doubt we'll find any safes with explosives in them there."

"We'll have to see," I said.

McGee consulted with Moore and radioed for Tylissa Booker to help close up and seal the crime scene. Then, the pair of us headed to our cars.

McGee took the lead as we made our way from Mountainview to a dilapidated area in Bloomdale. Liquor stores and the occasional pawn shop dominated the neighborhood. The few markets present had their windows covered with anti-theft bars that remained in place even during daylight hours.

We soon pulled in front of a building. The broken-down boarding house stood as a somber reminder of better days. It was once a bustling hub for travelers and tenants seeking temporary lodging. Now, the establishment seemed like a haunted relic, drowning in its own forgotten past.

Bill and I both got out of our cars and a crooked, weathered sign saying 'Rooms For Rent' greeted us as it hung precariously above the entrance. As we entered, the unmistakable scent of mildew and decay struck our noses. The once vibrant paint had long since peeled away, leaving behind only fragments that barely covered the splintered wood paneling of the house.

Inside the dimly lit foyer, stained and cracked linoleum floors did little to invite newcomers, the once shiny floors buried beneath a layer of grime. Bill and I walked up to a front desk where a disinterested woman sat on a stool looking at a small television set playing a game show.

The woman didn't look away from her television. "Yeah, waddaya want?"

Bill held out his shield and ID. "Police. I'm here to look through Worling's room."

This got her attention, and she faced Bill. She had the thin face of a smoker, brown hair that was matted and dull, and she glared at him with brown eyes full of malice. "You gonna get his shit out of there so I can rent the room? I can't afford to have it vacant."

"We're working on it, ma'am. You just have to give us a little time."

"Jeez, the bastard died days ago. I'm a small business, I can't have empty rooms—"

"If you could just get us the key, we'll only be a few minutes and then we're out of here," Bill said, keeping his temper in check.

The woman looked like she wanted to spit. She grabbed a key from a series of cubbyholes behind her, where it looked like she collected mail for residents.

"Get that room cleared as soon as you can," she complained. "I'm dyin' here."

"I'll do my best, ma'am," Bill said, and the pair of us headed for the elevator. Bill pulled out several blue nitrile gloves and handed me a pair. "Glove up. I don't want any trouble with evidence if we find anything."

On the fourth floor we walked down the narrow, creaky hallway, battered doors with rusty hinges guarded a series of cramped, poorly lit rooms. A pervasive smell of stale cigarettes and aged wood hung heavy in the air.

When we reached the correct doorway, Bill put the key in the door and, after a minor struggle, opened it. The room was even more depressing than the hallway, if that was possible. Dirty windows filtered the light. The scant furnishings were a testament to the quality of the location. There was a card table with an electric hot plate, a toaster oven, and a cube refrigerator under it. There was the one room, a bathroom, and a large closet. The unmade, sagging bed with threadbare linens was near the door, and a dresser with nearly unhinged drawers sat next to it.

"Another day in paradise," Bill wisecracked.

"Not much to the place, is there?" I pointed out.

"I think what little he had of value was at his office," Bill observed, opening the closet door. "This closet has some clothes, maybe a suitcase. You want to try your mojo?"

I sighed. "Might as well."

"Mind if I go out and try to locate a cup of coffee?"

"Check on the vehicles," I suggested.

"That as well."

"I'll be fine," I sighed. "I just need to see what I can find here."

"Should I get you some water? I know you need it after a reading."

I nodded. "Yes, please."

Bill locked the door behind him as he left.

There was a chair next to the bed, and I sat and closed my eyes, trying to relax.

Thoughts kept interrupting me as I tried to move into an altered state.

What if you can't find anything?

Your theory doesn't hold water...

Terry probably has nothing to do with any of this...

I moved past it by concentrating on my breath and releasing my need to be right. I didn't have a dog in this fight. If I found something, fine. If there was nothing to find, that was great. It wasn't my place to judge what I received, only to allow it in. It was my ego that wanted me to be important, but my job was to be aware of what there was to see.

I quickly moved into an alpha state, but then I went deeper, shifting my brainwaves down to delta, and then to the level closest to sleep, theta. I was striving toward theta, because that's when astral projection is possible.

I felt myself stand to look around the room, although my physical body remained in the chair. Glancing back, I saw myself sitting in the chair, looking like I was completely asleep. I merely shifted my mind so that I could take my spirit out for a walk. Astral projection always is a strange experience, which is why I don't do it very often.

I saw my ethereal form around me as I took a few steps away from my body. Nebulous and translucent, my astral self resembled my physical form, but with a faint, otherworldly glow. There was a silver thread connected to my body like an umbilical cord, but thinner.

I explored the scene. In this state, I possessed the ability to pass through objects and solid walls with ease, as though they were mere illusions.

I moved to the closet, which is where I felt a pull, and looked in it with a perception that could see more than the actual room. There were energetic imprints on many of the objects within. I not only sensed the energetic residue, but saw it as a spectrum of colors. This varied depending upon the emotion Alex Worling was feeling at the time he touched the object.

I was looking for something that he touched a lot and that glowed with colors that represented anger or fear, bright yellow for fear and red for anger or desire.

Since I was incorporeal, I hovered effortlessly through the scene. I didn't have to move things so much as move through them. There was an object glowing bright red in the back of the closet near the wall. I reached through the things in my way, and then my hand went into the wall itself.

It filled my mind with images.

I was looking down on a street from high above, on top of a building, or looking through the window up on a top floor. Down below me, I saw people lying on the ground in pools of red. In my hands was a high-powered rifle, with a long magazine and a scope on it, and I felt a sense of joy... of triumph.

I pulled back and found myself in the cheap rented room again, dazed and sickened by what I saw. I gently slid back to my body and carefully brought myself up to full consciousness.

I heard a key rattle in the door, and it opened to reveal Bill. He stepped in, holding a styrofoam cup of coffee and a bottle of water.

I slowly opened my eyes and tried to get used to being inside my body again.

"Any luck?" he asked, as he handed me the water.

I was still a bit dazed, so I pointed to the closet. "In the back," I croaked, my throat so dry I could barely talk. I opened the bottle of water and drained it. I felt bone-weary and realized I probably should have just done a reading of the room. Astral projection surpasses the boundaries of the physical world and allows me to see things hidden from others. But, it always wipes me out.

Bill put his coffee aside and went to the closet. He pulled things out of the way, putting them out on the floor. There was a box containing canned food, a battered suitcase, and another closed box with who-knows-what in it.

Bill looked at the back of the closet. "There's nothing here."

"The baseboard," I said, staying in my chair.

Bill glanced at me, frowned and knelt on the floor, reached into the closet, and pulled on the scarred wood trim at the base of the wall. He tugged and the entire piece came off in his hand, exposing a bag hidden in the wall itself.

"Okay, how the hell did you find this?" he asked, looking over his shoulder at me.

"I searched the room in astral form," I replied, feeling better from the water.

Bill reached back into the closet and pulled the heavy cloth bag out of the space in the wall.

"What have we here?" Bill asked as he placed it on the sloppy bed. He quickly opened a zipper and a gun barrel came into view. Mounted on the top was a heavy scope, and the glass glinted in the small amount of light. As he pulled it completely free of its cloth prison, I saw that folded down in the front were a pair of legs that the barrel could rest on while being fired.

Bill examined the weapon with a serious expression.

"What kind of gun is that?" I asked.

"I haven't seen one of these in years," Bill hissed. "It's a Barrett M82 — a fifty caliber sniper rifle."

The words sniper rifle echoed in my head.

That's what he wanted it for. That was his fantasy.

I looked over Bill's shoulder at the frightening machine. "I believe he was planning to shoot people from a prominent place."

"This would be the thing to do it with," Bill agreed. "It appears Mr. Worling may have also been a clear and present danger."

Which begged the question once again — how did the vigilantes know?

14. BATTERED BIAS

Bill had to remain at the scene while forensics came, as the high-powered weapon had to be fingerprinted and photographed at the scene. In the meantime, Bill reached into the secret hiding place and found a one hundred round box of fifty caliber cartridges.

More than enough for a killing spree.

I would have stayed with him, except he mentioned he saw Agent Montgomery at the MPD again, still going over case files on me. I left Bill without telling him where I was going, so there would be no one to stop me from confronting the smug agent.

In the car, I gave Jyanette a call.

"I'm about to head to my car," she said as she picked up.

"I've got to work on the case," I lied. If I told her I was going to confront Montgomery, she'd talk me out of it.

"Did something break?"

"Yes. We found dynamite in one of our victim's houses with the makings of a suicide vest, and a sniper rifle at another."

"You're kidding!"

"No. But from my point of view, the vigilantes could have just turned both of them into the police. Why didn't they just do that?"

Jyanette sighed, exasperated. "Because people like that don't believe in our system. They think everything is corrupt and only they can be the arbiters of true justice, as they are incorruptible."

"Sounds like I hit a nerve."

"It's just been a day. I'm still trying to get into my work groove again. I just had a meeting for a plea bargain my boss is insisting upon. This guy — Phillip Burke — is a piece-of-shit dealer and thief with an ego bigger than Manhattan. The whole thing just pissed me off. He'll be back on the street and we'll pick him up again a month from now, after he's done something worse than possession."

"I guess tonight might be a good night to come home late. Maybe after you've relaxed."

"Don't be too late, please," Jyanette implored. "You know I worry."

I pulled into the MPD lot. Though I had calmed a bit, my anger returned as I thought about the line of questions Montgomery used on Teddy Santos and Anna Sokolov.

It was one thing to turn my life upside down, but she had no business intimidating people who worked with me or were my students.

What I really wanted to do was send her back to Washington with her tail between her legs, but I doubted that would happen.

I let myself in the back way with my magnetic key card and walked directly into the main conference room.

She was there.

As she perused through a stack of files, she lifted her gaze from the one she currently had opened. Flipping over the legal pad she was furiously scribbling on, she stood up and neatly returned the folder to the designated box. Her dark tresses fell back as she straightened, preparing to continue her task.

"Doctor Wise," she said. "How can I help you?"

I didn't move any closer, even though the fact that I towered over her might be intimidating. I stood my ground and closed the door.

"By getting out of my life," I said. "It was low, even for you, to show up at the art museum to take photos."

"I wanted to know who would be there."

"Okay, since that doesn't sound probable, my second request would be to leave my friends alone." I fought to keep my temper in check and folded my arms over my chest. "You had no business talking to Teddy about Galland."

"Your Teaching Assistant learning hacking skills from an MPD cop?" she said. "I think that is relevant."

"My teaching assistant is a computer science major, and I'm lucky to have him. You made him feel threatened."

"If he has guilt about who he sleeps with, that isn't my problem," she scoffed.

"You don't get it. I know him, I know his family. Teddy doesn't want them to know his personal life, and your investigation doesn't require that information."

"I'll be the judge of what my investigation requires," she said, her chin up and her eyes defiant.

I forced myself to look away. A part of me wanted to meet her eyes, reach into her brain, and pull up the scariest, most horrible experience of her life and force her to relive it.

It would be so easy.

I held back, knowing that it was wrong. If I did that… violated her like that… I would be no better than the criminals I was trying to stop. The temptation was powerful. I forced myself to calm down, to think things through.

"Look, instead of nit-picking your way through those files, maybe it would be better if you went with me to a crime scene and see how I work?"

She did the smug smile again. God, I hated it.

"I told you, I don't believe in psychics."

"Maybe not, but I just found a suicide vest in a safe at the house of the victim in Mountainview. I also found a fifty-caliber sniper rifle in the rented room of that dead con man hidden behind the floor trim."

She narrowed her eyes with suspicion.

I went on. "Turns out they both held fantasies about blowing people up, or looking down from a high place and picking people off."

"And how do you know that?" she asked, her voice dripping with sarcasm. "Did you read their minds?"

"No, but I might have talked to their ghosts," I said.

She shook her head. "Utter bullshit."

"Fine. I will tell you what. There is a lawyer here in town whose office the Lieutenant and I want to go through. Why don't you go with me? We can take separate cars if you don't trust me."

"What will that prove?"

"I'll bet you I can find evidence to link the dead lawyer to the killers."

"Really?" she said, raising an eyebrow. "What's your bet?"

"If I find something, you buy me a cup of coffee. If I fail, I'll buy you one."

"That's it?"

"Well, I'd prefer to bet that you leave my friends alone, but I don't think you'd take it. I also would be nervous about what you'd ask for."

It was her turn to fold her arms. "I'd ask you to give up your work with the MPD."

This struck me for a moment. Now, at least I knew the goal of her investigation was getting me kicked out as a consultant.

On the one hand, I could give it up. It wasn't a paying gig and Jyanette would be happier if I wasn't getting myself into scrapes all the time. But I couldn't help but think about all the people who would never get justice if I wasn't there to help.

I tried to put on my poker face. "So coffee for now, and we'll work our way up to larger stakes."

She glared at me, but I saw she was thinking it through. Although I didn't like Agent Montgomery, I didn't for one second think she was dumb or bad at her job. I sensed she was smart and knew what she was doing. Confronting her was a stupid play, and I let my temper get the best of me. But if she came with me, and saw what I do, it might just turn things around. It might give her a chance to understand why I was a valuable asset for the MPD.

I pulled my phone from my pocket. "If it's a yes, I need to call Bill and get his permission and have him tell us where the keys are."

"Very well, I'm done for the day," she said and picked up the legal pad and put it in her leather messenger bag. "Let's go to your crime scene and you can show me what you do. We'll go in my car."

I quickly got Bill on the phone and he allowed entry to the crime scene and told me where the keys to the office were, and I could get them with no trouble. When I told him I was going with Agent Montgomery, this shocked him into silence.

Finally, he spoke. "Len, you will not do or say anything stupid, will you?"

"No, it's fine. We have a bet."

"A bet?"

"Yeah, she is going to watch how I work. If she thinks I am actually doing something, she buys me a cup of coffee, and if not, I buy her one."

"You're going to have to explain this to me later," he said, annoyed.

I left my cane in my van, as the last thing I needed was Montgomery playing with it and discovering the sword inside.

A few minutes later, I was in a black SUV with Agent Montgomery.

She had her own GPS built into the console and once I gave her the address; we were on our way.

Since we were having a moment of detente, I quietly asked, "By the way, there was a white van watching my house from the road last night. You didn't send someone to spy on my house, did you?"

"Not in a white van, Doctor," she said, not taking her eyes off the road. "Besides, you know I'm a one-woman operation. If I needed extra help, I'd have to contact the local FBI field office."

"That would be the FBI New Jersey Task Force."

"With your friend Kate Yearling — also she's a former lover, I understand."

I clenched my jaw. "It's gratifying that you're so thorough."

"I take my coffee black," she stated flatly.

We rode the rest of the way in silence.

She pulled the car into the lot in front of the five story office building on Bloomdale Avenue. The building had retail shops on the first level that were still open because it was not yet six PM. The pair of us got out, and Montgomery pulled two pairs of nitrile gloves from her glove compartment.

"I see you're prepared."

She handed me one pair, and we headed in the side entrance to take the elevator to the upper floor for Hallman's office.

As we rode up, Montgomery pulled on the gloves and asked, "Doesn't having a non-believer make it so your so-called powers don't work?"

She said powers like it tasted bad.

"It never has in the past. I'm merely going to see if I'm led to anything that will help my case."

"We'll see, won't we?" she said.

Both gloved up, we got to the office, and I pulled the key with its police tag. A large square of plywood covered the opening made by the battering ram, and a simple hasp with a padlock held the door closed and secured.

As I worked to unlock the door, Montgomery moved the yellow crime scene tape out of our way.

"Thank you," I said and flicked the wall switch to turn on the lights as we went in. I glanced around the room, the dusty volumes of archaic law books adorning the shelves, the leather bindings cracked and faded. Presiding over this murky realm was the centerpiece of the room. Hallman's imposing roll top desk sat in the middle of the room, crafted of dark, polished mahogany. Its burnished surface seemed to absorb what little light entered through the windows.

The desk's ancient exterior bore the scars of many ink spills and errant pen marks. Knowing Hallman, they were the aftermath of the deceitful documents he hastily created. The room was exactly the same as the last time I was in it. I saw the residue of fingerprint powder on the shiny handles of the wooden file cabinets. They loomed like silent sentinels, no longer guarding their corrupt master.

I tried to decide on my course of action, as my astral traveling in Worling's room tired me out and I didn't have my van with its supply of bottled water.

"So, what are you looking for?"

I turned the question around. "Are you at all familiar with the case?"

"Lawyer got shot. McGee said on his report it was the same guys that killed the con man in Bloomdale."

"Nice to know you're up to speed."

"Why did you want to come here?"

I pulled out the chair at the desk and sat down. "I have a theory about our killers, and I think Mr. Hallman had information about them."

Montgomery looked at me like I was stupid. "Shouldn't we be going through his file cabinets?"

With a smile, I closed my eyes and cleared my mind. I focused on anything hidden and put my attention on my breathing.

In… out, in… out.

I felt myself move into an alpha state, and I physically rose from the chair and peered around the room. The office shifted into sepia tones, and I saw Hallman at his desk. Sitting across from him was Terrence Garber. He was wearing a nice suit, and held a folder filled with papers in his hands.

Garber was speaking, but once again I couldn't hear anything they said. This annoyed me. Here was what could be the smoking gun, and I wasn't privy to the conversation. I watched the silent show, two men talking, but no sound emerging. There must be something here I could learn, as this moment created an energetic residue that I was receiving.

"What are you looking at?" a female voice said.

For a moment, it jolted me it wasn't McGee. Then, I remembered I was with Montgomery.

"I'm watching Hallman. He's doing a business deal with a suspect."

"What, his ghost?"

"No," I said as Garber handed the papers to Hallman, who got up and made his way directly through my body. "I'm seeing a moment with an emotional residue, a memory if you prefer."

I turned and followed Hallman to one of the file cabinets. He slid open a shadowy middle drawer and shoved the folder in about halfway back.

The pair of them faded from my view, as did the shadowy images of the office. I shut my eyes and gave my head a shake. When I opened them again, the office had returned to its regular colors.

"Come now, you expect me to buy that?" Montgomery said, her hands on her hips, staring at me in disbelief.

Ignoring her, I faced the cabinet and pulled out the middle drawer. I went through the folders, seeing if I could find the one that I saw Hallman put in there.

Danger...

I lifted my head and peered around the room. Everything seemed fine, but that was a pretty potent buzz. I sniffed the air and thought I smelled smoke. Worse than that, there was the scent of a sodden place where someone put a fire out.

"Now what?" she said impatiently.

"I'm not sure. We might be in danger." I focused on the folders again.

Danger...

I felt hot, as if they cranked the heat all at once, and the room was now stifling. My extra senses told me to get the hell out of there. My fingers flew down the folders, looking for the one Hallman placed there for Garber as sweat dripped into my eyes.

"You should get out. Something bad is about to happen," I told her.

"So you can destroy evidence?" she accused. "I don't think so."

Get out... Danger...

The buzz was louder inside my head this time, just as I saw the name 'Garber' and pulled out the folder.

LEAVE... NOW...

That final buzz screamed inside my head, and I turned and headed for the door, pushing the startled Montgomery in front of me.

"You take your hands off me," she threatened, as I pushed her through the door, only taking time to slam it shut behind us as we went.

She spun to face me. "Who do you think you are—"

I grabbed her and pushed her further into the hallway, ignoring her protests.

GET DOWN...

"Get down," I yelled as I pulled her to the floor, shielding her with my body.

Hallman's office door exploded outward with a flash of fire. A tremendous detonation rent the air. The repaired office door flew off its hinges and flew over our heads to land at the entrance to the stairs. I covered my head with my hands as debris fell down upon us. If we had been any closer, we both would be dead.

I rolled off the DOJ agent, my ears ringing as black smoke poured out of Hallman's office and flames glowed inside the room.

I coughed violently from the smoke, still lying on the floor, and through the hum in my ears I heard a loud alarm, some kind of bell going off.

I saw Montgomery sit up, debris falling off her clothes. She stared at me, then looked at the burning office. She got up, then moved on top of me, and put her knee in the center of my back.

"What are you doing?" I said between coughs.

She pulled my hands behind my back, not gently, and I felt handcuffs fasten around my wrists. A moment later she pulled me up on my knees. I stumbled to my feet, and she pulled me toward the stairs.

"The folder," I gasped. The hall was filling with the black smoke.

She let me go, then a moment later was back and pushing me to the stairway. She pulled me through the door and closed it. I stumbled and leaned against the wall to stay on my feet.

"I need my hands free," I croaked. "I can't go down the stairs."

"You are fucking under arrest!" she screamed at me.

I coughed again. "Are you insane? I just saved your life."

"You planned this, brought me here to put on this stupid show and act the hero. You think this would make me believe you're a goddamn psychic?"

"I don't care what you believe," I shot back. "We have to get out of here, and I can't go down the stairs with my hands cuffed behind my back."

She glowered at me, then turned me around, pushing my face into the wall painfully. With the cuffs off, I reached for the handrail and used it to support me as I started down the stairs. I went carefully down each step as I was still light-headed, and the ringing in my ears distracted me.

What had happened?

The office blew up, but how?

Was there a bomb in the office, cleverly hidden from view? Or did someone have a grenade launcher and shoot the explosive through a window?

My guess was they planted a bomb in the office — Tom Harrigan was an expert in demolitions from his combat training. I just showed up right before it was supposed to go off.

It was a locked door secured with police tape — how did they get in and set the bomb?

As we went, another fit of coughing overcame me, doubling me over. Montgomery pulled me upright and guided me along until she pushed open a door into the lobby, lit only by emergency lights.

Other people were evacuating as well. They were talking and lips were moving, but I only heard a murmur from the crowd as the loud alarm drowned out their words.

Even though I couldn't hear them, I sensed the panicked thoughts all around me. I allowed my mental barriers to fall away and refocused to keep them out of my head. Leading the way, Montgomery ushered me to the door, and we exited alongside the throngs of people congregating in the parking lot.

As I stepped out, smoke gushed out of the windows of the fourth-floor workplace. The detonation shattered the glass into smithereens, and a dense fog of grim smoke obscured the surroundings. The chaos was evident in the debris and remnants of the blast strewn all over the ground. It was a terrifying indicator of the sheer power unleashed within the office. No one expected it, and a sense of urgency weighed heavily in the air as the flames continued to spread.

I heard new sirens approaching and Montgomery pushed me along. She slammed me against her car, turned me around, and returned the handcuffs to my wrists. The other people headed to the outskirts of the lot, and some just got into their cars and drove off.

Police and a fire engine pulled into the lot, the sirens drowning out the building's fire alarm. The ladder truck maneuvered its way through the chaos, to extend a ladder skyward to the fourth floor.

Tylissa Booker stepped out of the MPD police car in the lot. She saw me and Montgomery and ran over to us just as I doubled over in another fit of coughing.

"I want this man arrested," Montgomery ordered.

She looked over at me, my suit damaged and me in cuffs. "You wanna arrest Doctor Wise? What for?"

Officer Galland had stepped out of the same police car and moved to take control of the scene. He helped guide in a second fire engine, and gestured to the onlookers to keep them back.

"He set off a bomb in that office," Montgomery said firmly. "He planned this."

"I gotta help Galland," Tylissa said and strode away.

Near us, the firefighters were spraying the damaged office through the broken windows, dousing the building with water to subdue the fire. They won minor victories, as some areas of the blaze seemed to shrink. In other places, the fire surged, fueled by the remnants of destroyed furniture and legal documents.

"The folder? Do you have the folder?" I asked.

"Yes, I have it," Montgomery said. "What's so goddamn important about it?"

"Does it have anything to do with 'flashes of future'?" I said.

Still annoyed, Montgomery opened the folder. "It's nothing! It's a stupid trademark application for—"

She stopped talking, her attention riveted to the pages open in front of her. After a moment, she looked up at me. She finally spoke. "It's a trademark request for a new software called 'flashes of future'." She turned another page. "Also a copyright application for software that is used as a predictive application."

"That's it," I rasped out. "That's what McGee and I need to get a warrant to go after our perp."

"You risked our lives for this?" she demanded.

At that moment, a vehicle I recognized pulled into the lot, a small red and blue rotating light flashing in its windshield. It pulled to the far end of the lot out of the way, and Bill McGee stepped out and jogged over to Montgomery and I.

"What's going on, Agent Montgomery?" Bill bellowed. "Why is my consultant in handcuffs?"

"He took us into that office," she said, pointing at the burning room. "Somehow he knew it would blow up, and he pulled us out at the last minute. It's a set-up."

He focused on me. "Are you all right? Your suit's a mess."

I said, "I was near the explosion. I've got ringing in my ears."

"Aren't you going to arrest him?" Montgomery demanded.

An ambulance pulled into the lot, adding its siren to the cacophony. I glanced at the building and the flames. They were consuming everything in their path, flickering and faltering under the relentless onslaught of water from the fire hoses.

Bill pulled his own handcuff keys and opened the cuffs, freeing my hands and handing the cuffs to Montgomery.

"Agent, I am going to have that ambulance over there take Doctor Wise to the hospital, and looking at you, I want you to go as well."

I pointed at the folder in Montgomery's hands. "Bill, the folder she has. It's the smoking gun. 'Flashes of future' is real and Garber created it."

Bill eyed the agent and held out his hand. With a frustrated exhalation, she handed it to him. Bill opened the folder, glanced at the papers, and nodded.

"Good work," he said, shutting the folder. "Now, both of you are going to the hospital."

"I'm perfectly fine," Montgomery argued.

"You both look like hell," Bill said. "And smoke inhalation can sneak up on you. Agent Montgomery, get in that ambulance with Doctor Wise."

He led the pair of us to the vehicle, and I was grateful to get into it and lie down on a stretcher. The adrenaline burst was wearing off and I could barely walk. The two EMTs looked us over and put oxygen masks on us both.

As the ambulance made its way to Mountainside Medical Center, Montgomery pulled her mask away from her face and said, "I still don't believe you're a psychic."

I pulled my mask aside and said, "I take my coffee with cream, no sugar."

We rode on in silence.

15. A MIND IS OPENED

At the Mountainside Medical Center, a doctor gave me a preliminary examination. I was told to clean the soot off my face and to change into one of those embarrassing hospital gowns.

I hadn't seen Agent Montgomery since we arrived.

As I lay in the bed with the oxygen mask on my face, I wondered why I had to be all but naked in a paper gown to be checked for smoke inhalation.

The ER doctor came into my room, writing on a clipboard. "Mr. Wise, I understand that you've had medical training."

I nodded. "Yes, at Johns Hopkins."

This made him raise an eyebrow, impressed. "Okay, so let me use the medical explanation. We've done a blood count and checked your carboxyhemoglobin and methemoglobin levels. We want to keep you overnight and on oxygen to err on the side of caution."

"Thank you, Doctor," I said. "I need to call my fiancée."

"Use the phone here in your room. No cell phones in the hospital." He examined the chart again. "You reported a ringing in your ears. Is that still prevalent?"

"No, it's fading."

"Probably a slight case of Noise Induced Hearing Loss. We'll add 60 mg Prednisolone to your IV. Then we'll check on it in the morning."

His diagnosis was sound. Prednisolone was a steroid and I read studies where doctors used steroids in Israel on military personnel for hearing loss.

They hooked me up to an IV. I didn't hurt as badly anymore and decided they'd added painkillers to my mix. I pulled the wired phone over and had to think for a minute as I tried to remember Jyanette's number.

A voice spoke up from the doorway. "You won't get me. I had to turn my phone off."

Jyanette stood in the doorway, a worried expression on her face. Her hair was in a bun and she wore a pantsuit, so she hadn't changed after work.

I smiled over at her. "How did you get here?"

"McGee called me, and your floor nurse let me come up."

She took me in a delicate hug, since I was wired up to machines, an IV, and an oxygen tank. She felt good, and I was thankful she was there.

"How are you?" I said.

"As usual, scared to death when you get hurt."

"You're not mad, are you?"

She sighed. "I spoke with Bill, and he said you saved yourself and that DOJ agent, and that you're a hero."

I was so glad to see my darling. "I did my best."

She held my fingers and rubbed the back of my hand. "Okay, now I want the truth."

Uh-oh.

"How long had your buzz been telling you to get out of that office before you actually left?"

Busted, once again.

I am the psychic in the family — how could Jyanette possibly know that I got warnings before I ran the hell out of there?

I sighed. "Maybe a few times. I left as soon as the warning was loud."

"That's the stuff I don't like," Jyanette said, her jaw set. "You've got this early warning system, and you just ignore it."

"I needed the folder I found. It's evidence."

She was unimpressed, and I could see my explanation didn't work. "And my soon-to-be-husband almost blown into pieces is not an acceptable way to get it."

"Sorry," I said, properly cowed.

She brought my hand to her lips and kissed it. "I'm not mad. I knew when I came back to you that this was part of the deal. But I prefer our wedding take place somewhere other than in a hospital. Can you work on that?"

"Yes, ma'am."

"And I heard you had a ringing in your ears. How am I supposed to nag you if you can't hear me?"

I stared at her in disbelief. "I hope you're kidding."

She broke into a huge smile. "No, I was just checking your hearing," she teased. "Now, I have to go home and try to sleep in an empty bed tonight."

"I promise I'll be home tomorrow and in one piece."

She raised one eyebrow. "I will do an inventory to make sure none of your parts got damaged."

"I look forward to it," I grinned.

She bent and kissed me, then headed out.

A nurse came in and injected something into my IV. It must have been benzodiazepine as well as the steroids, as I fell into a deep dreamless sleep. Like any drug or alcohol, it knocked out my psychic senses, which prevented images or thoughts from disturbing me.

I had a very peaceful night's sleep.

The next morning, I awoke to see the room filled with bright sunlight and a nurse next to my bed with something that resembled breakfast. I was ravenous.

A different doctor came by and checked my chart and said I could be released, so I called Bill and asked him to pick me up.

Within a few hours, dressed in my slightly singed suit, I was being pushed in a wheelchair out to McGee's unmarked police car.

"How are you feeling?" Bill asked as he pulled out of the lot.

"Better, thanks. Do you know what happened to my taser? It wasn't with my clothes."

"Yes, the hospital said you fell on it and smashed it. I think when you got knocked over by that explosion, you landed on it."

"Damn," I cursed. I focused on the more urgent situation. "Have you questioned Terrence Garber?"

"Not yet. We tried to reach him at the firm he consults for in New York. Turns out he's on a two-week vacation that started right before our first murder."

"The timing of that is suspicious."

"We thought so too, so this morning we got a warrant for his residence. He lives in his parent's place in Mountainview."

"I know it. I went there when I was dating Cathy. They lived in a mansion."

"It was an impressive place, I'll give you that. We went in with a warrant this morning and he wasn't there. However, we found his cell phone, and he had shut it off."

"So you can't track him by his phone. How about his car?"

"His regular car was at the house, but according to his neighbors, he's got an older car that he works on during weekends, which was missing. It's from the 90s and he'd spent months restoring it. But it doesn't have GPS or anything we can track."

"So he's off in the wind," I lamented.

"Very much like Tom Harrigan. We've had no luck finding his whereabouts, either."

"Do you want me to do a reading at the Garber house? Maybe I could find something."

"I would really like to find these guys and stop them before anyone else dies. Are you up to it?"

The rest I'd gotten in the hospital helped restore me. "I'll do my best."

"I should tell you — Agent Montgomery is meeting us there."

"What? How did she get involved in our case?"

"I thought you'd be pleased," Bill said, sounding surprised.

"Why would I be pleased? That crazy lady put me in handcuffs!"

"Len," Bill said, as if it were obvious. "If she's working on our case with us, she can't be investigating you."

I considered this as Bill drove. He had a point. Our case of the vigilante murders was taking up Agent Montgomery's attention. That meant she couldn't be putting my life under a microscope and bothering my friends and family.

"Did you talk her into this?" I asked.

"I spoke to her and suggested that if she really wanted to find the truth about you, working this case with us might provide her some insight."

I frowned. "And she agreed?"

"Wholeheartedly."

"That makes me nervous," I said. "Bill, there's no way I can ever convince her that what I do is real."

"Then you're no worse off than you already are. And it keeps her from bothering other people, right?"

He reached the same conclusion as me.

We drove in silence. All the problems ran round and round in my head as we pulled into the driveway for Terrence Garber's house.

I recalled a truly impressive, upscale home, just far enough away from the hustle and bustle of Manhattan. The house featured beautifully manicured gardens, a well-appointed courtyard, and impeccable architecture. The designers captured the essence of luxury living while remaining in harmony with its natural surroundings.

When I was last there, it offered both seclusion and privacy while boasting an unparalleled view of the iconic Manhattan skyline in the distance. It took full advantage of this vista, with floor-to-ceiling panoramic windows creating an enviable connection between the indoors and outdoors.

That was the way I remembered it when I visited with Cathy.

As we drove up the long and winding driveway, it was still a luxurious abode characterized by a mix of traditional and contemporary design. There were stately elements, such as classical columns and ornate moldings with sleek, modern touches.

It was obvious from the unkempt lawn and the overgrown hedges that things had changed. There was no external defacement, but it wore the look of neglect. The building appeared to be burdened by a lack of attention and care, despite no one causing damage to it.

It saddened me to see such a magnificent structure ignored for so long.

I couldn't help but wonder what happened.

And then it occurred to me. Cathy died, the Garber's passed, leaving Terry alone, the only remnant of that family.

And here I was trying to track him down and put him in a cage.

I told myself I wasn't responsible for his choices. His choices were his own. But it was little comfort.

I followed McGee into the house, where everything was familiar. Mr. Garber had died three years ago, and Mrs. Garber just before I returned to Mountainview. From all appearances, Terry had not maintained a thing since their passing.

Just off the foyer, I walked through a lavish living room featuring a stunning marble fireplace and rich hardwood floors. Floor-to-ceiling glass doors framed the unparalleled view of the city skyline. Padded chairs and a large sofa sat in muted colors, all the same as my last visit nine years earlier.

The adjoining formal dining room was equally extravagant, with a table that could easily accommodate twelve guests. Above the table hung a graceful chandelier. The furniture was solid wood and finely made, though I noticed a layer of dust on tables that Mrs. Garber would have never allowed. Not that she did her own cleaning — she had two women who came daily to clean and cook. My guess was that Terry hadn't maintained their services.

Like the dust on the tables, there was evidence that no one vacuumed or did the simple housekeeping necessary to maintain the rooms.

I walked past the large open kitchen, which was completely unchanged, but it all seemed to have the same feel of deterioration. The curtains were getting old and needed cleaning or replacements. The refrigerator held little, and taking a peek out on the veranda, it looked like the furniture sat outside all winter.

I felt tears in my eyes. I remembered sitting out on that veranda and talking with my soon-to-be in-laws about the wedding. Recalling myself out there holding hands with Cathy and speaking excitedly about our plans.

"Feeling nostalgic?" a woman said.

I turned without thinking, and I believe the look on my face was so intense, Agent Montgomery actually backed away.

"Don't fucking go there," I hissed. I walked back down the hall, with every intention of walking out of that house and never coming back.

"What location would work best for what you want to do?" Bill asked.

"I can't do it," I said, still heading for the door and fighting to keep my composure.

Bill put his hand on my shoulder. "Tougher than you thought?"

I stopped and shook my head. "It's devastating for me, Bill. In this house, I still feel Cathy and her parents. They're still here in my memory. But Terry? It feels like he was never in this house. It doesn't reflect him at all."

"Len, you can leave. I won't think anything of it."

I took a deep breath and gritted my teeth. "No, people could die if I do." I tried to clear my head as an obvious question occurred to me. "He did cybersecurity. Did you locate a computer?"

"Is it safe?" Montgomery said from a nearby doorway.

I felt sheepish. "Agent Montgomery, I want to apologize, I—"

"Save it, Doctor." She didn't look angry. In fact, she looked composed. "That was the first time I felt you'd been honest with me since we met." She turned. "I found the den, and it looks like a computer had been there. Come look."

I glanced at Bill, who shrugged. We followed her past the kitchen and into the small office off the main downstairs hallway.

I stopped in the doorway, recalling the night I was here with Cathy. Her father took me into this den alone. I remembered the older man sitting at his desk.

"Len, sit here." He pointed to a chair as he sat in a black leather office style chair that creaked as he leaned back. "I just want to talk, man to man."

"Yes, sir," I said, not knowing what to make of this.

"We raised Cathy a good Catholic," he said. "Now, you're talking about her converting to Judaism. I worry Cathy may feel overly influenced by you."

I wanted to laugh. My Cathy was a woman who knew her own mind and had no trouble expressing it. I merely replied, "Really, sir, we discussed it at length. It wasn't a simple decision for either of us."

"How so?" he asked, his eyebrows raised.

"I talked to her about what converting would require, and we also discussed what converting to Catholicism would require of me. We had some deep theological discussions, and she gave me books to read, and I gave her books of my own. We both knew it was a decision that would affect the rest of our lives."

"You came to this decision mutually?"

"Sir, Cathy growing up Catholic had a lot to do with that. I've tried to be a good person and live according to my faith. I also have respect for your traditions. They made your daughter the woman she is. All we want is to raise children that become good people. All I want is for Cathy to be happy."

He grew serious and watched my face. "That's what I want, too."

I stood in the office looking at that empty chair and found my eyes were wet again. I peered around the room and noticed a distinct, musty scent in the air. Dust settled upon every surface, casting a dull sheen over once vibrant wood and leather furnishings. Cobwebs crept along the corners of the room, as if silently reclaiming this space for the creatures who now called it home.

There were other ghosts here, but they were the ghosts of my memory, and some of those still haunted me.

Bill startled me back to awareness. "You okay, Len?"

Montgomery added, "You looked like you went into a trance when we stepped in here."

"You have no idea," I muttered and moved to the desk. I saw a rectangular pattern interrupting the dust on the desktop.

"There was a laptop there," Montgomery said.

"Easy to take if he needed to leave in a hurry," I pointed out.

"Do you think he was planning to run off the entire time?" Bill asked.

"Find him, and you could ask him," Montgomery suggested.

I sat in the chair. "Let's see if I can get something."

"Do you need me here to guide you?"

"I don't know what I'm looking for," I said.

McGee nodded and headed for the door. "Coming, Agent?"

"I thought I'd stay for the show," she said, and glanced at me. "Unless I'm going to ruin your aura."

"It's fine, but I won't be interacting with you."

"Just let me know if something is about to blow up," she countered. "With a little more warning this time."

Bill shook his head and left the room, and I closed my eyes. Pushing aside any concerns I had about the past, or Agent Montgomery, I focused on what I needed to do now: locate Terry and find these men who were killing people.

The way this house pushed at my memories made me work to shut out the surrounding room. I had to clear my mind, put my attention on my breath, and find Terry. I let myself move into an alpha state and rested there, seeing what would come.

The mists within my mind faded, and I looked down at a strange scene. I was in a dark room, and there was a head sitting on a table. It looked like someone beheaded a man and stuck his neck on to a metal pipe.

As the image became clearer, I saw it wasn't a real head after all, but some kind of casting. It was made of plaster and molded or sculpted. The pipe that came out of the neck went all the way through the top of the head. The face appeared vaguely familiar with its closed eyes, but I couldn't place it.

There were several self-standing metal shelf units against the far wall. Each one was about six feet long and four feet wide. On the eye-level shelves were two-gallon bottles of a clear liquid that read: Uni-Sil XS 0020 Part A.

Nearby was the same type of bottle, also with a clear liquid that had the same code numbers and Part B.

There were also large plastic containers that read: Disposable Mixing Cup- 5 gallons. On the next shelf there were many small plastic containers that had powders of many colors, and also carried odd names, like 'flocking pigment.'

On the lowest shelves were large blue forms in the shape of a man's head and shoulders, like odd blue shrouds. Bolts and wing nuts went around an extended edge of them, and I struggled to think what use they had. There were at least five of them all in a row on the bottom shelf. They were three dimensional and I could easily have put any of them over my head and shoulders.

The image faded, and I found myself back in the den. I opened my eyes and tried to understand what I had seen. A warehouse with molds that looked like someone's upper body?

If the vision was trying to give me some information, I could not fathom what it was.

"No luck?" Montgomery said from another chair. I glanced at her, and realized I'd forgotten she was there.

"Something... a warehouse. I don't know what it meant."

"You gonna buy me my coffee now?" she taunted.

I looked at the spot on the desk where the laptop had been. The perfect clean rectangle with dust all around it. What had happened to Terry, that he cared so little about his surroundings that he stopped doing basic cleaning?

I placed my hand on the spot where the laptop had been and closed my eyes. I focused on finding Terry, getting a glimpse of where he went.

A brick building appeared in my mind. It was obviously an old warehouse, of which there were many in parts of Mountainview and Bloomdale. The unique thing was that the building had a row of yellow bricks running just under the cornices on the roof. The building was older and dirty, but the yellow brick was easy to see.

The image faded, and I wondered if that was where he'd gone, or if it was the building that housed the strange molds and decapitated plaster head I saw.

"Anything else?"

I shook my head. "Nothing I can offer."

"I'll give it to you. You sure make it look good. If you have nothing, then I'll go back to the MPD and continue where I was with your files."

"Would you mind giving me a ride to the precinct? I left my car there."

She eyed me with suspicion. "Might as well."

She wouldn't care about what I saw and wouldn't help me, even if I told her my vision. This would have to be done alone.

I had to find that building — before anyone else got hurt.

16. OBSCENE OBJECTIVITY

Harper drove me to get my minivan still parked at the MPD.

"I don't think you tried to blow me up."

"What convinced you?" I said.

"McGee showed me the preliminary Fire Marshall's report. He said it was a good sized device with a timer. I doubted that you could have brought that in with us."

"No hard feelings, then?"

"I also don't think you knew about the bomb by some premonition. From the blast radius, he decided they set the device in the corner near those file cabinets where you were. I think you saw it on the floor and pushed us out of the room."

I nodded. "You're welcome."

"If you were actually psychic, you never would have let us into that office at all." Looking smug, Montgomery brought me to my van. "Keep me in the loop about these vigilantes. I might help."

I got out of her car and into my van, and watched Montgomery as she parked her car and went inside the MPD.

I pulled out of the lot and drove back to Hallman's office to see the aftermath of our brush with death. I pulled into the parking lot in front of the blackened former office with the glassless window frames.

If I didn't get that warning…

My abilities had saved me once again — the strange mental powers that began the night Cathy died, when I saw a demon in the middle of the road and crashed our car.

Had it been worth it?

The answer that immediately came to me was that it had not. The life I planned died that night, along with my lost love. I didn't feel I could ever balance the scales of Cathy's loss against any good I could do in this world.

Perhaps that was why I took these chances and tried to solve crimes. Perhaps I felt it was my penance for killing the woman I loved.

Maybe Jyanette was right to worry that my attempts at playing the hero would endanger me — and us.

I realized that to make my relationship with Jyanette work, it would require that I leave my guilt about losing Cathy behind. She wasn't the love of my life, Jyanette was. As Jyanette said, the universe had to go to a lot of trouble to get us together.

Warehouse…

The buzz pulled my attention away and startled me. I realized I had a much more powerful way to find the vigilante's hideaway.

I could allow myself to be led.

It meant driving around looking at buildings by myself. What if I stumbled upon the bad guys or found the missing Terrence Garber? Isn't that what I'd just been telling myself not to do?

It was the middle of the day, and I didn't think they would be in some lair making plans. If I found the building, I could text McGee the address. That solution made sense, and I drove out of the lot to follow my instincts.

The warehouse districts in both Mountainview and Bloomdale were near the railroad tracks.

I was interested in one specific building, the one with the row of yellow bricks near the top.

Driving down the streets, I headed down to meet the train tracks, as most of the older warehouses in town were located near the train. I passed through some middle-class neighborhoods, then down into an area of older buildings. Several buildings being boarded over and unused surprised me. In most of Mountainview, they'd replaced the older warehouses or renovated them into office space.

I continued down side streets, always keeping near the train route, and moved out of Mountainview and into Bloomdale, then back. I passed a building that was once a restaurant. The owner covered its first floor brick construction with fancy wood paneling, which now stood faded from sun and neglect.

With the train lines on my right, I passed a vast warehouse with no signage, and the next block was filled with large Victorian style houses.

I went about two and a half blocks when the street abruptly stopped at a dead end with a large chain-link fence closing off the end of the road.

Behind the high fence, there was a building blocked by a large dump truck sitting near a set of tall, locked chain-link gates, blocking a clear view of the structure. Beyond the train tracks, I saw a skating arena constructed on the site of a former warehouse.

I pulled to the side of the road so I didn't block anyone trying to get down the street. With cane in hand, I walked to the pair of six-foot-tall gates that opened inward. A large, heavy chain with an impressive lock held the gates together and immobile. Further along, the fence was only a few feet tall, built on top of cinderblocks filled with cement. I peered around the dump truck, and my eyes rested on a brick warehouse — with a row of yellow bricks along the top.

Bingo.

There was a battered white metal sign reading:

Private Property

No Trespassing

The building itself was quite large, with several regular doors, as well as oversized overhead doors for deliveries. Were the people I sought using part of this space?

I went back to my van and, using the GPS, I pinpointed where I was and texted the address to McGee.

In a corner of the fence was an old stump from a long-removed tree. If I climbed up on that, I could easily jump over the part of the fence right next to it. My additional concern was how I could get out, especially if I had to do so in a hurry.

Wearing jeans, a long sleeve shirt, and my damaged sports coat from the explosion, I had not attired myself in clothing for spy work. Then again, it was only early afternoon, so people would see me walking around anyway.

With the use of my cane, I pushed myself up onto the stump. It's amazing how much difference it makes to have a right knee that can bend. I stepped onto the fence, and then jumped down, but the sleeve of my sports coat caught and a part of the cloth ripped. I cursed under my breath at the small triangular rip in my right sleeve.

I stepped past the huge dump truck, and I now saw a sign on the building. It was old and discolored.

GARBER INDUSTRIES

I stared at it in disbelief — this made perfect sense. Terry and Cathy's father made his money in land development, including construction. This must have been the location of the construction side of his empire when he was alive.

Why hadn't I suggested McGee look for land owned by the Garber family? Then it occurred to me that maybe it wasn't part of Terry's inheritance. Maybe the site was owned by the corporation or had long since been sold to a developer.

I crept toward the building, glancing up to see if there were any cameras. None came into view, which was good.

They couldn't see me coming.

The entire facility looked like an abandoned warehouse. There were several such buildings along the train lines in this part of New Jersey.

I tried the first door I came to, which was locked. What did I expect? An open door and an invitation into the evil den, where the bad guy would answer all my questions as he monologues about his brilliant plan?

I considered going back to my van to wait for McGee.

I was driven to keep going, moving from door to door, looking for one that might be open or have a flaw that might allow access. I had my cane with its twenty-four inch blade and I had used it to finagle a few locks in my time.

When I reached the far side of the building, I noticed a back gate that operated by a recently installed winch and chain mechanism. Next to the gate, there was a car. It was one of those little hatchback vehicles that was good on gas and looked to be an older model.

My eyes went to the side of the building and noticed a single sturdy metal door, freshly painted, which seemed out of place on the older building. It was complete with a small square window conveniently placed at eye level.

I moved to the car and lay my hand on the hood. It was warm to the touch.

Someone was here.

Move, now…

Acting on the buzz, I hurried to the corner of the building, shifting position to be out of sight from anyone who came out of the metal door. I couldn't really hide since it was still broad daylight.

I heard the heavy door open and I slid back against the wall. If whoever it was took even a quick glance around, he would easily spot me.

I needn't have worried. The guy headed straight to the car, got in, and started it up. The chain-link gate rattled and slowly opened as he started the car.

I stayed flush against the wall as the guy drove off. As he pulled through the gate, it closed again. I stayed where I was in case he could glimpse me in his rearview mirror.

The man looked familiar: average height, sandy hair, body of someone who works out. Why was he so familiar to me?

Then it hit me.

In the dream where I saw Tom Harrigan as the shooter and Terry as his associate, this was the third man.

In my vision of the events, the third man had powerful arms, but a gut that this man didn't have. The fellow I saw in the vision looked completely different, bald and jowly.

My vision and that strange dream showed me dissimilar people, which is why I dismissed the dream.

That man was the third guy from the dream, not the one from my visions.

Curiouser and curiouser.

With the car out of sight, I left my hiding place and moved to the door. It was indeed heavy steel, and the small square of glass was reinforced with wire, so even shattered, I couldn't reach in.

There was a metal doorknob and above it, a deadbolt lock. I gently grabbed the doorknob — locked.

I sighed. I was so close. Then a buzz filled my brain.

Spare key...

I looked around, trying to see what could have caught the attention of my extra senses. Everything looked completely normal for a parking lot, and then I noticed that a rock on the side of the building seemed to glow.

I picked it up, and it felt lighter than it should have. When I turned it over, there was a panel on the bottom. It was nothing but plastic. I slid the panel to reveal a key.

I unlocked the door and returned the key to its hiding place and put it back where I found it.

I stepped into the darkness, pulling the door closed behind me.

The first thing I heard was a dull hum, like an air conditioner running on high. The only light was coming in through the small square at the window, and it took a moment for my eyes to adjust. There were doors on both sides of a hallway that must have been where the construction company had its offices. I proceeded slowly down the hallway, my cane in hand, ready to use it as a weapon if needed.

The entire place had an odd smell — a powerful odor that was vinegary, and extremely astringent. There was also an ozone scent, like a lot of electronics, all working at once.

A door to my right was making the loudest hum. The door opened to a room filled with servers on large metal racks running from floor to ceiling. The room was in darkness except for the hundreds of blinking lights on the multitude of servers and three lit monitors on a desk.

The room was warm, and the sound was coming from several large fans built into the ceiling sucking out the hot air.

The desk was next to one wall with monitors, two keyboards, a mouse, and a touchpad. It had a very comfortable looking wheeled leather chair, and I knew why Terry didn't have a desktop computer at home. This was where he was doing his data mining.

I closed the door and continued down the hall, where the ozone smell faded and the vinegar one increased. I was trying to allow my abilities to lead me, but I probably already saw enough.

At the end of the hall, I turned to my right and opened a door. It was the dark little room I had seen in my vision, with supplies on industrial metal racks and that odd beheaded plaster cast on the metal pipe.

I looked at the plaster face. It appeared to be a life casting of the very person I saw drive off a few minutes ago in his car. The head was hairless; the ears covered with something like a bald cap when they made the casting.

But why?

My extra senses were not giving me any helpful information. They guided me here, but I still knew as little as when I first arrived.

On the metal racks were the same strange blue shrouds. They had a cloth-like appearance, but they were hard plaster bandages. There were five of them, and each one was some kind of mold.

But a mold for what?

In one corner of the room was a washer and dryer, and on the wall above them was a solid plank with wooden dowels holding several full-face gas masks.

Whatever they used for the molds must involve some caustic chemicals and the masks were necessary to breathe during the process.

Backing out into the hall, I closed the door behind me. I headed directly across to another door and opened it. Feeling around for a light switch, I fumbled it on.

Fluorescents blinked overhead, and I saw faces staring at me with dead eyes.

I cried out in shock. My knees almost gave out on me and I was grateful I had my cane to keep me upright.

It was the three men from my vision, the ones who committed the murders. Beheaded, their disembodied faces hanging with open mouths on top of a round table in the middle of the room.

Behind them, lighted mirrors glowed against the wall, reflecting the back of their heads.

After a moment, as my shock faded, I realized they were not staring at me with dead eyes — styrofoam filled their eye sockets.

An armature held the heads up and when I touched one it felt cool, and a lot like skin, but it was a very flexible and lifelike type of rubber or silicone.

It was a mask.

More than just a mask, as I studied it. Someone put each hair on the head individually, as if growing out of the flesh.

I pulled the head of 'shooter guy' off the supporting form. It came up easily and then flopped over and hung loose, the head distorting when nothing supported it anymore.

These were indeed masks. But they were incredibly high-quality ones that completely covered the head and neck. There were flaps of fake skin that hung down to be tucked into clothing and complete the illusion.

This explained why I thought the shooter's mouth moved oddly, and why the faces I saw appeared out of place. My special senses were trying to tell me the truth, which is why I had the dream where I saw their actual faces.

Hanging from several pipes were three jumpsuits, two larger and one smaller. Each had a small patch that read: Maintenance. Since I did not see these in my visions, I wondered what they were for.

I also examined the lighted mirrors around the room. They had chairs in front of them, like make-up mirrors used in theaters. There, each of the three men could put on the masks and adjust them. Each mirror had a small ledge built out of the wall, and on it were different makeup products: a flesh-colored foundation, eyeliner, and more.

They must make the masks themselves — that explained the molds, the chemicals, and pigments. Since Terry was the computer guy and Tom was the shooter, it was logical to assume that the third man could be the artist who made the masks. This made sense of the blue molds I found. Those were what was used to cast the head coverings. There was probably also a mold for the belly the third man wore at the shootings, which again made me think the trio looked far different.

I pulled out my phone to call McGee.

When the screen opened, I saw I had no signal bars at all, and words claiming 'No Service' scrolled along the top of my phone.

I broke out in a sweat. Moving to the correct app, I checked to see if my text with the location went out to McGee earlier. I quickly pulled up the last text to see a red mark on the display.

It failed to send.

No one knew where I was, and I had contacted no one as backup. I didn't need extra senses to know I needed to get the hell out of there right away.

Slipping my phone back into my pocket, I replaced the mask on its support. I turned off the lights and was about to run back into the hall.

Suddenly, above the hum of the computer fans, I heard a sound.

Remaining in the darkened room, I closed the door to just a crack and peered down the hallway. I was just in time to see three men enter the building, talking quietly.

It was the sandy-haired man from the car, along with two men I recognized easily: Tom Harrigan and Terry Garber.

I leaned back into the darkness of the room, watching them, my heart pounding. Terry and Tom were not only involved in the crimes, they were the ones who committed the murders.

If I didn't get out of here, I would be next.

17. FALSE PROPRIETY

My mind flashed with a quick buzz.

Danger…

Like I didn't know. Sometimes the timing of my precognition isn't much help.

What could I do?

The three of them walked into the room of servers, leaving the door open. I couldn't hear what they were saying over the hum of the exhaust fans. That hallway was the only way to the exit door, and if I tried to escape, they would see me. Trying to outrun them was a foolish notion. Even though I could now bend my leg, I still didn't have the leg strength to outrun Tom or even Terry.

I glanced at my watch. Almost three PM. I was supposed to be meeting Anna Sokolov at Mindy's Diner. I couldn't even use my cell phone to call or text her — then it hit me.

Anna and I had a way of communicating that didn't need cell phones or any technology at all.

We could use telepathy.

She and I easily communicated while in the same room, and there was a time when she sent her thoughts to me long distance.

But that had been when the people who abducted her frightened her out of her wits. Would it work now?

If being frightened helped, I was pretty scared myself.

I silently shut the door and stepped away from it, being careful not to bump the table with the masks. I moved a chair to behind the door. If someone came in, I was in a dominant position to push against the door and slam it against whoever it was.

I sat in the dark room, closed my eyes and reached out, letting the protections around my mind come down and opening my mind.

Anna…

I felt myself moving through a misty place, reaching out to wisps of consciousness, trying desperately to connect, to touch my mind to hers. I pictured her face strongly in my mind.

Anna Sokolov…

I didn't sense any response, and it worried me. I concentrated harder.

Anna, please hear me…

Len…?

I felt the small voice almost more than I heard it. My heart raced, and I had to stop myself from becoming too excited. I needed to stay in an alpha state for this to work. I forced myself to take deep, slow breaths, and reached out with the image of Anna firmly in my head.

Yes, Anna, it's Len Wise. Can you hear me…?

I saw Anna in the diner. She was in the back room where we practiced, with papers laid out in front of her. Next to her was a coffee mug and a carafe of coffee.

I can hear you. Where are you...?

Anna, I am in trouble...

I sensed the panic rise in her.

Stay calm. I need you to contact the Mountainview Police Department...

I felt resistance.

I can't. They'll think I'm a crazy kid...

I couldn't contact anyone but her, so she had to be the one to make the call. Then, an idea struck me.

Do you still have the business card of that DOJ agent? She will listen to you...

I didn't know if Agent Montgomery would believe Anna or not, but at least Anna had met her and had her number. She might convince the agent.

Again, I sensed doubt and a mix of emotions, fear, excitement, and concern about me.

I can try that. Where are you...

Tell Agent Montgomery I am at the old Garber Construction Company warehouse at the end of Canal Street. Can you remember that? Canal Street...?

Canal Street...

Her resistance was fading, and a sense of resolve was stirring within her.

I am hiding in the warehouse, and I need help to get out...

Panic filled her mind, blinding and off-putting.

OH GOD! ARE YOU IN DANGER? OH GOD...

Her thoughts were bursting with emotions that made it almost painful for me. I had forgotten that with teenagers, emotions are still so raw and powerful. I sent feelings of calm along with my thoughts.

I'm all right so far. You must call her right away and tell her about Canal Street. The brown steel door is the correct one. Tell her…

I will…

From sheer exhaustion, I ended the communication. I think I blacked out for a few minutes. The strain of using so much mental energy wore me out and I was semi-conscious for a while. It didn't appear that anyone had come in or out during my communication with Anna or for however long I was not conscious.

I was still not safe. Even if Anna got through to Montgomery, it didn't mean the cavalry was on its way. I just hoped that Montgomery had the wisdom to bring backup.

I heard voices out in the hall and cursed under my breath. Drained and thirsty, I knew well that pushing myself like that was exhausting, and I didn't have the strength for a second attempt.

I listened, hoping that I might hear them if they drew close to my door. From the tone of their voices, it seemed like they were standing out in the hall arguing about something.

The voices grew louder and I heard them more clearly. I moved the chair back where it belonged, and slipped back into the corner to hide better, as they sounded like they stopped right outside my door.

"When I agreed to this, it was only because the program pointed us to people who were about to commit a major crime that we could prevent."

I knew that voice. It was definitely Tom Harrigan.

He went on. "It wasn't part of the plan to have me set that bomb in Hallman's office!"

"He's right," said a voice I didn't recognize. "Hallman wasn't a threat to anyone but you."

"He was a threat to us all," Terry said, and he sounded angry. "The blackmailing bastard figured out from the copyright papers for 'flashes of future' and what it did. He put two and two together. He would have brought us all down."

"Our agreement was that we would only take out major threats that the police couldn't stop," the third voice said.

"Dan's right," Tom said.

Dan. At least I now knew all the players.

Terry continued. "So far, it's gone according to plan. If they have any camera video of us, they only saw the masks."

"What if Len Wise is really a psychic?" Tom pointed out.

"You actually believe that crap?" Dan challenged.

"He convinced a lot of guys at the MPD," Tom replied.

Terry interrupted. "Even if he is, the only faces he could have seen are the masks."

He had me there. Except my abilities knew better.

"We have only one last target," Terry proclaimed, "and it's set for tonight."

Tom grunted. "Then you sell the program and we split the money."

"A pity we can't use the case histories to show that it works," Dan added.

"No need," Terry assured. "Once that bomb goes off, the DOJ will clamor for the program. It has to be a big event to get the

DOJ to shell out the money," His voice grew fainter as the three of them walked away, still talking.

I was weary, but I couldn't help but wonder what they'd planned. I tried to think of ways I could find out, and the image of Jyanette with her face blown off filled my mind.

A cold sweat covered me.

I closed my eyes and focused on the image. I needed to see where this would happen. Terry said a bomb would go off. Where was it going to be set?

My mentor, Dr. Kohl, said that my abilities tapped into energetic residue at crime scenes that I interpreted as a vision. Here were three minds putting out their intentions. I needed to sense what they wanted to do.

I stayed focused on the image of Jyanette, even though it frightened me. Suddenly I saw she was lying on a floor, and the surrounding room filled in, solidifying in my mind. There were large machines ripped apart and a steel shelving unit had fallen to the floor, spilling reams of paper and black toner. The explosion burst through a wall, misshaping a doorway. Plaster and broken metal studs lay in pieces, burning, and smoke was everywhere.

I stood in that hall looking down at my darling, and around me I saw other dead people on the floor. A man in a suit was among them, ripped apart by the blast. Another wore a uniform and I saw that patch on his arm. It read:

Essex County Court
Bailiff

The realization washed over me. This was part of the Essex County Courthouse. With Jyanette there, it had to be offices. Her offices.

A bomb in the prosecutor's office? It made sense. That was where Jyanette worked. But why? What criminal conspiracy could happen there?

Terry said the operation was tonight. What could I do? For me, the safest strategy would be to stand here and wait to see if they go.

My only other option was to fight if they came into this room. I could smack at least one of them with the door, maybe strike another with my cane. My taser was gone, destroyed when I fell on it. I would be in trouble if Tom had a weapon. The bullets they used in that gun could blast through the door without even slowing down.

I also knew that, eventually, Dan was going to come into this room to check on the masks. I hoped they would leave the building and come back. Surely their plan was for late at night?

I focused on my breath, keeping it nice and steady. Panicking would not help. I still had time to stop them, if I could just get away.

I stood there for what felt like hours, as time became meaningless. Standing alone in a room in the dark and only hearing the murmur of voices above the roar of exhaust fans made time creep by impossibly slowly. Shifting from foot to foot was not helping, and my right leg was aching from the unforgiving concrete floor.

I finally dared to move to the door and carefully turned the handle. I opened it up a crack so I could once again peer down the hallway to check on the trio.

From what few snippets of conversation I could hear, I sensed they were back in the computer room, and I watched for any movement.

My leg continued to hurt, and I would have to sit down soon, or my leg was going to give out on me. I leaned more heavily on my cane and watched soundlessly.

Tom was the first to step out of the room. He glanced down at my end of the hall and then in the opposite direction at the door. He was wearing a light coat and long pants, and I didn't see the bulge of a weapon either near his shoulders or hip. He faced the computer room and announced to Dan and Terry, "Are we going to get dinner or what?"

I looked at my watch. It was almost five o'clock. I contacted Anna at about three-thirty. Where the hell was Agent Montgomery? Of course, Montgomery needed to assemble a team, and that might have taken a while. There was also the possibility that Anna hadn't convinced her. Now I was too exhausted to attempt to contact her.

If they went out to dinner, I would have my chance to escape.

Dan pushed past Tom and headed my way. "I need to check the uniforms, make sure they're ready."

Leaving the door open the small amount it was, I hastened back to my spot where the open door would hide me. I stood against the wall and waited.

He burst through the door and swung it open. I caught it and pulled it to cover myself, slipping into the gap as far as I could.

The fluorescent lights flashed on, and Dan came into the room. He wasn't trying to be quiet at all, and I could hear his footsteps as he made his way to the jumpsuits.

I stood still, the doorknob in my left hand, trying to make sure he didn't glimpse me in one of those damn make-up mirrors. Keeping my feet pulled back, I hoped he wouldn't catch sight of my shoes under the door. I kept my breathing as quiet as I could, but I was pretty sure he couldn't hear me over those fans down the hall in the computer room.

I didn't know what he was doing as I couldn't see him, but I assumed he checked the coveralls and maybe even the masks. I was ready for him to finish up and head out. All I had to do was release the door handle the moment he touched it, and pray he'd turn the light out without looking back.

I heard him near the door and felt the knob quiver as he took it. I let it go and held stone still.

The door swung — in the mirror across from me, Dan looked right at me, and our eyes met.

"What the—?" He grimaced in stunned surprise.

I threw myself against the door, slamming him between the wood of the door and the frame, and he cried out. I yanked the door open, and he dropped to one knee. I slid my cane down in my hand, swung the stick, smacking him in the head with the heavy metal cobra, and he fell out into the hall.

I slammed the door shut, moving as fast as I could, the element of surprise still in my favor. Grabbing a chair, I forced it under the doorknob, which jammed it to block the door.

I backed up and felt something on my neck, jumped and spun around, only to find I walked into the coveralls hanging from the plumbing.

There was a pounding at the door, followed by the thumping of someone slamming themselves against it.

The chair held the door closed.

I hit the catch on my cane, and the twenty-four inch blade slid out of the wooden shaft.

What was I planning to do, stab them?

Probably not. If they broke a hole in the door, I could certainly damage any part of their anatomy they tried to shove in. Looking at the masks, I got another idea of just how useful this blade could be.

Another loud noise came from the door as someone, probably Tom, threw himself against the door a second time. The door made a cracking sound this time, and I knew it could not hold for long.

Staying out of the way of the door, in case a gun was the next attempt, I yelled out, "Stop it, right now! I have a knife and I'll cut up these masks if you don't stop."

I stepped to the first mask, again making sure to not be directly in front of the door. I grabbed it by the neck of the styrofoam head and put the blade of the sword against it.

"Leonard?" Tom asked urgently from the other side of the door.

"Yes, Tom, it's me," I said. I was breathing hard again.

"Why don't you come out here and we can talk about this?" Terry said.

"I know you're out there too, Terry," I said. "I have a better idea. Why don't all of you surrender before the police get here?"

Terry chortled, a disgusting, rueful sound. "If the police were coming, they would already be here. We know there's no phone service at this location. That was one reason I picked it. How were you planning to contact them? Smoke signals?"

"I'm in here with these masks of yours and these maintenance uniforms. In a minute, I'm going to slice and dice, and you guys won't have your precious disguises."

"Don't be hasty," Terry said, alarmed. "Len, we're doing a public service."

"A public service?" I repeated, disbelieving. "Committing murders?"

"We're stopping people before they commit atrocities that will kill dozens of people," Terry said. "Like you, Len. It's a matter of predicting the future, finding the criminals who will commit terrible acts before they do it."

"And blowing up the Essex County Prosecutor?" I yelled. "You consider that office a terrible threat?"

He was quiet, and all I heard was the noise of those damn exhaust fans in the distance. Apparently, my vision was correct, and it was their intended target.

Terry finally spoke. "At ten o'clock tomorrow morning, the Essex County Prosecutor is meeting with a criminal named Phillip Burke. The guy is a low-life drug dealer and petty crook, and they're going to work out a plea bargain which will allow him to be released from custody the same day."

I frowned. How could Terry know such things with such detail? That name — it was the one Jyanette told me about that morning.

The case she was working on.

Terry continued. "Within a week, Burke will attempt the robbery of a bank here in Mountainview. As part of the threat, he will have plastic explosives so the police don't storm the building. However, he is unfamiliar with the explosives. He will accidentally detonate them prematurely, take out the bank, and most of that city block."

I was stunned. "You cannot know that."

Terry continued. "The blast will kill everyone in the bank and several nearby stores. It will burn down ten buildings and kill upward of a dozen residents who live in apartments above the stores. I know it, because he already purchased the explosives and hid them where the police cannot find them."

"Then go get the explosives if you know where they are!" I yelled. "With your plan, you will kill people in the prosecutor's office!"

"I don't know where Burke is keeping the explosives. Tomorrow is the only time I am assured of his location before he attempts the bank heist."

I decided on another tack. "Terry, you have many other choices. Contact the police, let them know what you have. You cannot take the law into your own hands."

Terry snorted that disturbing laugh again. "Says the man in our warehouse, threatening me with destruction of my property."

"You left me no choice."

"And society left me no choice," Terry replied angrily. "I've been trying to explain to police for months, warning them of potential threats my program predicts. They ignored me, told me to leave them alone. I found it necessary to create a team of like-minded people who could get the job done."

I shook my head and looked at the masks. "Well, you'll have to do it without these masks."

The one I'd grabbed was the bald man Dan had worn. I pressed the sword blade against the face and sliced it. It felt odd, like I was ripping through actual human flesh. A line appeared on the face where I sliced, and the silicone rolled away exposing the styrofoam head, which I also sliced into.

As I lifted the sword again, a buzz flashed through my mind.

Get down, now…!

I fell to my knees just as a deafening explosion rent the air. As debris fell on top of me, I shielded my face. The force of the explosion blew the mask I cut completely off the table. It glared up at me from the floor with a large hole in the middle of the face.

That could have been me!

A large hole gaped in the middle of the door. My ears were still ringing from the noise, but I saw a canister the size of a soup can fly through the opening and bounce onto the floor. It issued smoke and a steady stream rapidly filled the air.

Tear gas!

My eyes were already stinging, but I didn't have a gas mask or some way to stop the flow of the mist that rapidly filled the little room. I lay on the floor with my hands over my head and coughed.

Suddenly, hands were grabbing me and roughly pulling me to my feet. They dragged me from the room.

They had me, and there was nothing I could do.

18. EVEN-HANDED BOUNTY

The gas temporarily blinded me, and I blinked, coughed, and moaned as they dragged me to a chair in another room.

I continued coughing as they duct taped my arms to a chair as I sat there choking, blinking, and fighting the urge to throw up.

My hearing was slowly returning, and I heard Tom bark at me. "Lean your head back and keep your eyes shut."

I did as I was told, as there wasn't any point in fighting. I jumped a bit as I felt water run over my eyes. It was cooling and refreshing and helped to stop the terrible itching.

I straightened my head, coughed, and opened my eyes.

Terry Garber towered above me, one of the gas masks hanging loosely from his neck. I sat in one of the heavy metal chairs in the computer server room. They restrained both of my arms with layers of duct tape. The room was warm, humming from the machines and exhaust fans.

Terry held the sword from my cane in his hands, examining the blade.

"Were you planning to use this?" he smirked. "We're lucky you only hit Dan on the head and didn't run him through."

I growled, "Killing's your thing, not mine."

These few words caused me to fall into another fit of coughing.

"Might be a poetic ending if I stabbed you with your own sword," Terry mused.

I coughed in reply.

Tom came back into the room, his own gas mask in his hand. He used a moist towelette all over my hands and face.

"Do those things really work?" Terry asked.

"We used them with gas training in the service," Tom explained. "These special wipes stop the burning and itching."

He wiped all over my face with the heavy towelette, and it brought relief with it. He then held a plastic cup of water to my lips and tipped it as I drank.

"Thank you," I croaked once the cup was empty and removed.

At least if Terry was planning to stab me, I wouldn't itch so much.

"How are the masks and the coveralls?" Terry demanded.

"We're lucky that room had an exhaust fan as well," Tom reported. "The gas is out of the room and it won't spread through the warehouse."

I wished I'd known that when they set the gas off.

"The coveralls are fine," Tom went on. "When we blew the door, Dan's mask got hit by the bullet and it's unusable."

"Pity you missed the doctor. That would have saved us several problems," Terry said, and pulled my phone out of my jacket pocket. "Check on Dan, I'm going to take care of his phone."

Tom nodded and headed out. Terry took my phone to the desk, and using a small tool, he removed the SIM card. He then put it into a card reader connected to the computer.

"The phone doesn't get a signal," I said.

"I know, and I'm going to make sure it doesn't," Terry said, and put the phone back in my pocket, minus the SIM card.

Without the card, my phone was useless.

Tom came in. "Dan's coming around from the blow on his head, but he's unsteady on his feet."

"His job is to drive the van and monitor the police band. He'll be fine, even without his mask."

"We'll wipe down the masks inside and out. We don't want any of the tear gas chemicals close to our eyes."

"You don't have to do this," I said, my voice coming back. "You can report this Burke guy to the police."

"Along with ourselves?" Terry stepped closer, my sword still in his hand. "Wise, shut the hell up, or we'll gag you."

Not wanting to be gagged, I did as I was told.

Terry and Tom stepped into the hall to speak. Despite the explosion and the sound of the exhaust fans overhead, I caught some of what they said.

"Leave him here until tomorrow. Once we go—" Tom was saying.

"Won't work. He knows it was us. He's seen us," Terry hissed. "Why are you defending him? He killed my sister."

"Len saved a bunch of people the day the crazy therapist made me try and blow up the MPD. He stopped me and didn't hurt me, even though I tried to shoot him."

"According to him," Terry scoffed.

"He testified at my trial. If he hadn't, I would be in prison right now."

"We need to focus on the mission," a third person said.

Dan, with a lump on his head, joined them in the hall, glanced at me through the open door, and then closed it, leaving me alone in the server room.

I sat there, my arms tightly bound, still blinking from my exposure to the gas. I gazed around the room and tried to think. They hadn't taped my legs down, so I could push the metal chair over. I might even stand, but there was little else I could do.

I was in serious trouble. I was the only one who saw their actual faces and could connect them to the murdered men. Terry insisted they kill Hallman because he'd figured out that Terry was involved in the slayings. I doubted they could afford to be any more merciful with me.

They were putting a bomb in the Essex County Prosecutor's office, and Jyanette would be there. She was the lawyer assigned to meet with this Burke guy.

I had to do something.

Where was Agent Montgomery?

I thought about Jyanette, and how she scolded me about going in on my own. Once again, she was right. I should have let other people know where I was going before I went. But who knew I would hit the jackpot?

Suddenly I heard a loud noise over the computer fans that sounded like the front door being thrown open. My heart pounded in my chest as I heard a female voice raised above the others.

Was I about to be rescued?

The server room door opened and Dan walked in with a sour look on his face, followed by Tom and Terry. Last of all was Agent Harper Montgomery. She didn't have her weapon drawn and she seemed to be casually chatting with Terry.

My excitement turned to fear.

"How did he even get in here?" she said, looking angrily at Terry.

Dan glared at me. He had a holster around his waist with a pistol in it. "He must have gotten in while I was out."

"Great! Somehow he contacted that brat at the diner and she called my goddamn cell number. I had to drive over to that greasy spoon and convince her to let me handle it."

"You should have brought her with you," Terry said coldly.

"Oh great. Let's kidnap a teenager while we're at it!" Montgomery complained. "Like you three haven't done enough stupid over the last week."

"You wanted proof the program worked," Tom said. "We took out a suicide bomber and a mass shooter."

"The deal was only to take out Burke at the prosecutor's office," Montgomery complained. "I didn't ask for proof by executing a pedophile or a conman."

"So, we gave you more than you asked for," Terry said.

"Who cares if scum like that was taken out?" Tom said, his jaw tight.

"It brought attention we didn't need. The deal was you take out Burke and that bomb in the DA's office would allow me to green light the DOJ to use 'flashes of future'. Then we four retire with the money."

"Oh, yeah?" Terry said, annoyed. "Your job was to keep Wise busy, yet here he is.

"I was doing it, and then you almost blew me up in Hallman's office."

Terry shook his head. "I asked Tom to take out the office, get rid of anything that linked Hallman to me."

"It was on a timer," Tom said. "It wasn't our fault you and Wise went there."

"If you wanted to test that sample of the plastic explosives I provided, a heads up would have helped," Montgomery snapped. "You drew attention from the MPD I didn't want, and now Wise found the warehouse."

Terry glared over at me. "How the hell did he even find this place? And how did he contact the girl?"

Montgomery looked at me as well. "He must have phoned her."

"Impossible. Cell phones don't work here," Terry said.

She bent to be eye to eye with me. "So, Len, how did you find this place?"

I met her eyes and wanted to push my way into her head, but I forced myself to glance away. "I had a vision of the warehouse at Terry's house."

"You expect me to believe that?" she grunted. "I was there. You got nothing."

I kept my expression as neutral as I could. "I found this building, didn't I?"

Terry stepped over. "How'd you get in? You gonna tell me you just made the door open with magic?"

I raised my head and glared at him. "No, the fake rock with the spare key made things pretty easy."

His mouth fell open in surprise.

I lowered my eyes to the floor. "That's a pretty low-tech system for a high-tech place like this."

Montgomery took charge. "Look, we don't know who else that girl might have spoken to. We need to move out now."

"We can't just leave Wise here alone," Dan said.

Montgomery's jaw set as she glared at Dan. "Fine, what's your job tonight?"

Dan frowned. "I stay in the van and scan the police band. I warn Tom and Terry if the police show up."

"Easy enough. You stay and watch Wise. I'll go with these two and stay in the van."

"That wasn't part of the plan," Tom said.

"Yes, and plans change," Montgomery said. "Now I have to cover your ass. If anyone discovers me in the van, I can pull out my DOJ identification and bullshit my way out of it. Now, you guys need to gear up."

Tom and Terry nodded and headed out the door and down the hall.

"I want to leave in ten minutes," Montgomery said and sat in a chair.

Dan, with the red lump on his head where I struck him, looked disgruntled. He faced the monitor and stayed quiet.

Montgomery pulled out her phone. "He's right, doesn't work at all."

A few minutes later, Tom and Terry appeared in the doorway. They were wearing the masks and the coveralls. They appeared as their false personas: Tom in the short-haired mask with the rugged face and Terry as the balding man with the mustache. Tom carried a shoulder bag, and I worried about what he had in it.

"Okay," Tom said, the silicone mask's mouth opening and closing as he spoke in that strange way that it did. "Let's head out."

Montgomery glanced at me, and then said to Dan, "You keep an eye on him."

"What are we going to do with him?" Dan asked, without getting up or trying to conceal what he was saying.

Terry peered down at me through the eyeholes of his own mask. "We'll take care of him tomorrow. I want to keep him alive until after the bomb goes off and takes out his fiancée."

"Bastard," I grumbled.

"I want him to know the pain of losing someone he loves," Terry said. "Just watch him for now."

"What should I do if he tries something?"

The mouth on Terry's mask stretched, and it looked like he was smiling. "Shoot him. Try to only wound him if you can. I'll figure a place to dump him tomorrow. But I want my revenge."

I certainly didn't like the sound of that.

The three of them headed out of my view down the hall, and I soon heard the main door open and close.

Dan glared at me. I continued to observe the floor. The only sound was the noise of the exhaust fans and the clicking of the servers. Finally he said, "So, you're a police psychic? That's bullshit."

"Those masks you made really fooled me. The MPD has sketches of those faces."

This made Dan laugh. "Yeah, Terry did it because of cameras, but Tom kept saying we had to worry about Len Wise. And then you show up right here."

Police...

I felt the buzz and was unsure of it. There was no way the police could know where I was or rescue me. However, I've learned to listen to those buzzes, and I had to be ready to make a move if fate offered one. Dan still had that gun strapped to his waist, and I didn't want to be shot.

"I asked you how you found this place?" Dan asked, and he wasn't laughing anymore.

"I told you, my abilities led me here."

"Through your psychic powers?" he scoffed. "Look, Wise, I'm not a kid, and I don't believe in psychics, mind-reading, or any of that bullshit."

There was a loud noise at the end of the hall, and both of us turned our heads to the doorway.

"What the hell was that?" Dan jumped to his feet. He moved to the hall and stood watching the door. There was another loud crash, and Dan pulled out the pistol and aimed at the door.

Must move now…

The buzz flashed through my head, and without thinking, I rocked forward onto my feet. I was off balance, but seeing it as my only attack, I charged wordlessly toward Dan.

I fell against Dan, the top of the chair hitting him in his midsection and slamming him against the wall. The gun flew from his grip just as the police knocked the door off its hinges with a battering ram.

Bright lights shone in, blinding me, and cries of "Police, nobody move," filled the corridor. I lay on top of the fallen Dan, the chair still attached to me, or rather me to it.

McGee's voice said, "Thanks for the assist with the takedown. Now maybe you'll allow us to help you."

19. PREJUDICIAL PLAN

Officers helped untangle me from Dan and set me upright, and Bill cut the duct tape to free my arms.

They pulled Dan to his feet, handcuffed him, and escorted him out of the building.

"You okay?" Bill asked as the team behind him swept down the hall, checking the other rooms. They were all dressed in black with bulletproof vests and semi-automatic weapons.

"Knocked around a bit," I said, clenching and unclenching my fists to get the blood flowing, and yanking the remains of the tape off of my sleeves.

Bill helped me to my feet, and my right leg gave out on me, but Bill caught me before I could fall. "Not as stable as you thought?"

He helped me back into the chair. "Bill, it was Montgomery. She was here. She's helping them."

"Really?"

"I need my cane, and it might be in two pieces," I said, panic in my voice, hoping Bill understood the reference. The State of New Jersey considered my cane a weapon with its hidden blade. The people with him were obviously police, but not from the

MPD. It looked like Bill commandeered a State Police SWAT team.

"I'll get right on it," Bill said. "Where should I look?"

"The room down the hall with the wig forms and the make-up mirrors."

Bill stepped into the hall. A man wearing all black with a balaclava over his face and a helmet approached.

"We've cleared the site, Lieutenant. We found blasting caps and what looks like C-4 in one room."

"Thank you, Captain," Bill said and headed past him down the hall.

The big man came into the room, pulled off the helmet, and lowered the balaclava to reveal his short crewcut of silver-grey hair, and the firm jaw of a lifetime warrior.

"Captain Albertson," I said, pleased to see a familiar face.

"Len Wise," he said, shaking my hand. "Been a while since I've seen you. I heard you only take help from the FBI these days."

"I'm surprised to see you," I said. "Your SWAT team doesn't come into our neck of the woods very often."

"Bill found out I was in Bloomdale, contacted me, and said he needed some serious backup. When Bill told me what he needed, the men and I came right here." He looked around at all the blinking lights and the exhaust fan on the ceiling. "What is this place?"

"This room is a server farm," I explained. "But this is the killers' base of operations."

"I take it there is more than just the one guy?"

"Yes, and I know where the other men are going, and what they have planned."

This made Albertson grin. "Of course you do."

Bill walked into the room with my cane in his hand, all of its parts reunited. He also carried a fleshy deformed face in his other hand. He held out the cane for me. "Here you go, Len."

I took the walking stick and I leaned my weight on it.

Bill laid out the silicone mask on the desk. The chest, ears, and bald head were undamaged, but there was a big hole in the front with chunks of the face missing.

"What the hell is that supposed to be?" Albertson asked.

"The key to this entire case," I reported. "Bill, Captain, the killers are Tom Harrigan and Terry Garber."

"Officer Tom Harrigan?" Albertson exclaimed, frowning. "I thought he left New Jersey."

"He came back." I quickly explained the false faces and the basic concepts as I understood them and Terry's 'flashes of future' program. I kept my suppositions to a minimum and stuck to what facts I knew.

As I spoke, I located the SIM card for my phone, still in the card reader, and reinserted it into my phone. I powered it up, and it appeared to work, though I still didn't have a signal.

I explained Terry used his program to locate people about to commit major crimes and brought in Tom Harrigan as the triggerman. Dan made the lifelike masks. I clarified they killed Hallman to protect themselves. Then I dropped my biggest news: that Agent Montgomery was with them right now to help them plant a bomb in the Essex County DA's office tonight.

"Len, you're sure it was Montgomery?" Bill said.

"I saw her discuss the plan in this very room," I said. "Some criminal named Phillip Burke is meeting to discuss a plea bargain. According to Terry's program, they'll set the guy free and he will blow up a bank and kill dozens of people. We have to—"

"Wait," Albertson said. "I still don't understand why they want to set off the bomb. They want to kill some guy before he commits a crime? How can they be sure?"

"Bill and I found the makings of a suicide vest at a murdered man's house and a sniper rifle in a rented room of another victim," I explained. "Garber and Harrigan killed them because he predicted they were going to commit mass-murder. Terry took the law into his own hands."

"And they want to blow up the District Attorney's office in Newark?" Albertson asked, stroking his chin. "How can they get in there to plant the bomb?"

"They had copies of maintenance uniforms," I explained. "With Terry's computer skills, they probably have a floor plan for the building and fake ID to get in." I turned to McGee. "Bill, we have to get to the DA's office and stop that bomb! Jyanette—"

Bill raised his hand to cut me off. "I know your fiancée works for the DA. Captain, can you go with us? Maybe call in the bomb squad?"

Albertson nodded and pulled a cell phone. "On it."

He headed down the hall. I hoped he had a better chance at getting a signal than I did.

"Why didn't you call me?" Bill said, now that we were alone.

"My phone didn't get a signal."

He nodded. "I was at the station when I got word of where you were."

"Did Anna call you? Montgomery claimed she called her."

"How did you talk to Anna?"

"She and I don't need a phone."

Bill nodded. "Like when those guys kidnapped her, and you two communicated—" He tapped his forehead.

"Yes. Anna has a powerful talent, and I owe her my life."

"Be sure to let her know that."

"I will when I'm not worried about a bomb."

Bill looked at me. "I want to get moving to catch these men in the act. You're riding with me."

I frowned. "You want me along?"

McGee grinned. "Len, I have faith in bomb-sniffing dogs, but I want you there to make sure we actually find it."

In the parking lot, the compact car that Dan used earlier was still there. There was a SWAT step van parked just past the dump truck, and the gate at the Canal Street entrance stood open as someone cut the chain, leaving the lock hanging from it. McGee had parked his unmarked police car on Canal Street, just past mine.

I went to my van first and got two bottles of water. Checking McGee's car, I found it unsecured, so I got into the passenger seat to give my leg a rest. As I drank the first bottle of water, I watched as Albertson got into the back of the step van. Leaving several men at the warehouse door, the van headed off.

I wanted to call Jyanette to reassure her, but I still had no service.

I wrote a text instead, hoping the damn machine would deliver it when it found a signal again.

I'm fine.

Got delayed in a place with no phone service.

I'll be home late. I'm with McGee.

I pocketed the device, hoping once she got the text, it would soothe her.

I spent the previous night in the hospital, snuck into a warehouse, got shot at, gassed, and tied up. Now we were going to head to Newark to find a bomb.

No wonder I was tired.

McGee got into the car. "The MPD is coming to help secure this place. Albertson and his men are on their way to Newark. We'll meet them there."

He drove past my van as he headed up Canal Street.

"Did he get through to the bomb squad?" I asked.

"He's working on that. His men found several bricks of C-4 in the storage room in that warehouse you were in."

"I heard them talk about it. Plastic explosives?"

"Looks like it. He's having the bomb squad send a vehicle here as well, to analyze and dispose of it. But our prime concern is Newark."

I nodded, recalling the time Harrigan almost blew up the MPD with a brick of C-4. He worked demolitions in the

Marines, so he knew how to handle the stuff, but this time he was not under the sway of a crazed hypnotherapist. This time he was doing it of his own volition, motivated because he was saving lives by killing.

Terry sought for years to create a program to predict criminal events. Was part of the reason because of Cathy's death? Had he, like me, felt wracked with guilt that he couldn't prevent the death of his much-loved sister? I learned to live with my feelings — I needed to, in order to learn to use my abilities. I had to move on, because there was no other choice.

Mark Twain said, "History doesn't repeat itself, but it often rhymes." Forces were aligned that could take Jyanette's life as the accident took Cathy's, and once again, I was the epicenter for the events.

Once we reached the highway, McGee put on his lights and siren. He placed the revolving bubble on the roof of the unmarked car and pushed the speed of the vehicle up to eighty.

My phone rang. It was Jyanette.

"Jyanette, I can explain—" I began.

"I just got your text," she said. She didn't sound angry, but concerned. "Can you tell me what's going on?"

"I can give you the basics. I tracked our bad guys to their lair, and my phone didn't work there."

She exhaled heavily as annoyance crept into her voice. "You went in and confronted them by yourself?"

"Jyanette, McGee and I are on our way to stop a bomb. If you want to yell at me, it will have to wait."

"No, I don't want to yell at you, but we have to talk about having backup again. Provided you don't get blown up tonight."

"I'll do my best to avoid it," I said. "I love you."

"And I love you. Though if you didn't make me worry so much, I would appreciate it."

"See you later. I'll try not to wake you if I'm late."

"Wake me, I don't care. If you're not in a hospital, I'll be fine with losing sleep."

I ended the call.

"Sorry to say, she needs to get used to this sort of thing," Bill commented.

Now it was my turn to sigh. "How does Laura cope with your job?"

"As best as she can. The spouse of a police officer is always worried about receiving bad news. It's a strain on the spouse and the relationship. It's one reason divorce is so common in my line of work."

Bill stopped the siren as we pulled off the highway and onto the ramp that took us into Newark. The prosecutor's office was part of a huge courthouse complex built over the last twenty years. We headed off the ramp and onto the city streets. Newark is a strange mix of neighborhoods, with abandoned buildings on one side of the street and restored Victorian houses opposite.

"I still don't understand what Agent Montgomery is playing at," I said. "She said she supplied them with the explosives and went with them tonight to listen to the police band from their van and warn Terry."

"Maybe there's more to it than you think," Bill said. "Think about it. If she's working with them, why did she almost get blown up with you when Hallman's office went up?"

"I don't know. She told them she was keeping an eye on me."

We drove down Elizabeth Avenue, past the small businesses in two- and three-story brick buildings. Older houses stood next to newer urban renewal projects. We passed warehouses and event halls as we made our way toward the center of the city.

Once we turned onto Doctor Martin Luther King Boulevard, the buildings got taller and newer. Soon we reached an intersection where a large, curved white building was across the street. On the wall in large letters and lit by a spotlight was the moniker:

Essex County

Dr. Martin Luther King

Justice Building

It wasn't just one structure, but a collection of unique buildings. It took up several blocks, including the courthouse, the prosecutor's office, the Newark Police, and even holding cells for prisoners.

We pulled off the street and into a large parking area. There was a separate four-story parking garage, but the lot, often full during the day, was empty now except for a group of emergency vehicles. Bill turned off his flashing lights, as there were more than enough vehicles with lights blazing in alternating red and blue.

One vehicle was familiar: a white, oversized Humvee-style armored truck. It stood emblazoned with 'Essex County Sheriff', and in smaller letters, 'Bomb Disposal Unit'.

Albertson beat us there, and was already taking charge. He was talking to an African-American man with short cropped hair in a black padded outfit with a tactical vest that read: Bomb Unit.

I immediately recognized the man as Technician Moore, who helped remove the dynamite at the pedophile's house.

Bill jumped out of the car, and I followed more slowly, being careful with my right leg and thankful for my cane. By the time I caught up, Bill was talking to Albertson and Moore.

Albertson glanced over at us as I approached. "I'm glad everyone knows each other. Moore was telling me he'd already seen you a few days ago."

I offered my hand, and Moore took it in a quick handshake and said, "Captain Albertson tells me you're the reason we got this lead."

"Yes, sir," I said, catching my breath.

"That's twice in one week," Moore said and seemed impressed. "The dynamite was your call as well."

"Here, we think the perps are still onsite," McGee said. "They're dressed like the cleaning crew."

"Right now the Newark PD team is evacuating the building, checking IDs on everyone as they exit," Albertson said. "The building security team is helping."

"I would assume there are few people here at night," I said.

Moore looked stern. "Just security and the cleaning crew. Security says they didn't see anyone who wasn't a regular."

Albertson exhaled heavily. "I'll be honest with you, gentlemen. We've got ourselves a clusterfuck of jurisdictions going on right now. There's the Newark PD, the county sheriff's people, and my SWAT team from the state. There's too many people who don't know each other, and that's going to be hard to control." Albertson eyed Bill and Moore. "I hate to pull rank, but I'm going to ask that everything go through me."

"To be honest, Captain, I'd be glad if you did," Moore said, looking relieved.

I looked at McGee. "This is like the attack on the MPD."

McGee looked unsure. "What does that have to do with this?"

"Last year, there was a strategic attack on MPD," I said, to explain the situation to the others. "A lot of guys got shot and the building almost blown up. When the FBI brought in a SWAT team, there was a sniper waiting to shoot them."

Albertson frowned. "You think they're going to attack the team?"

"If they know there are police searching the building, they might take drastic action to get themselves out of there, and they have explosives." I scanned the parking lot with the flashing lights and the multiple vehicles. "Your presence is hard to miss."

Albertson looked me over from head to toe. "I take it you're about to advise something, Mr. Consultant?"

"I think if you get the police and the security out of there and let McGee and me go in, we can locate the bomb and disarm it."

20. DOUBLE DECEIT

"Excuse me?" Moore said. "My partner, Technician Carter, can work in a bomb suit and we have a robot with us. One of them should go."

Albertson noticed Bill's reaction to my suggestion. "A robot? Show me that, will you?"

They headed to the back of the van, leaving Bill and I alone.

"Are you out of your mind?"

"I know how organized Terry is," I said. "He has a pre-selected place they would put the bomb, and I had a vision where I saw the aftermath. I can find it. We need to hurry, and a search team will slow us down."

Bill shook his head. "This is the exact thing Jyanette complains about you. This is you playing hero."

I frowned. Bill had a point, but I pressed the issue. "Bill, I saw Jyanette dead in that hallway. Believe me, if I see it again, I will know it."

Moore was returning with Captain Albertson, talking quietly as they drew close.

Albertson spoke first. "You want to have just the two of you go in?"

"Captain," I began, "I think the perps have a way out. McGee and I can find the bomb, and quickly. But other people will slow us down."

"You're faster than a bomb-sniffing dog?" Moore asked, incredulous. "How are you going to do that?"

Bill cleared his throat. "Doctor Wise has… a unique talent for finding hidden things."

"Moore, I know this all looks strange to you," Albertson said. "But I've seen what the Doctor can do, firsthand." He faced me. "You'll both wear body armor, you got it?"

McGee and I exchanged a glance and nodded.

"Okay," Albertson said, getting on his phone to the NPD. "Moore, can you set these two up?"

"Yes, sir," Moore said and took us to the back of the van. The door was open revealing a machine that reminded me of the lead character in the movie, Wall-E, with mechanical arms and a camera head. Moore pulled out a pair of tactical vests marked "Bomb Disposal" and handed them down to McGee and me.

Albertson spoke to the commander of the Newark PD and asked them to pull back.

"Lieutenant, do you need a belt holster for your sidearm?" Moore asked.

"Yes sir," McGee said. "The shoulder holster might slow me down."

Moore handed McGee a leather belt with a weapon harness. "Will you carry radios?"

No radio…

I spoke up. "No, sir, no radio. I believe they're listening on all channels."

Both McGee and Albertson stared at me for a moment.

"He's right," Bill finally said. "Anything else?"

"You can't have your cell phones on. They might set off the bomb," Moore explained. "That's standard operating procedure."

Bill and I both pulled out our cell phones and shut them off.

"Do you have the specs of the building?" McGee asked.

Moore retrieved a tablet. "I do, sir." He pointed at the series of lines on the tablet. "You go in there and take the elevator to the fourth floor. That entire level is the prosecutors' offices."

The floor plan featured several offices and meeting rooms as well as open spaces with cubicles.

"We should start there," I said, taking the tablet from Moore and pointing at the meeting rooms. "If they planted a bomb to take out someone meeting with the prosecutor or an ADA, these would be the logical choice."

"Let's move out," Albertson said, loud enough to be heard. "I want radio silence until we are sure that we render any explosive device harmless."

As a group, we headed toward the lobby of the nine-story building.

We moved through a revolving door, where a security guard waited. Albertson approached him and spoke in hushed tones. "Your men all cleared?"

"Yes sir. I was watching this entrance, as you requested," the security officer reported.

"Okay, clear out. No radios."

The man nodded and left, and McGee and I headed to the elevator on our own.

Stairs…

I stopped McGee. "We have to take the stairs."

McGee frowned. "You sure? You've started limping, and I noticed you're using your cane a lot right now."

"No choice," I said and pointed to the nearby stairway door. "I'll be okay."

This didn't please McGee, but we headed through the door, which exposed a dark and poorly lit stairway of unpainted concrete. We mounted the stairs slowly and quietly. The additional weight of the heavy bullet-proof vest and my exhaustion made the trek arduous. The muscles in my right leg cried out in pain. I moved my cane to my left hand and used the heavy metal railing to pull myself up.

It took minutes of climbing until we reached the fourth floor.

McGee cracked the door and looked out. "It's clear." He let the door close and whispered, "Where are we going once we go through the door?"

I shut my eyes and reached out with my mind, trying to get a fix on the vision I had of the blown-up room, and the dead bodies on the floor. I sensed something not too far away.

I whispered to Bill. "Head out to the right, at the end of the hall, go left."

"You should lead," he said.

He cracked the door again and peered down the hall. "Okay, go," he whispered.

I stepped out, my cane in my right hand, helping to support my leg as I limped down the hall, Bill right behind me. The offices to our right and left were all dark. We crept to the end, turned left, and kept going. Bill held his service weapon with both hands, pointing it at the ceiling, his finger on top of the trigger guard.

I moved down the hallway and raised my left hand to stop. The walls had a familiar look to them. They were not the destroyed walls I glimpsed in my vision, but the walls and the nearby open office door struck a chord. I knew it was the doorway that would be destroyed. I felt along the wall until I touched a switch and pushed it up. I backed quickly out of the doorway as the lights flickered on. Bill moved past me and into the room, the gun pointing up and down as he scanned.

He lowered the weapon and said, "Clear."

I breathed a sigh of relief and stepped into the room. Several large copy machines filled the space. On the wall was a steel storage unit that held multiple boxes of paper, toner, and replacement cartridges for the apparatus. All of it was familiar, except now the machines were undamaged and the storage rack was still standing.

There was one office chair on wheels in the room.

"Anyone nearby who might jump us?" Bill asked.

I closed my eyes and reached out, trying to sense any danger in the surroundings. I sensed nothing that posed an immediate threat.

I opened my eyes and released a pent-up breath. "No one near, but we should stay on our guard."

Bill scanned the room. "Why are we here, then?"

I let my instincts lead me as I gazed around the small utility room. "This is the epicenter of the explosion. There's something in this room."

I moved away from Bill toward one copier.

That bottom cabinet of the machine drew my attention like a magnet, and my mouth went dry. I pulled the wheeled chair over so I could sit and tried to locate the catch on that cabinet. My hands were shaking, and I was sweating, even though it wasn't hot in the building.

I gently opened the door.

"Anything?" Bill said.

"I don't know…" I croaked.

There, laying between two reams of paper, I saw a block of dark material. It seemed to be constructed of four smaller plastic covered rectangles, with straps binding them together. On the plastic wrap were the words Charge Demolition. On top of it was a digital display that was counting down in bright red LED letters, with wires from the display into the brick.

I gingerly slid the chair back and whispered, my eyes fixated on the device. "I think we have a bomb."

"Move back," Bill said quietly as he knelt in front of the cabinet. He pulled a small flashlight from one vest pocket and shone the beam into the enclosed space.

I looked at the display. The numbers were indeed running backwards, counting down, but the device wouldn't go off for over eight hours. I sat stock still in the chair and watched as Bill examined the wires and the block of plastic explosives. He moved the flashlight to different points to check the way they attached the wires to the block.

There was something wrong. If this bomb went off, if you touched it or discovered it, my psychic abilities would sound off like a car alarm. I recalled when I was in Hoffman's office, and the warning kept getting louder and louder. I was getting nothing at all, no warning, no impressions, nothing.

Bill lifted the block and looked under it, and then cursed under his breath.

"What, what is it?" I demanded a bit too loudly.

"Give me a minute," he said and pulled the wires out of it, the display off the top, and put the block of what looked like plastic wrapped clay on the floor.

He faced me. "Do you think there is another?"

I closed my eyes and reached out, still confused that I didn't get a warning while Bill handled the C-4. "I don't think so."

Bill nodded and pulled out his cell phone, turned it on, and called Albertson.

"We got it, bring something up to contain it," Bill said and listened, frowning. "Could you repeat that?" He listened again. "Okay, we'll stay here then." He ended the call and looked at me, his eyes blazing. "They checked the blocks of C-4 in the warehouse. They're inert."

"What?" I blurted. "Does that mean they were fake?"

"Appears so."

"Is this one phony as well?"

McGee shook his head. "I don't know. Moore is going to come up here and test it."

"How do they do that?" I asked.

"The fastest way is a chemical spot test. That's what they did at the warehouse, and that stuff was just clay. Did you get anything about it, your special way?"

I was totally confused. "No, nothing. I have no explanation, unless neither Tom nor Terry knew. Tom said Agent Montgomery supplied the C-4."

"Is it possible she gave them fakes?"

I thought back to the way she was interacting with the trio back in the warehouse, but I couldn't be sure which side she was on. If she gave them fake explosives, it could all just be a DOJ sting operation. But the explosion in Hallman's office had been genuine enough.

"Bill, I don't know. I got all those warnings about radios and using the stairs—" I stopped talking and gazed at the ceiling.

"What? What is it?"

"If someone had the frequency, they could listen in on the police and SWAT team bands, right?"

Bill appeared surprised by my question. "Sure. So what?"

I glanced back at the hall we walked down. "The elevator has a camera?"

"Probably. What does that have to do with a fake bomb?"

I pushed myself to my feet. "Is there any way we can open a door and look down at the roof of the elevator car without moving it?"

Bill considered this for a minute. "Security has a key that can open the elevator doors in case anyone gets trapped."

"Can you get it? And tell Albertson and his men to keep away from the elevator and maintain radio silence."

"Len, the bomb's disabled and maybe a fake. He should let everyone know."

"Terry's a hacker, and he could be nearby listening in to the chatter on all the police frequencies," I said. "We don't want him to know we found his bomb, and we certainly don't want him to know it was a fake."

Bill nodded in agreement, as I had a point. "Why the elevator?"

"I'm not sure, yet. But if we can look at the roof of the elevator car, I think we'll find our answers."

Bill headed back down the hall to the stairs. I knew he would make much better time than I would, tired as I was.

Now alone, I took this as an opportunity to get a better reading on the building and the threat we were facing. I was extremely tired from the long day. Without a doubt, my exhaustion was affecting my abilities.

I shut my eyes and focused on my breath, trying to relax and let go of my fears.

In… out, in… out.

I slipped down into an alpha state, and I opened my eyes to the room, now shifted into grays, blacks, and whites, like an old motion picture. Before me, a translucent Terry was standing, still wearing his balding silicon mask. Tom was crouched by the copier with his own mask over his face and head.

Tom was putting the final touches on the fake bomb as he slid it into the cabinet.

"You'll be able to activate it remotely?" Tom was asking.

This was one of those times I heard people speak in a vision.

"Provided my amplifier works," Terry said. "It's connected to the hall camera. I won't turn that on until the morning, or if anyone comes up the elevator."

There were lights flashing from the window in an office across the hall. Terry looked out the window, facing the parking lot.

"Police," Terry said, and glared back at Tom. "We have to move."

"Is our route clear?" Tom worried.

"It should be," Terry said, and pulled out a tablet. "I'll send security to help the police. We'll just stroll out that emergency exit where I disabled the alarm."

Tom grabbed Terry's arm. "How did the police know to come? You said you took care of the cameras and motion detectors."

"Maybe they're just checking."

"What if Wise got a message to them?"

Terry looked stunned. "He's tied up back at the warehouse. We have to stick to the plan. I need to keep the van close to monitor our cameras."

Tom nodded. "Then let's move out."

The pair of them headed down the hall, and the scene faded, just as Bill walked through the door and color returned to the room. He held up a very long metal key with a chain hanging from it.

"Got it," he announced. "I spoke to Albertson, and since the bomb's disabled, he's willing to hold back until we say otherwise."

"Where's the elevator?"

"It's on the first floor. If we go down to the second, we can open the door, look down the hoist way and see the roof of the cab."

"We need to get out of this hall anyway," I said, rising and heading to the door. "There's a camera here, but it's not working right now."

"Why would they have a camera in this hall?"

I looked down the hall and back up at the copy room, the memory of the floor plan in my head. "I think the plan was that the officers were going to bring Burke up that elevator. Terry could monitor it and watch for him. Then, on their way to a meeting room, the group would walk past that copier room and Terry could see them from a second camera, and detonate the bomb."

"But it's a fake," Bill argued.

I stopped at the door to the stairs. "I don't think Terry knew that."

We headed down the two flights of stairs to the second floor and found our way to the lone elevator. Bill quickly unlocked the sliding door and it opened, exposing the heavy steel cables that ran to the elevator cab. The roof of the car was only a few feet below where we were standing.

"There!" I said and pointed. Sure enough, on top of the elevator was a small device with an antenna. The unit had a red blinking light on it. "What is that?"

Bill shook his head. "A wireless router. It probably allows our bad guys to use the elevator's camera. That way he could see if the —"

At that moment, the elevator made a loud hum; the cables moved and the large counterweight slid quietly down its track as the cab rose.

"No, no!" I yelled, to no avail. The cab rose past our open door and kept going up to the fourth floor.

"You stay here," McGee said and took off in a dead run for the stairs as I looked up, helpless to stop the machine.

Not listening to my friend, I headed for the stairs as fast as I could and started up them at a pretty good pace. I had to make sure that Terry didn't activate the camera he mentioned in my vision.

By the time I reached the fourth floor, I was panting hard and relying on my cane to keep me going. I headed past the elevator to the hallway and heard voices ahead of me.

"I'm sorry, Lieutenant, but once our dog got here, I received orders directly from the governor to bring him up."

"We need this area sealed off. We don't know what else the perp hid," Bill complained.

I turned the corner, where McGee was facing off with Moore, who had a dog by his side. Moore was now in full gear with heavy pads that covered his legs and arms, and a helmet with a face protector. The dog stood about twenty-four inches tall with a coat that was short, dense, and mahogany in color, with a black mask and ears.

Both men turned to me, stunned into silence.

Camera…

My eyes were pulled to a spot near the ceiling as the buzz flashed through my brain. A tiny red LED lit up, and I knew Terry was staring right at me.

"I have my orders, Lieutenant," Moore said.

"Look, we have to—"

An alarm went off in the copy room. Not a loud one to evacuate a building, but the simple sound coming from a cheap clock. Moore's dog ran into the copy room.

There on the floor were the remains of the fake bomb, the digital display and its parts, but now an alarm was coming out of the device that suddenly ended. Bill picked up the clock and turned it over, and I noticed for the first time the small pack connected to it and the hanging wire that acted as an antenna.

"He saw us," I said.

Bill held the unit, staring down at it. "What?"

"Terry put a camera up in the hall that he could turn on and off. He saw Moore and the dog in the elevator and turned it on just as I came around the corner. I saw the light go on."

Bill was still looking at the display in his hand. "So he sent a signal to set off the bomb?"

I nodded. "And now he knows that the bomb's disabled."

"That doesn't help us," Bill murmured, putting the display back on the floor.

"I think Terry is still nearby. He needed to be close to monitor the equipment."

Bill pushed past me. "Then we have to move."

21. FOCUSED OBJECTIVITY

"Dammit, we have radio silence!" he yelled as he pulled out his phone to call Albertson while stepping out into the hall.

I just sat down in the wheeled chair I used before, too tired to follow. The dog, which I guessed was a Belgian Malinois, had his nose down, checking around the copiers. He moved to the small display on the floor, took several steps back, and promptly sat.

Moore went to one knee and picked up the display.

"What does it mean when he sits?" I asked.

"It means he's found something that smells like a bomb," the man said simply. "My guess is that someone connected this display to explosive materials at some point."

I rolled the chair over to pick up the square of clay. "This is what they connected it to."

He held it out to the dog, who ignored it and sniffed around the room instead. "Yeah, even though someone labelled this C-4, I don't think it is. I have a container near the elevator to seal it up and take it out."

From his TAC vest, he withdrew a plastic container containing a Petrie dish, a short scalpel, a small saltshaker, and two bottles with eyedropper tops. He slit the plastic on some of the brick and scraped off the clay into the Petrie dish. Next, he added a few crystals from the shaker and a few drops from the eyedropper. With the scalpel, he blended the mixture together.

"What are you doing?" I asked.

"Testing it. I'm mixing the clay with thymol crystals and a few drops of sulfuric acid." He held up the other eyedropper in his heavily gloved hand. "Now I add a little ethyl alcohol, and it should become a bright rose color if it is really C-4."

He dripped the alcohol onto the mixture, and it did nothing, just remaining an ugly gray. He put a lid on the dish, sealed it, and put the kit away. "Yeah, it's totally inert." He looked over at the broken display on the floor. "I wonder what was the point? A bomb scare?"

All I could do was shrug.

"I gotta check the other rooms up here," he explained. "Orders from the governor."

"Do what you have to do, " I said. I leaned back in the chair and closed my eyes to rest them.

Wise...

I lifted my head, but I was no longer in the copy room.

I was in a van.

Looking over, I saw Terry still wearing his mask. From where I was, I had to be in the passenger seat.

"This is all Wise's fault," Terry said, the mouth of his mask moving in that odd way. "How did he escape?"

"Look, Garber," a female said from where I sat. "We need to get you out of town. Let me make a few phone calls and I can get the DOJ to lock down that warehouse so the police can't touch it."

Harper Montgomery.

She went on, "Then we'll figure out a deal to get your program set up in Washington—"

Terry pulled the vehicle into the parking lot of a used car dealer and pulled behind the building, where he stopped the van and shut off the lights. I heard police sirens growing louder and saw the flashes of police lights as two cars went by.

Terry unbuttoned his shirt, and tugged the false face off his own. Terry's hair was damp with sweat, and he held the face mask and glared at it.

With a curse, he threw the deflated mask into the back of his van. I looked back to see the flashing lights of machines and surveillance equipment in the back with a chair, apparently bolted to the floor, in front of a desk.

He grabbed a bag from behind his seat and pulled out a brick-shaped object with a timer display on top and wires leading to the brick. He placed the brick with the timer back behind him again.

"I have one more thing to do."

"Look, I can't approve of—" Harper attempted.

"Then get out," Terry growled. "I'm going to take from Wise what he took from me." Terry started the van.

I saw my point of view change to the door, and it opened to let me out. I stepped to the ground and shut it, and as I watched, Terry drove away.

"Len, did you fall asleep?" a voice demanded.

Startled, I raised my head to find myself back in the copy room of the prosecutor's office, my head spinning from what I saw. It took me a minute to realize it was Bill standing in front of me.

"Bill?" I croaked.

"Moore cleared the offices with the dog. There is no other bomb here, just the fake we found. He's sealed it in a metal container and is taking it downstairs."

"Bill, Terry knows we were here."

"So what? You said he was nearby. Right now the Newark Police are cordoning off the area. If he's anywhere within a ten-block radius, we'll capture him."

I attempted to rise from the chair, but my leg gave out on me, and I fell back. Bill grabbed me and helped lower me down. If not, I probably would have knocked the wheeled chair right over.

"You don't understand," I said, finding my voice. "There was a white van outside my house days ago. I thought it was Agent Montgomery spying on me, but it was Terry. He knows where I live and he's determined to take revenge."

Bill stared at me, as if trying to understand. "Your house? Who's there now?"

"Both Jyanette and Mrs. Higgins," I said. Bill pulled away, but I clung onto him. "He's got another bomb!"

"A fake like here, or is this one real?"

"I don't know."

"We have to get a move on. Len, let's head to the elevator—"

"The elevator?"

McGee shook his head. "It doesn't make any difference now. Come on!"

Once I arrived at the first floor, I found the small lobby was under siege, with the full SWAT team in charge.

McGee found Albertson and explained our dilemma.

"Bill, we're spread too thin as it is," Albertson complained. "Plus, I've got to coordinate everything through the County, the State, and the Newark PD. Now the governor got himself involved!"

They turned away from me to look at the large entrance doors as Tom Harrigan walked through.

I froze, my breath caught in my throat, and I wondered why I didn't get a buzz of danger. Then I saw he was being escorted by a uniformed officer of the NPD.

Tom's hands were behind his back. The officer had put him in either handcuffs or restraints.

The officer was the first to speak. "Sir, this man surrendered himself to me. He claims to have knowledge of the bomb."

"Captain, this is Tom Harrigan," Bill reported, his eyes blazing as he glared at his former compatriot.

Albertson nodded, his mouth a tight line.

Tom saw me and merely nodded in recognition. I attempted to look stern, but I was too shocked to do it well.

"Terry's gone crazy," Tom admitted. "He has an agent from the DOJ helping him."

McGee nodded. "You freely admit you're a part of this, and that Terry Garber is your confederate?"

Tom shook his head and looked at the floor. "All of it was Terry's idea."

"Like we haven't heard that one before," Albertson muttered.

"We know about 'flashes of future'," I said. "How did you get involved?"

"He sought me out. He said he could prove that there were people planning big events, but he could stop them with my help." Tom looked stricken. "But after the lawyer's office, and you almost getting killed, I knew it had gone wrong."

"What was your part of the plan tonight?" McGee asserted.

"I was supposed to get an Uber or a bus back to Mountainview while he stayed close and watched the cameras." He raised his head and looked at me. "He told me to go back to the warehouse and kill Len."

I moved close until I was inches away from his face. "He's heading to my house right now, and he's got another one of those bombs."

Tom couldn't meet my eyes. "He has my gun as well."

McGee took my arm. "Captain, we're heading to Len's house. Get the van's license plate number from Harrigan and put out an APB to stop him."

"I'll do it."

We headed straight for Bill's car, and he checked his cell phone as we went. He activated the lights and siren, using the radio to contact MPD and demand all available officers to move out and shut off my road. He followed it with my address.

He then glanced at me. "I have to make one stop along the way."

I drank the extra bottle of water I'd left in the car, as I pulled out my phone and turned it on to call Mrs. Higgins and Jyanette.

Although I powered it up, my screen was blank. I stared at it, dumbfounded.

"My phone doesn't work," I said.

"What?" McGee said. "It worked when you spoke to Jyanette before."

I shook my head. "Terry took my phone away and pulled the SIM card when they tied me up. I put it back in and my phone worked before."

"That means he probably cloned it."

"Cloned it?"

"A hacker can make a copy of your phone, and if he wants, he can shut down your phone, so that calls and texts only go to the clone," McGee explained.

I did not know where McGee was going and yet the road he was driving looked familiar.

"Bill, we'd go a lot faster on the Interstate," I said, worried.

"Sorry, Len, this takes priority," Bill said, rushing down the road.

He turned into a used car lot that looked familiar and pulled around back, where Agent Montgomery stood waiting.

He pulled right up to her, and she yanked open my door and glared at me. "Get in back, Wise."

I was completely dumbfounded, but stepped out of the car to tower over her, my cane in hand like a weapon. "You're working with them!"

She placed her hands on her hips and shook her head. "Before you make a total ass of yourself, get in the back."

I stood my ground.

"Len," McGee said. "Please get in the back."

I stepped around Montgomery, yanked opened the back door, and got in as Montgomery replaced me in the passenger seat.

"He's heading to Wise's house," she said as McGee pulled the car out of the lot, and hit the lights and siren.

"We know," I barked.

"Really, how?" she asked.

"I saw you in the van, talking with Garber," I said.

She glanced over her shoulder in annoyance, unimpressed. "Oh, really?"

"He did," McGee said simply. "Len told me what went down, even before I got your text."

"Text?" I said, surprised. "You two are working together?"

McGee sighed. "Len, I couldn't tell you. Montgomery works deep cover. The DOJ assigned her to find Garber and set him up so they could take him down."

"Three people have died," I shouted.

"That wasn't part of the plan. I didn't know that Garber was planning those hits," Montgomery said. "My part of the plan was to get Garber a sample of C-4 for testing, and then give him the fake stuff. He was planning to detonate it tomorrow, so an FBI task force under the auspices of the DOJ was going to raid him and his warehouse then. I had it all set up." She glanced back at me. "Until you stumbled across his warehouse and messed up the entire plan."

I looked at McGee. "You knew about this?"

"Len, I was in the dark as well, until the pair of you almost got blown up at Hallman's office," McGee said. "Then Captain Harris got a call from the DOJ and brought us in on the mission. I spoke to Agent Montgomery at the hospital, and she explained everything to me. But no, I didn't know the C-4 was fake. It looked genuine enough to me."

"That was the point," Montgomery added.

"Len, I was under orders to not tell anyone," McGee said.

"Even me?"

"Even you," Bill said, glancing at me in the rearview mirror.

"I thought you were psychic," Montgomery jeered. "Doesn't that mean you should've known of all this?"

"So, you haven't been investigating me?" I said.

"Not really, no," Montgomery admitted. "I found reading those case files interesting, though. Garber wanted me to keep you busy."

"By harassing my students and friends?" I said, my temper rising. "By following me around?"

She made that infuriating, smug smile again. "I had to make it look good, didn't I?"

"Len, look," McGee said. "She's the one who let me know where you were tonight. I got the address of that warehouse from her and she told me to assemble a team and wait forty-five minutes. She's the reason I got you out."

"And since the entire operation was going to shit, I had to improvise, go with Garber, to be a witness to the fact that he planted the bomb. I couldn't tell you not to go to Newark."

"You knew the bomb was a fake?" I asked.

"Yes. I didn't have any way to stop you from going there to disarm it. It was going fine until he saw the dog go up in the elevator. Then he activated the hall camera and saw Wise. Some psychic! You didn't have enough sense to hide before it came on."

"Why didn't you stay with him?" I demanded.

"Because he is bent on revenge and has a gun," Montgomery said. "The last thing I wanted was a shootout in his van. I got out and texted McGee to pick me up."

"I need to warn Jyanette, but my phone doesn't work," I said.

"It doesn't matter anyway," Montgomery said, her eyes on the road. "By now, Garber will have deactivated your fiancée's phone and your landlady's."

"He can do that?" McGee said, staring straight ahead.

"Afraid so." She turned to look back at me. "Can't you just talk to them in the ether or something? Like you did Anna?"

"I have no way to call Jyanette or Mrs. Higgins," I worried, fear gripping my heart.

"If we can get there, tell him the bomb is no good. I should be able to talk him down," Montgomery said.

"I can get a police sniper in and take him down," Bill said.

"No, I want him alive," Montgomery said. "We know his program is good, and the DOJ is going to have it."

I stared at the back of Montgomery's head. I despised this woman. She'd let people get killed by these madmen, and even though he was seeking revenge, she still wanted to take him alive so she could get her hands on 'flashes of future'.

I needed to do whatever was necessary to save the people I loved, and I wouldn't let her stand in my way.

---

22. VAIN VIRTUE

I tried to not focus on being scared for two people I loved, but attempted to think about how I could take Terry Garber down peacefully. I honestly didn't want Terry to get shot, but I didn't want him shooting anyone at my house, either.

Bill was talking back and forth on the radio and driving. I was too scared to watch the road, because we were going far too fast for me. Once we got off the highway, he slowed down on the streets of Mountainview, and McGee shut down the siren as we wove our way through the back streets.

A call came over the radio with our car code and McGee grabbed the mike. "Yeah?"

"LT, Officer Galland is 10-23, with 10-53. Officer reports a possible 10-79, repeat a 10-79."

"Shit," McGee cursed. "Keep back, form a perimeter and do not engage, repeat, do not engage. We're coming in 10-80."

He hung up the microphone and glanced at me.

"That didn't sound good," I worried. "What did it mean?"

It was Montgomery who spoke. "It meant Galland is at the location, and the street is closed down. 10-79 means that it is a hostage situation. Our arrival is 10-80, which means with no lights and no siren."

"Nice to see you know your ten codes, Montgomery."

McGee hit the switch and the dome he'd placed on the roof shut down, leaving our headlights as the only illumination.

I have been afraid before. Demonic creatures appear to me in visions and in the real world, people have shot, beaten, and battered me. I even faced moments when I thought I had no chance and would die.

It was nothing to what I felt at that moment.

It felt like the foundations of my world itself came crashing down all at once, and utter helplessness, which stole away my hope and will, overwhelmed me.

Montgomery seemed to sense my concerns and spoke quietly. "We'll be there in five minutes. I'll talk him down."

"How do you talk down a madman?" I croaked. "Worse, a madman who thinks it's all about justice."

"Don't let him get in your head, Len," McGee advised. "You need to get into his."

It seemed I'd been a fixture in Terry's head for the last nine years. I was sure his original desire was a good one. He wanted to predict and prevent crimes, save lives. It became corrupted by his own ego and his decision to not merely predict events, but to stop them himself. Being tech-savvy and aware of the proliferation of cameras, he'd involved Dan to make the full head covering masks. To get a man experienced with a gun and demolitions, he convinced Tom of the righteousness of his campaign and the infallibility of his predictions.

My intervention at the warehouse must have pushed his buttons in all the wrong ways. He stopped being interested in saving lives and transformed into an avenging angel who would take the lives of those he judged unworthy. Seeing me on camera at the prosecutor's office, the pinnacle of what should have been his victory, made me the focus of his unbridled rage.

I had to push past my fear and anger and focus on stopping him. I closed my eyes and reached out with my mind, centered my attention on that task, pushing down my sense of panic.

I was trying to touch his mind, sense where he was and what he was doing. I focused my attention, and the mists cleared.

I was looking at a bomb.

I was so shocked by this image, it almost pushed me out of my altered state. I tried to see what was around me. The bomb was directly next to the door for my private entrance to my house.

I was looking through Terry's eyes.

Down on the ground, there was a small rectangle of what looked like modeling clay, and a lit up display on top. It was not counting down, which was good. His point of view shifted as he went from kneeling to standing up.

I saw the gun in his belt, and a small slim device that sported a rigid wire antenna. I guessed it was a radio detonator for the bomb.

He looked at the house, and I saw that all the lights were off. I knew that Mrs. Higgins and Jyanette were not asleep, so where were they? Terry headed back toward the large white van, and I glimpsed Mrs. Higgins' little car and Jyanette's Honda.

If both cars were there, then they hadn't left. Had they shut off all the lights and gone to bed? If they were in my part of the house and that bomb went off, it might kill them.

I brought myself out of the trance and spoke. "The sample of C-4 for them to test. What did it look like?"

Montgomery glared back at me. "Two ounces, about four inches long and two inches wide, about the size of a candy bar. Why? They used it at Hallman's office."

"No, they didn't," I said. "When I saw you in the van, Garber was playing with a brick of the stuff. But he just put a bomb at the door of my house, and he's changed out the brick for something the size of a candy bar."

"That can't be," Montgomery said. "This is some kind of trick."

"He has a deadman's switch," I told her.

"We're here," McGee said.

We reached my street and there was an MPD vehicle blocking the road.

Bill turned to me. "I think we should leave the car here and approach by foot."

I felt my jaw tighten. "It doesn't matter. He knows we're coming."

"Still, if we approach over the hill and into—"

"Bill, he has a bomb with real C-4 next to the entrance to my part of the house, and a radio detonator on him. Not to mention an enormous gun in his belt."

Bill grabbed the microphone from his police band radio and said, "Galland, report. What do you see?"

"No lights on, LT. I see three vehicles, including the suspect's white van," Galland dutifully reported. "I believe the suspect has been walking around down there, but he's keeping to the shadows."

Another voice broke in on the police frequency. "The lieutenant has arrived. I assume you brought Leonard Wise?"

It was Terry's voice.

"Here is what you will do," Terry went on. "Send Len down to me, or I will blow up his house and anyone who might be inside."

Bill and I exchanged a glance. "I can't let you do that," he hissed.

"I don't think we have a choice. Mrs. Higgins and Jyanette are in there."

Bill shook his head. "Even so—"

"Bill, I can stall him."

"Hello?" Terry said impatiently. "I know you can hear me."

Bill pushed the button on the side of his microphone. "If you set off that bomb, it could kill you as well."

"Doesn't matter," Terry answered. "As long as it kills anyone in the house, I don't care."

"Bill, let me go talk to him," I pleaded.

"Len, you go down there and you're walking into your own murder. If I had a police sniper and could take him out—"

"I want that man alive," Montgomery insisted.

I ignored her. "Look, Bill, I've been able to get inside his head. If I can get close, I might influence him to surrender peacefully."

"Does any of this look peaceful to you?"

The radio crackled, and Terry was back. "I need an answer, and I don't intend to wait until you bring a SWAT team here."

Bill's lips drew back in a snarl as he pushed the button on the microphone. "Okay, he'll come down. We can't get past the roadblock, so we have to let him out here. It might take him a few minutes to get to you."

"I'll be watching you," Terry said.

McGee hung up the radio. "I have an idea."

"I'm open to suggestions."

"You get him to talk while I sneak down that way," Bill said as he pointed at a copse of trees on the property. "I can use those trees. He won't see me."

"He said he'll be watching," I worried. "He might have drones or binoculars or something."

"If I stay low and go fast, he won't see me."

"He won't see us," said Montgomery.

"No one asked you to come, Agent," Bill said.

"Two of us with guns is a better choice," she said.

I shook my head. "I still don't like it."

The light went on in the vehicle when I opened my door. I stood, my cane in my right hand, helping to push me to my feet. Galland had his gun drawn and was resting his arms with the weapon on top of the roof. He aimed at the white van in my driveway.

I heard the door on the driver's side close, and knew I had stalled enough for Bill and Harper to get out of the car so the vehicle hid them. I slammed my door and the light in the car went out.

With my cane in front of me, I followed the road until I reached the top of the driveway. Taking a deep breath, I descended the driveway toward the circular roadway in front of the house where the white van waited.

I was running potential scenarios through my mind. Could I get into the van and overpower him? Not likely. My Aikido skills are superb for hand-to-hand combat at close range, but not against a gun. I would have to reach out to him, see if I could find the spark of the man I once knew.

I arrived at the van and looked at the house. All the windows were dark and even the lights outside were off. It looked dead. Could he already have gone through the house and killed Jyanette and Mrs. Higgins? No, my psychic senses would have known. I had to have faith that they were still alive and that I had the power to save them.

I knocked gently on the back of the van.

"Open it, slowly," came the reply.

I exhaled heavily and carefully opened one side of the pair of doors. The overhead lights were not on in the van, but the many LED lights from the computers and other machinery cast a pale glow. I easily saw Terry in the dim light. He sat in the chair that was bolted to the floor but swiveled it to face me. In one hand was the small device with the antenna. In the other hand was the pistol with the armor-piercing rounds pointed directly at me.

"Open the other door as well. That way, you can't duck behind it."

I hit the pair of latches at the top and bottom of the second door and opened it, slowly. "That wouldn't do me any good. You'd just blow up my house."

A small smile appeared on his lips. "Glad to see you know what's at stake." He lifted the hand with the device and its tiny glowing light. "Do you know what this is?"

"I assume it's a radio controlled detonator."

He glanced at the device in his hand. "You are correct, but it is also what is called a dead-man's switch. I'm sure you're familiar with such a device."

I was sweating profusely. "Yes. As long as you hold it closed, it won't explode. But if anything happens to you, you release the switch, and the bomb goes off."

"Very good," he quipped. "Then you know what is at stake." He leaned back in the chair. "I am curious. How did you escape from the warehouse? And get a police escort as well?"

"I learned a few tricks from Houdini," I replied, trying not to sound like I was mocking him. "The police captured Dan at the warehouse, and Tom surrendered to the Newark Police."

That surprised him. "What?"

"Tom thought you were going too far," I reported, keeping any emotion out of my telling. Then I stopped talking, wanting to make sure I didn't enrage Terry. His plan was falling apart, and I wanted him to know it, in the hope he would surrender peaceably. I didn't want to rub his nose in it, just tell him the facts.

Terry looked at his feet. "I figured out that the C-4 that bitch gave me was fake — except the sample. That's what I have at your side door."

"Look, Terry — it's over," I implored. "You got carried away, but more killing and destruction isn't the solution."

"Shut up!" he snapped. "You will not lecture me."

"Terry, I know you blame me for Cathy's death, and I'll be honest with you, I blamed myself for years. You don't know what happened in that car. While I lay there, with both legs broken, and Cathy's life bleeding away, I saw the life we should have had together."

He frowned at this. "What are you talking about?"

"They say when you die, your life flashes before your eyes. Well, I saw the life we were supposed to have. Getting married, having babies, fights and fears, and us going into old age together. I saw the life that I should have shared with Cathy. It was all taken away from me that night, and I spent years in a bottle after that."

He rose from the chair. "Don't sell me on this. Here you are, alive, a professor, getting married, while my sister lays in the cold ground."

I held up my hands and limped a couple of steps backward, holding my cane up in my right hand. "Terry, you need to end this before anyone else gets hurt. I don't want to die and I don't want you hurt, either."

Terry stepped to the opened doors of the van and scanned the hill above the van to make sure we were indeed alone. He lowered himself to the ground, the gun still pointed at my head.

I slowly lowered the cane to lean on it so I didn't collapse, my right leg no longer able to support my weight.

"Losing Cathy changed my life," he complained. "I didn't feel close to anyone after that. I focused on my work with computers. Then my mother passed away and finally, my father. If you ask me, it was the grief of losing Cathy that killed them both. Meanwhile, you were in California, and couldn't care less."

"What could I have done, Terry?" I said, trying not to sound defensive. "The thing that connected me to your family was Cathy, and she was gone. I didn't want to be a reminder of that pain."

"Move over that way," Terry said, gesturing with the gun. "In case they have any snipers. I want you between me and the police up there."

I moved as he instructed, which put his back to my section of the house. The dark windows framed him in silhouette.

"You know there are no snipers," I said. "You've been monitoring the police band."

"You can't be too careful," he snarled. "You see what I was trying to do? I was trying to stop horrendous events."

"Before they happen?" I observed. "Terry, I'm sure your program is amazing, but you can't judge people before they commit the crime."

"They were already criminals!" he shouted. "Even that worthless lawyer, Jacques Hallman. I could show you all the times he broke the law to fix things for his clients."

"Then you show the evidence and get him disbarred. You don't kill him and blow up his office!"

"You don't get it. I was tired of being in the background. It was time to do something, and I had the means."

"And yet, here we are," I said and gestured around us. "This isn't about justice, Terry, and it's not about stopping crime. The only reason you're here is for revenge."

His face shifted, and he seemed to take on demonic features in the dim light outside my home. I knew my ploy had not worked, and now I would pay for it.

"Nietzsche said, 'It is impossible to suffer without making someone pay for it; every complaint already contains revenge.' Now, Doctor Wise, I shall have mine."

He raised the pistol and pointed it at my head.

There was nothing I could do, no place I could hide. I only hoped that my sacrifice would save Jyanette and Mrs. Higgins.

I jumped as I heard the report of the gun, and it surprised me when I felt no pain. The noise was not as close as it should have been.

Terry had the oddest look on his face, and even in the darkness, I saw a dark patch blossoming on his white shirt. He fell forward, and I moved to him as fast as I could, grabbing his left hand and the dead man's switch.

I kept the switch closed as I looked into Terry's eyes. He was obviously in a great deal of pain, and I glanced around, unsure of where the bullet came from.

I met Terry's eyes. "You didn't have to do this."

He coughed and muttered. "Yes, I did."

Through an incredible show of strength, he smacked me on the side of my face with his pistol. The blow stunned me and I saw stars.

Overcome, I released his left hand just as he dropped the detonator.

"You lose," he croaked.

I heard the alarm, the same sound I heard in the prosecutor's office, when Terry sent the signal for the fake bomb to detonate.

I covered my head as the night sky came alive with the bright light and fire of a loud explosion.

I looked up. The explosion was not at my house, but in the woods several hundred yards away, near one of the stone walls that encircled the house.

Bill McGee stepped out of the woods with Montgomery, her weapon still in her hand.

"You stalled long enough for me to get the bomb away from the house," Bill explained. "Sorry, I couldn't let you know."

The outside floodlights came on around the driveway and lights in the house came on. Jyanette and Mrs. Higgins burst out the main entrance.

I looked down at Terry. He was dead.

"Dammit," Montgomery said.

Bill moved to the ladies. "You two all right?"

"We're fine," Jyanette said breathlessly. "We barricaded the doors and shut off the lights before he arrived."

I looked up at my love. "How did you know?" I said.

"It wasn't me," Jyanette said and put her hand on Mrs. Higgins' shoulder. "It was Margery. She stormed into our bedroom and told me to get dressed while she shoved a chair under our door. Then she got me to help her move the desk in front of it, turn out all the lights, and barricade the front door."

"Mrs. Higgins," Bill said. "How did you know what was coming?"

Mrs. Higgins shrugged. "Joost a feelin' I had. It was a good thing I did, too."

I looked over at Mrs. Higgins, grateful for her. I forgot that when it comes to psychic ability, Mrs. Higgins had her own gifts.

"We kept the house dark," Mrs. Higgins explained, "and dinna make any noise."

"As long as you're all right," Bill said. "The police will be here to take your statements."

"And the coroner," I said sadly. I looked up at Montgomery. "You saved my life."

She nodded, holstering her weapon. "I hoped you might talk him down."

I pushed myself up with my cane and took both Jyanette and Mrs. Higgins in my arms. We were all crying.

I didn't end up spending the night in the hospital for once, even though Bill saw the bruise on the side of my face and wanted me to go. We stayed in the house as a forensic team showed up and went through the white van.

Mrs. Higgins, trooper that she was, made coffee and brought out steaming cups and some of her amazing baked goods to the officers that swarmed our driveway and home.

Jyanette and I sat in the living room, holding hands, and not saying very much. We were both tired, but the relief that both of us were alive tempered the violence of the night.

She touched the sore spot on my face repeatedly and gently. "That's going to be quite a bruise."

I sighed. "I know, and we're going to my parents for Passover tomorrow."

"That will be fine," she said.

"How so?"

She sighed. "Len, whether or not I like it, you always show up at your parents' house bruised and beaten."

"Yeah, sorry."

"If you didn't, they might think there was something wrong."

I stared at her in disbelief, and she smiled. I grinned, which hurt.

Finally, at about five in the morning, they were done. A town truck hooked up the white van to take it to the pound. Everyone left.

I took a long hot shower, and we dragged ourselves off to bed.

When I got into bed, I expected Jyanette to be asleep. But she lay in bed naked, and her arms came around me, pulling me on top of her.

We made love, slowly and gently, reassuringly. I didn't realize how much we needed it. It was a reconnection and sharing of our bodies that renewed our attachment and our love.

We both fell into a deep sleep.

EPILOGUE

We slept until noon, and upon waking, I checked my phone. It pleased me that my phone screen lit up and looked normal.

There was a message from Officer Galland to let me know he located the clone of my phone and deactivated it. There were also texts from Bill, Captain Albertson, and Agent Montgomery requesting I write up my eyewitness account of the events of the previous day.

I finally showered and shaved, grimacing at the obvious bruise on my face where Terry hit me with the gun. I considered covering it with make-up, but Jyanette's products certainly wouldn't work with my skin tone.

Jyanette went to the kitchen to see Mrs. Higgins, while I sat at my desk and wrote my witness testimony on my laptop. Knowing all the right terms for a police report, I typed it up quickly. I just finished when there was a knock on the sitting-room door of the house, my private entrance.

I opened the door to see Agent Harper Montgomery there, holding a styrofoam cup.

"May I come in?" she said in a businesslike tone.

I let her in and indicated my laser printer. "I'm printing up my witness account right now."

"You can just email me a copy. I wanted to let you know the DOJ has taken over the warehouse, and we took custody of Dan and Tom."

"So, you got 'flashes of future' after all. You probably can't make it work without Terry."

"The DOJ has people with impressive computer skills," she bragged. "We'll get it to work."

She seemed undaunted by how everything went down. "You won't like my account of events. I question all of your choices."

"Not unexpected," she said, nonplussed. "My report will contain proof that it was your involvement that made the operation go wrong."

"So, I blame you, and you blame me?" I said.

"I also commend your bravery facing those men, and your attempt to talk Garber down. I also state that I believe you to be an asset to the Mountainview Police Department." She held out the cup. "Here, I owe you."

"What's this?"

"Our bet. Coffee with cream, no sugar."

I reached out and took the cup. "So you believe I'm psychic?"

"No," she said, narrowing her eyes as she observed me. "But I believe you have some kind of deductive intuition that makes you a valuable asset. I'm going to give you this one."

Jyanette walked in from the hall, stopped in surprise at the doorway, staring at our guest. "Agent Montgomery? I thought you'd be on your way to Washington."

Montgomery smiled. "I am. I just had to settle up with the Doctor." She met my eyes and said, "Until we meet again."

She left, and Jyanette shook her head. "Something about that woman just ticks me off."

"Me, too," I said as I turned to her. "I have to drop off my statement and do a few things before we head to my parents. Do you have to go into the office?"

"No. I was supposed to work out that settlement with Philip Burke today, but someone planted a bomb in our offices, so I have the day off."

"Are you going to let him off with probation? Terry predicted that in a few days, he's going to blow up a bank and kill dozens of people."

Her eyes grew wide. "Really? No, I won't give him probation and I never intended to. Mr. Burke will not blow up any banks or anything else, because I am making sure he's put away for a long time."

"Glad to hear it," I said, and grabbed my printed statement and headed for the door.

I had a lot to do in the next few hours, and it required I run to the MPD and talk to Bill, then head over to GSU to see Jon Baines. It took some finagling, but I convinced both of them to do what I requested.

At three in the afternoon, I headed over to Mindy's Diner.

Carl was at the cash register and happy to see me. Anna was pulling a waitressing shift, and I saw her walking about, wearing one of the pink and white outfits the waitresses wore. When she saw me, her eyes lit up, and she waved.

Carl said, "She has been worried about you. You should go talk to her in the banquet room."

I looked over at Anna, scurrying about. "Is that all right?"

"Yes, my wonder man. I will get another waitress to cover her tables. Go talk."

I stepped into the back room, and after a moment, Anna came in. The girl threw herself into my arms in a dramatic hug.

"You're all right, you're all right," she said and there were tears in her eyes.

"I'm fine," I said, and carefully extricated myself. I held her by her shoulders and met her eyes. "Thanks to you."

I was so scared…

I received the thought, but kept talking. "Everything's fine, in fact, more than fine." I pulled some paperwork from the brown envelope I carried.

"What is this?" Anna asked as I handed her a certificate.

"I had a talk with Lieutenant McGee today, and he is awarding you a certificate of Public Service for your help with the Mountainview Police Department. Specifically, helping me."

This surprised, but also confused her. "Um… okay."

I smiled. "You don't fully appreciate what this means. Since you got this certificate, it demonstrates your commitment to the community, and it was what you needed for this—"

I pulled out another certificate.

"You are officially being awarded the Presidential Award Scholarship, a full scholarship that will include a stipend. That, and your work for me as my Teaching Assistant—"

She shrieked. "I got it?"

I smiled as wide as I could. "You did. You are definitely going to Garden State University next semester. Congratulations!"

Once again, she threw herself into my arms and it was all I could do to avoid being knocked over.

"Thank you, thank you," she gasped.

"You earned it. Now, I've got to go to my parents' for Passover. Will you be able to finish your shift?"

"Are you kidding? I'll float through it. Thank you, Len." She reached up and kissed my cheek, then backed away, turning beet red.

"I'll see you next week for our practice session," I assured her, and headed for the door.

I sensed the thought as I got into my van.

I love you…

I finished getting ready, and Jyanette came to watch me as I put on my tie. She looked amazing, wearing a black outfit that showed off her figure, but had long sleeves and a high collar, so it was appropriate to wear for a religious event.

We were on the road by four, knowing that the seder would start at five.

Jyanette was very attentive, always touching my arm or my leg, as if to reassure herself that I was there and mostly undamaged.

"Do you think there was anything to Terry's program, 'flashes of future'?" she asked.

My eyes were on the road as I exhaled heavily. "I don't know. There was the suicide vest and the sniper rifle, so the pair of victims were considering acting out on their fantasies. But he said the prosecutor wanted to meet with Phillip Burke and release him."

She nodded. "However, I altered the course of events by rejecting the plea deal. Also, while you were out, I talked with the prosecutor regarding your remarks about Burke. As a result, the police searched Burke's residence and discovered multiple explosive devices. He will face federal charges for possession of explosives along with his other current offenses."

"Terry said Burke had the explosives, so he was right," I said. "Even so, it was only a computer program, but people can change. Even with Worling and Barton collecting weapons, it might have been a fantasy that they never acted upon. Predicting human behavior is not possible."

Jyanette asked, "What do you think will happen to Tom Harrigan?"

I shook my head. "The DOJ has him under wraps. Same with Dan, the mask maker. They'll pump them for information, but then they'll put them somewhere where they can't tell anyone about Terry's invention. I mean, they were involved in what we could label a terrorist attack."

We soon arrived in Copeland, and I pulled into the winding driveway of my parents' house and parked my van.

My mother met us at the door. "Thank goodness you're here. We can get started."

"Sorry, Mom," I replied, feeling guilt swell up. How did she do that so easily?

"Oy, gevalt!" she blurted. "What happened to your face?"

Jyanette spoke up. "He was fighting bad guys again, Mrs. Wise."

"Well, make him stop!" she complained, then turned to Jyanette, all smiles. "Good to see you, darling."

"I'd love to get him to stop, Miriam."

"You're a woman. Use your feminine wiles."

My mother and Jyanette working together? That thought chilled me.

The family was all there at a big folding table that took up most of the living room. My twin brother Thomas and his fiancée, Julia, my sister Rayna and her husband, Mark, as well as my two nephews, Judah and Ben. My father sat at the head of the table near the seder plate, which was decorated with the different symbols of the holiday.

We quickly found our places at the table, and the ceremonies began. A Passover seder recounts the freeing of the Jewish people from slavery in Egypt. We are required to drink four cups of wine or grape juice, and recount the story of the Exodus, as well as eat matzah.

Lots of matzah.

I relaxed and enjoyed the familiar narration and blessings and joined in with the traditional songs. We went around the table so everyone read parts of the Haggadah, the book we used to do everything in the correct order.

I was so pleased to be with my family, and Jyanette brought a new energy to the festival, asking several questions that my father delighted in answering. It was a joyous night, with the ceremonies, and more important, everyone coming together. We involved both Julia and Jyanette, who would soon become members of the family.

I needed this after the days of pursuing men who thought the only solution was to take the law into their own hands and kill whoever they thought was a danger.

It was uplifting, because the story tells us that if we can make a difference in the world, we must try. We all shared a night with friends and family, and a belief that there was a higher force for good in the world.

I felt I was finally letting go of my past feelings about Cathy, and that I was ready to move into a new life and a marriage with Jyanette.

I also vowed to use my abilities to help bring true justice into the world.

Every chance I got.

FREE PREVIEW

RITUAL IN THE MIND

DOCTOR WISE BOOK 12

ARJAY LEWIS

MIND
BENDER
PRESS

FREE PREVIEW

I t had been quiet overnight, but now the men came again with their tools and began pulling down the walls — her walls.

Why wouldn't they leave her alone?

The constant pounding of hammers, the shrill screeching of power tools, and the ceaseless chatter amongst themselves was enough to drive her to madness. It seemed they had no regard for her in this place.

She hated this room, but she'd grown used to it over the years, became used to the solitude, where she simply drifted. Now it was suddenly a battleground of noisy invaders. They relentlessly tore down walls, the room filled with dusty debris and the incessant clatter of hammers and saws. Her sanctuary, her ethereal abode for years was being invaded.

It wasn't just the noise and destruction that angered her; it was their ignorance as well. They scoffed at the mere mention of a presence, dismissing the tales of haunting as nothing more than superstitious nonsense. They carried on with their work, convinced they were the sole inhabitants of this space. They did not know their actions disturbed the delicate balance between the physical and spiritual worlds, and she hated them for it.

Someone new came in, so much like the man she hated. His fancy suit and perfect haircut angered her. He spoke to the workers, laughing and joking.

She wanted to strike out at him, but it was daytime, and she was too weak in the light.

Among the group of workmen, a burly man showed him their unexpected find. He held out an old Colt 45 Peacemaker, like an iconic relic.

As the man turned it over in his hand, she saw layers of dust and neglect tarnished its weathered exterior. It had remained undisturbed for fifteen years. The once vibrant nickel-plating had decayed, giving way to patches of rust, but the gun's timeless elegance still held a charm that transcended its deteriorated state.

But there was more.

To her, the weapon glowed with an aura of dark energy, like a black ring surrounded it, as if it contained a secret power. She knew what it was. That handgun had been the instrument of her death. The cold metal delivering the fatal shot that left her trapped in this place all these years.

Death — after she had experienced terrible things.

Fear gave way to anger, and she felt a renewed energy. She glared at the weapon, her soul filled with fiery determination.

She would find the owner of that weapon, bring him here and take her vengeance upon him, upon all who did the awful things to her, and she would use that very weapon to do so.

The man in the fine suit smiled and took the weapon with him, leaving the men to their work.

She followed him as he went down the stairs and into the hotel. She sensed the glow of the weapon as if it were a beacon, pulling her onward.

She would have her vengeance.

TO BE CONTINUED IN

RITUAL IN THE MIND

DOCTOR WISE BOOK 12

AUTHOR'S NOTE

We meet again, postulant of the odd.

Justice In the Mind has some nice plot twists for me. Being a person who has done elaborate make-up techniques that include facial prosthetics and the like, I find the rapid growth in production of lifelike silicon masks interesting, and I wanted to incorporate it into a story.

What I wrote about is possible: there was a man who have successfully robbed banks wearing such a mask. This made the photographic evidence useless in tracking down the robber. However, once the police realized it was a mask, they found the manufacturer and looked for the people who ordered that specific mask. The police captured him.

By having my bad guys make their own masks, it made tracking them impossible, and added to the reason that could even fool Len's psychic senses.

Add to this, Agent Harper Montgomery shows up to be a thorn in Len's side, investigating the investigator. I loved their interplay, and I felt Harper was the perfect bureaucrat: smug, condescending, and resolutely sure she was right.

I have plans for her to appear in a future Wise book, but you'll have to wait for it.

Coming up next, *Ritual In The Mind,* which includes a visit to Vegas and Len's brother Thomas getting married, as well as a death at a séance.

—Arjay Lewis

ABOUT THE AUTHOR

Known as the "Wizard Of Odd," Arjay Lewis is an actor, magician, and multi-award-winning author.

I write tales of the strange and the horrifying.

I have spent my life as an entertainer, amusing people as a street-performer in the 1970s; a Broadway and casino artist in the 1980s; a party performer in the 1990s and 2000s; a cruise ship performer in the 2010s.

Stories have always been in my mind, and I have been writing since the 1990s. My reason to write is simple: to entertain. I write the type of books that I like to read: murder mysteries, strange tales of unnatural gifts, odd happenings and horror.

Please visit my web site and sign up for my mailing list to be "in the know" for upcoming books. Visit me on Facebook, Twitter, or my Amazon Author page.

And thank you for reading. You are the reason I write.

www.arjaylewis.com
www.facebook.com/arjaylewis
www.twitter.com/arjaylewiswrite
www.amazon.com/Arjay-Lewis

ALSO BY ARJAY LEWIS

Doctor Wise Series
Fire In The Mind
Seduction In The Mind
Reunion In The Mind
Haunted In The Mind
Devotion In The Mind
Asylum In The Mind
Specter In The Mind
Vengeance In The Mind
Echoes In The Mind
Infection In The Mind
Justice In The Mind
Ritual In The Mind
Vanished In The Mind

Horror
The Muse
Kept In The Dark
The Vanishing
Digger

Romantic Suspense
(with Debra Snow)
A Study In Murder

NYPD Wizard Detective
The Wizards Of Central Park West
The Vampires Of Greenwich Village
The Werewolves Of Washington Square

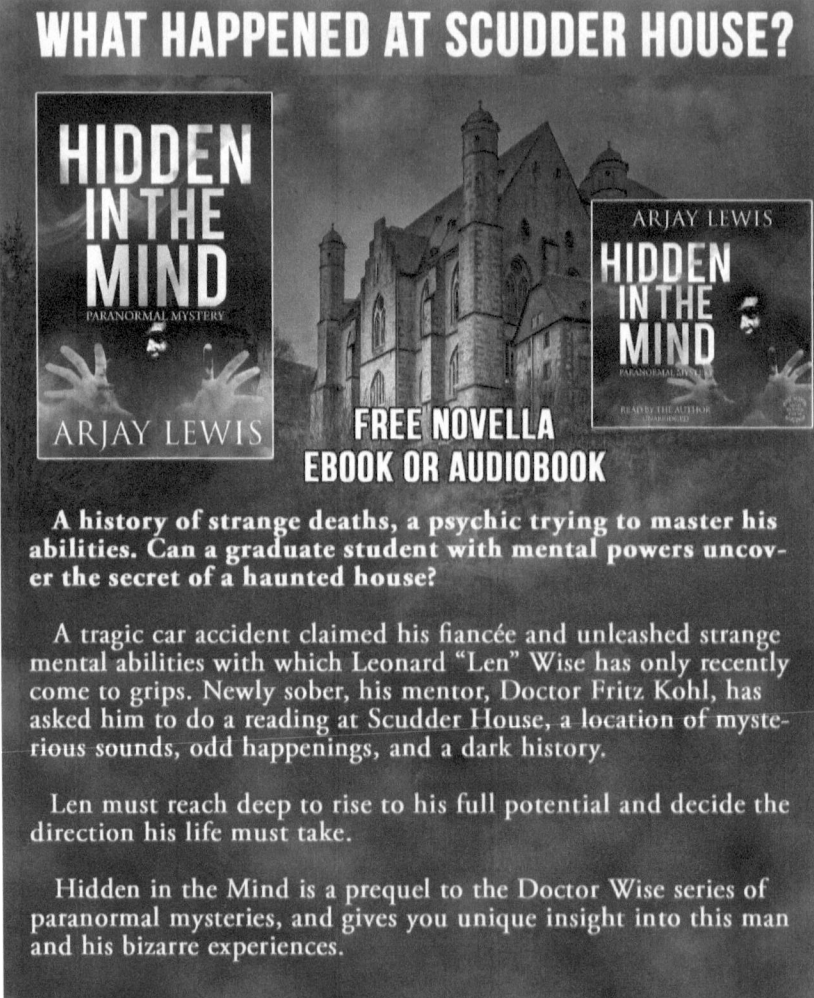

FREE NOVELLA

VOWS

AND OTHER TALES OF THE MACABRE

For those who enjoy a good scare, here is a collection of stories designed to give you nightmares. These stories that have been published in *Weird Tales, H.P. Lovecraft Magazine Of Horror, The Ultimate Halloween,* and *Sherlock Holmes Mystery Magazine.* If you tried to get them from their original source they would cost over $20.00. But you get them for FREE by signing up for Arjay's Newsletter

VOWS: A story of devotion that extends beyond death itself.
SIREN: A Sci-Fi fantasy of a condemned prisoner lost in space.
THE DARK: A guard sees creatures in the night...are they really there?
DREAMCATCHER: A walk in the woods...but you are not alone.
THE TRAVELER: What do you do if your flight is delayed...forever?
INTO THE ABYSS: A makeup artist gets the dream job...at a price.

www.arjaylewis.com/free-stuff.html